THE
SNAKE TREE

UWE TIMM

THE
SNAKE TREE

Translated by Peter Tegel

A NEW DIRECTIONS BOOK

© Kiepenheuer & Witsch 1986
Translation © Pan Books 1988

All rights reserved. Except for brief passages quoted in a newspaper, magazine, radio, or television review, no part of this book may be reproduced in any form of by any means, electronic or mechanical, including photocopying and recording, or by any information storage and retrieval system, without permission in writing from the Publisher.

Manufactured in the United States of America
New Directions Books are printed on acid-free paper.
First published clothbound and as New Directions Paperbook 686 in 1989

English language edition first published by Pan Books Ltd., London in 1988

The story of Cabeza de Vaca and the description of the discovery of the Iguaza Falls are taken from Eduardo Galeanos' book *Origins, Memories of Fire 1*.

Library of Congress Cataloging-in-Publication Data
Timm, Uwe, 1940–
    [Schlangenbaum. English]
    The snake tree / Uwe Timm ; translated by Peter Tegel.
        p.   cm.
    Translation of: Der Schlangenbaum.
    ISBN 0-8112-1101-0 (alk. paper). —ISBN 0-8112-1121-5 (pbk. :
alk. paper)
    I. Title.
PT2682.I39S3513   1990
833'.914—dc20   89-14496
                                                 CIP

New Directions Books are published for James Laughlin
by New Directions Publishing Corporation
80 Eighth Avenue, New York 10011

Our impotent endeavours belong as much to the universal order
as our successful ones.

Denis Diderot
on the wall of his cell
in Vincennes

THE
SNAKE TREE

East Lansing 2/13/90

Für
Gabriele Hahn
herzlich

[signature]

One

The concrete steamed. There was still rainwater on the tarmac and the storm clouds through which they had flown towered blue-black in the west. The plane had made a smooth landing after a bumpy approach when gusts of wind had shaken it, and had taxied to the airport building. When the doors opened the oppressive, humid heat and the smell of kerosene and algae forced its way into the cabin. Wagner thought he could smell the river and the swamps nearby.

He was the first to get out and go over to the arrivals hall, a small, low, dilapidated building. After a few steps his shirt was already soaked in sweat, his trousers stuck to his legs. The conveyor belts at the luggage counter were rolling empty. He leaned against a column and lit a cigarette. Smoking, he watched the passengers crowd to the conveyor belt, some business men, engineers and managers, a few women, their hair carefully done, brunette and suntanned. He was a little disappointed as he had imagined them differently, bolder in appearance, with more Indian features. In their suits and dresses, in which they appeared so astonishingly cool despite the heat, they might just as well have been in Rome or Madrid. Only the passengers who had come with him from Frankfurt and changed planes in Buenos Aires stood out: pale sweaty faces after a twenty-two-hour flight.

Yesterday in the early morning he had taken a taxi to Hamburg Airport. What was left of the snow that had fallen in the night lay grey, dirty at the roadside. At breakfast he had gone over with Susann all the things that she would have to see to in the next few days. Sascha had whined a little at first because they were not letting him come to the airport, then quietly drank his cocoa and wanted to know, were there parrots where Wagner was going. Wagner promised to write immediately and tell him, then got up, ordered a taxi, carried his cases to the door, checked his documents again, and went into the garden. He stood on the terrace and looked into the greyness from which a soft rain was falling. The logs he had cut for the fire lay carefully stacked against the wall of the house. The little wooden hut he had built for Sascha under the pear tree would remain unfinished after all. The windows were missing and the door had only been temporarily hung. He shivered. He had gone back into the house. A little later the bell had rung. The taxi had arrived.

There was sudden movement among the waiting passengers. The first pieces of luggage appeared on the conveyor belt, among them his big aluminium case. He lifted it from the belt and waited until the other, somewhat smaller, case had come.

Berthold had recommended putting a ten dollar note for customs in his passport. Then that tiresome unpacking and packing again could be avoided. But company management had told him not to worry, producing the company letter with the work permit would suffice.

At customs Wagner stood behind an older woman. He had already noticed her in Frankfurt because she wore a broad-brimmed straw hat of the kind travellers usually brought back from South America.

She was now arguing in Spanish with the customs official

while he unscrewed various bottles of pills and with serene composure emptied them onto the table, where laundry and articles of clothing already lay scattered.

The official made a brusque gesture: the woman should pack her case. He came to Wagner, read the company letter and chalked a mark on the case. Wagner could go through.

At the exit those waiting for the arriving passengers pressed forward. Among them he noticed a big man with reddish blonde hair who held up a piece of cardboard with the inscription: Wagner.

Wagner waved to him. The man forced his way through those waiting and said something that sounded like 'good morning', and held out a hand, a very large fleshy hand, to Wagner. He threw the cardboard notice into a bin, then reached for the two heavy cases and carried them almost effortlessly from the airport building.

They crossed to the parking area. The asphalt yielded softly underfoot and over the car roofs the air shimmered. Sweat ran down Wagner's forehead, through his eyebrows and burning into his eyes. He regretted not having put a cotton handkerchief in his pocket as his paper one was nothing now but a small ball of fluff.

On scaffolding outside the arrivals hall a neon sign metres high wrote his firm's name bright red against the sky and then put the firm's oval logo round it in yellow.

The chauffeur opened the rear door of an alpine white Mercedes. Wagner stepped into an agreeable coolness and let himself drop onto the upholstered seat. The air-conditioner hissed quietly. The chauffeur put the cases in the boot, walked round the car, reached into his jacket and put the Mercedes star on the grille.

They drove along a wide concrete road. To the right and left stretched a landscape of greyish brown dried grass in which stood a few tousled palms and dusty eucalpytus. Between them lagoons with a dense growth of reeds from which herons rose ponderously, startled by the noise of the motor. At the edge of these swamps were long white strips like snow that suddenly flew up in a cloud of white: butterflies. At the roadside the wind spun clouds of dust and drove rags of paper and plastic rubbish across the highway. From time to time there were houses by the road, small whitewashed buildings with interconnecting roofs. There were many lorries and a few coaches. Once the chauffeur had to drive round a dead horse on the road from which the bluish black intestines had been squeezed from the anus. A little later the smell of the rotting carcass was in the car.

Suddenly the chauffeur began talking to Wagner in a language he at first took for Danish or Dutch until he understood a word now and then and slowly realized it was German, a very peculiar dialect he had not heard before. Wagner would have preferred the man not to know a word of German, then he could have indicated his willingness to communicate with his meagre Spanish, and then fallen asleep. Instead he sat leaning forward straining to hear so that he could grasp the meaning of these very strange sounding words. As far as he could make out the road should have been built by a German firm, but had been prevented by somebody or other. Evidently a local firm had then built the road which – the further they drove from the airport – gaped with ever wider and deeper fissures, veritable canyons that the driver always crossed at their narrowest point. He obviously knew the way well as he aimed for these spots, then everything rattled.

'Is a burn,' the man shouted, 'is a burn.'

Wagner started. 'What?'

'Is a burn,' the man shouted and gesticulated.

'Oh, yes,' Wagner said.

But the man persisted stubbornly: 'Is a burn it all.'

Wagner leaned forward and looked to where the man was

pointing. Now in the greyish brown grassland he could see a creeping wall of flame that was sending up a small yellow-brown cloud, behind it an expanse, burned black, in which trees standing singly burned like torches.

Wagner asked the driver where he had learned his German. The driver told him, if Wagner understood correctly, that his great-grandfather, a tanner from Hessian Hanau had immigrated here and settled in what in fact was a small remote place, Salta, at the foot of the Andes. Despite marrying into the local population the family had kept its German.

And that was how, even if only spoken by this one family, an Andean-Hessian dialect had come into being.

'But childen no speakin German, is pity pity.'

The driver braked, drove onto the hard shoulder, got out, stood in front of the car and peed.

Wagner kept feeling he was going in the wrong direction. At home he had taken care to memorize the exact route that led to the site on a map. He had imagined a more hilly landscape. But above all they were driving in a southeasterly direction, instead of northwest. The thought flashed through his mind that he was being kidnapped just as one of his two predecessors at the site had been, but when he looked at the Andean-Hessian speaking driver the idea was ridiculous. As they drove on Wagner asked if the road led to the sea.

'No,' the driver said, 'inland' (he said: 'Indelund').

'But we're going southeast,' Wagner said.

'No, nordwest.'

Wagner decided that during their long isolation the family had reversed the points of the compass. Wagner pointed to the sun: north.

'No, sout,' the man said.

With a gesture Wagner described the course of the sun.

'No,' the man said, and indicated another direction.

Only then did Wagner realize that here he had a different view of the sun. He would have to mentally adjust.

Two

In the late afternoon they reached the city. Wagner had slept almost four hours. When he woke they were driving through a reddish brown dusty plain in which the rain had washed deep channels. They came to a cement works, next to it stood four-storeyed box-like houses, new buildings that looked like ruins. Clearly the workers at the neighbouring cement works lived here. The houses stood in a valley where the water had remained after the recent rain. Women waded barefoot through it; a man, barefoot and with trousers rolled up, was balancing on a board by a house entrance. Children paddled from house to house on petrol cans tied together. What idiotic planning, Wagner thought, to build houses on this low ground. A few hundred metres further they would have stood on dry land.

They drove past shacks and small makeshift houses and came to the older part of the city. The houses here were mostly two-storeyed, with voluted columns on the roof balustrades. They had probably been built at the turn of the century. To a large extent the plaster had fallen from the facades, ledges were broken, slats missing from the wooden shutters. Palms loomed from the courtyards, powdered grey with dust from the nearby cement works and ragged like gigantic lavatory brushes. In the

13

shade in front of the houses women sat darning and cleaning vegetables. An old grey-haired woman sat at a pedal sewing machine on the pavement. A horde of children were fighting over a football.

They drove past a square at the centre of which stood an equestrian statue in copper, a man on a rearing horse thrusting his sabre into the sky.

'San Martin,' the driver said, 'liberator statue.'

Behind the square were three, four newish tall buildings. The driver stopped outside the first, where the setting sun was reflected on the honey-coloured glass, got out and opened the car door. At the same time a man in a beige suit came from the entrance to the building, ran down the wide white marble steps, and from a distance already held his hand out to Wagner.

'Welcome,' he called, 'to this wilderness,' then with exaggerated firmness squeezed Wagner's hand and said: 'My name is Bredow. I thought it best if we were to go immediately to your place, then you can change, have a swim, and if you feel like it after your long journey come to us for a meal.' Bredow sat next to Wagner in the back and spoke to the driver in Spanish.

The director of the foreign department in company management had expressly drawn Wagner's attention to the division of authority on this project. He was responsible exclusively for the technical side, here he was totally independent. But all other matters, business, and particularly negotiations with the authorities and the country's administrative departments, were Bredow's exclusive responsibility. Bredow had already managed several projects (he had emphasized 'managed' and later it had annoyed Wagner not to have asked, who then was the manager, he or Bredow), and he had also already lived in the country for fifteen years and had excellent relations with officials and departments. Without that nothing worked. Wagner's predecessor had behaved like a bull in a china shop,

14

it was hardly surprising he had had a nervous breakdown. Wagner took this as it was intended, as a warning.

Bredow had strikingly transparent, bright blue eyes, but the deep tan of his face was the sort usually only seen with dark-haired people. His long light blonde hair was combed tightly back to the nape of his neck where it curled up again, as if set free.

They left the city and drove west toward the setting sun. From the otherwise bare reddish brown plain a hill, covered in trees and shrubs, rose like an island. Houses and villas were visible amidst the green. On the left of the road men and women came towards them in an endless stream.

'Servants,' Bredow explained, 'and gardeners; they've finished work and they're on their way home to the city.'

At the foot of the hill the road was closed by a barrier. Two soldiers with submachine guns stood guard. One of the soldiers sauntered to the car. Bredow had lowered the window and now called out something in Spanish. The soldier laughed, said something and went to the barrier, which he raised.

'Well, this is the Green Hill. You live at the bottom right by the wall. Our house isn't far. The really well-off people, the so-called rancid families, live at the top.'

The road was wide and carefully asphalted. The stones at the edge had been painted phosphorescent white. Though it was only just getting dark there were lights everywhere: houses, garden walls, paths, lawns and even individual trees in the gardens were all illumined.

Wagner asked if one could walk over to the city at night. 'No, better not. And you do have a car. The firm of course only allows a Ford, but it does the job.' The chauffeur stopped at a large, brightly lit bungalow.

They got out. Suddenly there was silence but for the melodious song of a single bird. Wagner stood in the twilight with the noise of travelling still in his ears, a noise that had accompanied him for more than thirty hours and reverberated like an echo. It had grown a little cooler. The air was filled with the heavy scent of flowers that Wagner strangely enough also thought he could taste, sweetish. The bungalow door opened and an alarm wailed briefly. A hand drew back. The alarm was turned off. Then an old woman in a white overall appeared. On her unusually large, bare feet she wore plastic sandals.

'This is Sophie,' Bredow said, 'the friendly spirit of the house.'

The woman shook hands with Wagner and stared at him out of blue, motionless, almost lifeless eyes.

'Welcome,' she muttered and shuffled back into the house. The chauffeur followed her with the cases.

'She's from Entre Rios,' Bredow said, 'there are many Russian Germans there who came from Russia in the twenties, after the revolution. Somewhat old-fashioned in their views, but hard working and honest, which can't always be taken for granted here.'

Bredow led Wagner through the house; five rooms, an enormous living room, outside a veranda. The rooms were furnished, massive chairs, cupboards of polished mahogany.

'Not exactly Italian design,' Bredow said and tapped a cupboard, 'but solid carpentry and above all made in this country.'

'Six rooms. All I can do is lock them or perhaps open a boarding house.'

'Or preferably a brothel.'

Wagner looked out at the illumined garden, large limp leaves, a closely mown lawn, a banana tree from which a bunch of fruit hung heavily, lush shrubbery, behind it: darkness. Wagner went through the rooms. The bedroom was filled with glossy white, built-in cupboards, in the middle stood an enormous brass double bed. Two bright transfers were stuck to the window that led to the garden, two smurfs. Because of them the room lost some of its unfamiliarity. He would sleep in this room, Wagner said, not in that fortress of a marriage bed.

'Makes no difference to me,' Sophie murmured and dragged Wagner's travelling bag into the room.

'I'll go home now,' Bredow said. 'You're having a meal with us, in about an hour. You've already seen our house, the number's easy to remember, 333, the battle of Issus.'

Wagner accompanied Bredow to the door and said goodbye to the chauffeur. He watched Bredow walk to his car. There was a deliberate economy to all his movements, a saving of energy, and a friendly calm spread from him. This was not a man who needed to fight for recognition, with whom you engaged in trench warfare over trivial details.

Sophie was in the process of dividing his things among the numerous built-in cupboards of the house. It would have been far simpler to put everything in the cupboard of what had been the children's room but the woman had her set ideas, so slowly socks, trousers and shirts disappeared into the house.

He asked for his swimming trunks and she shuffled off, mumbling something to herself. From now on he would have to ask for every article of clothing. He went into the garden, on the grass which felt like a bristle under his bare feet.

The swimming pool was a good ten metres long and ended in a grotto built of natural stone from which a small waterfall rippled. Lit from below, the water cast its reflection onto the extensively overhanging, large leaves of several thick-stemmed plants that grew as densely as if the jungle had been right here behind the pool. Wagner swam and dived. Above him shone the foliage of an immense tree, its trunk shaped like a bottle. A night bird sang, its song a delicate melodious whistling ending always in a curious frog-like croak. Unless there were two animals answering each other. Wagner lay down on a white wooden bench covered with a towel. He lay here in the dark and felt the tickling drops of water run from his skin.

He had accepted immediately on being asked if he would take over a building project in South America.

The director of the foreign department had phoned him at his office on the site at Lüdenscheid. Company management had been considering who might take over the project and had decided on him, Wagner, firstly because he had almost finished his power station and because Wagner's deputy could take care of the inspection in three weeks. Also (and this was the reason he had been the first to be asked) they could rely on Wagner to set this rather messy project back on its feet. A paper factory in the middle of the jungle. It was not an easy undertaking and the firm so far had been unlucky in its managers. The first had been kidnapped by the guerilleros and later set free, though only on condition he left the country. The second had fallen ill three weeks ago, or rather, he had had a nervous breakdown. The man had obviously suffered a great deal because of the climate and not gained organizational control. Working conditions naturally were not comparable to those in the Sauerland and naturally there were any amount of incalculable problems. Quite apart from technical matters, one needed to be capable of both organization and improvisation. But perhaps just that would tempt Wagner. At any rate it was something different.

Wagner said: 'Yes, I'll take over. When must I be there?'

'Next week. We're already behind.'

Wagner again said: 'Yes,' at the same time surprised at the ease with which he accepted without any hesitation, thereby upsetting all his plans. Because after the inspection of the power station and a four week holiday he was to have built a sugar factory near Uelzen. He could get to the site in a forty-five-minute drive from his home. And after two years of weekend commuting he could at last have lived at home again. All of them, Sascha, Susann and himself had looked forward to this and made plans.

'A decision has to be made quickly,' the director said, 'but not this quickly. I can give you a day to think it over.'

'No, there's no need.'

'It won't be easy for your wife.'

'No, it won't be easy, but we'll manage.'

'You can take your family with you. There's a German school in the capital.'

'We'll see,' Wagner said.

They arranged a meeting at the central office in Düsseldorf for the following week. Then he could be briefed on the project.

He wondered whether he should phone Susann immediately. But in any case he was flying the next day, so he thought it better to tell her at home. But how would he explain to her that he had immediately and without giving it much consideration accepted this crazy job? He couldn't even explain it to himself. And yet not a single doubt arose in him over his decision. That day and the next, even on the flight home with all those exhausted men, he kept trying every possible answer. The duty to work for a change in an underdeveloped country, to put his knowledge and experience to use there. She would only laugh, after all they had known each other for eight years. And it wasn't the money either. The director had admittedly named an astonishingly high sum, but he and Susann had always agreed that what they earned, she as a teacher and he as a manager, was sufficient. Despite the payments on the house which they had built three years ago, more than enough remained. But then, he said to himself, even as a child he wanted to travel to the jungles of South America, and he had told Susann that, but as an explanation for his quick decision it was a childish excuse. That left him with only the argument of his career, of what he hoped to be one day, manager of a major building site abroad, like Berthold who had built the pilgrim airport in Jeddah. And yet he knew there was more to it than that.

He had come home on the Friday evening, as always Susann was cooking, Sascha sat at his game of Double Trouble. Wagner had meant to tell her immediately about his new project but with Sascha pleading, would he please come and play, he postponed it. As always he tried to somehow avoid winning, or at least not too quickly. Sascha could not lose, and he usually ended the game either because he was losing or saw that Wagner was letting him win. But it was extremely difficult to deliberately lose at this game without Sascha noticing. As if he were being punished Wagner always threw the numbers that allowed him to advance and that brought that nervous look to Sascha's face. Suddenly he was fidgety, suddenly he didn't want to play anymore, suddenly you could see him gripped by deep disappointment. All week he had looked forward to this moment, this game of Double Trouble with Daddy, and now every bad throw of the dice disappointed his expectations.

Later they ate together and everything was exactly as Wagner had anticipated. Wagner told a story about a foreman who, after eight bottles of beer, if he was in a good mood, would eat the glass. You could actually hear the glass crunching between his teeth. Sascha always roared with laughter as if he had never heard the story before. After he had put Sascha to bed and read to him he had gone down to the living room where Susann was sitting on the sofa, her legs crossed. He had sat beside her and pressed her to him as if to press from her all the bodily intimacy he had been missing all these days, until she gasped for breath, laughing. Then he had said – and had really needed to pluck up the courage – that he had accepted a project abroad, a paper factory. The completely unexpected had happened. Susann was not in the least upset, she wasn't even surprised. She only said, 'six months go by quickly.'

After hesitating a moment, he said: 'It'll be about a year.' 'We'll manage that too.' It was as if she were trying to encourage him when he had in fact already decided. 'We can't possibly take Sascha out of school. He had enough problems starting school.'

'No,' he said, 'that wouldn't be a good idea.'

It was, Wagner now felt, a more far-reaching goodbye than he had originally supposed. They were separating for a year and neither of them resisted.

Later that evening Renate and Berthold had dropped in. Berthold was only two years older than Wagner and had already managed three projects abroad. He immediately said: 'It's a suicide mission. Conditions being what they are, it could hardly be worse: a military dictatorship, guerillas, corruption, incompetence, and then the heat. If you get this built, then in future you choose what to build, if not, you'll plunge into the pit. Because one thing's certain, your predecessor will be building small private houses on the Lünerburgér Heide until he's pensioned off.'

While talking about his new job he had looked at Renate. She was surprised and she was unable to hide her surprise, and Wagner hoped neither Berthold nor Susann would notice. He avoided talking alone with Renate that evening. They had all drunk to the new job. They had been unable to find the place in an atlas.

Not until the next morning, when he told Sascha he would be away in the jungle for a long time, did Wagner begin to feel how much his decision would change their lives. He immediately promised to bring Sascha arrows and quivers from the Indians. But this did nothing to lessen Sascha's grief because the steamboat they were going to build together would not be built, nor the intercom, and for a long time there would be no game of Double Trouble. Sascha had burst into tears and had a crying fit. He was so inconsolable that for the first time

Wagner doubted his decision and felt as if he were running away. Even now the memory of Sascha's grief tormented him.

Bats shot through the air. In the lamplight heavy insects reeled. In the distance he heard the deep barking of a dog. In the neighbouring garden someone was talking in a broad Texan accent about the cultivation of various kinds of maize; the voice could have been a woman's, but also a man's. Wagner got up so as not to fall asleep. He swam again, then put on jeans and a white shirt. He asked Sophie for the car key. The car was in the garage, a grey Ford Falcon. The car was as good as new. His predecessor had been given it by the company two months ago.

Wagner drove up the asphalt road to Bredow. Bredow's wife opened the door. Christi, as she introduced herself, a large red-haired woman with an athletic, almost muscular body. She was wearing a dress with a blue flower pattern and high heeled shoes. Christi led Wagner through the house. The armchairs, tables, chests of drawers, cupboards and chairs were all of light walnut, made in Denmark.

Christi said, being Danish, Wagner would have to excuse her rather faltering German. But she spoke German almost without an accent.

There was some old Swedish glass in a corner cupboard, in front of the windows linen curtains in pastel tones. Tasteful and expensive.

Bredow came in, large barbecue fork in one hand. He had taken off his jacket and rolled up the sleeves of his light blue shirt.

'You know', he said, 'one has to make oneself comfortable here, otherwise one can't bear it for long, that's why we always move with all our furniture. Most of the things are Christi's. All I brought to the marriage was a letter.' He pointed with the barbecue fork to a framed letter hanging on the wall. From a blue ribbon hung a medal. A handwritten letter to Bredow's ancestor from Tsar Alexander the First after the battle of Leipzig. 'He had advanced with a Prussian regiment and thereby saved a Russian corps. That's all that's left, the rest stayed in the east, the Russians took it back home.'

Wagner went with Bredow into the garden. The grill was there, an Asado.

'The steaks in this country are unique. They taste different. That's because the cattle graze all year and are not given concentrated feed.'

He cut into the meat and tested how well it was done. The blood gathered in the cut. 'For a bachelor life's not easy. In the city, if you want to call it a city, there's one cinema and one nightclub and neither, as you can well imagine, are of an international standard. Social life is confined almost exclusively to the houses here on the Green Hill. There's quite a large German colony, but naturally they live on the far side of the moon. You're sure to get to know them soon. They'll invite you. Go. Think of them as museum pieces. Discussion is pointless. Fall out with these people and you can be damned lonely if you know no Spanish.'

They ate on the veranda and drank a Burgundy with the meat. 'Why didn't you bring your wife?' Christi asked.

His wife had stayed behind, Wagner said, as she hadn't wanted to take their son out of school, he had made a great effort to settle in.

'The German school in the capital is very good. And they have their own boarding school. Our children are there.'

'How old are they?'

'Ten and twelve.'

As Wagner looked at Christi in surprise, she laughed. She'd run into Bredow when she was eighteen. Her father had been a diplomat in the country at the time.

Christi wanted to know, why had Wagner put himself forward for the job.

'Simply that I wanted to work abroad for once.' Wagner was constantly surprised that people seemed satisfied with this explanation. Of course they suspected other reasons, just didn't ask what they were. Shouldn't at least Susann have asked?

As Bredow made no reference to the project Wagner asked him, were they making progress.

'Things are taking their course,' Bredow said and cut at his steak.

'Are there any problems?'

'No, at least none other than the usual.'

'And what are the usual?'

'You'll see. I'll drive you there tomorrow.'

Three

 At five in the morning Wagner drove to the site. Bredow had called for him at his house and drove ahead in his BMW. First north, along the country road, then they turned onto a narrow asphalted road that had been built by the firm. The deep impression of lorry tyres was visible everywhere along the roadside. The lorries had to give way to each other on the narrow road. The asphalt surface of the road was covered in red dust. Bredow drove quickly, from time to time hooted as if to reassure himself Wagner had not fallen asleep. Wagner had turned down all the windows, the airstream ran through his hair. The green bulge on the horizon, the rain forest, slowly grew bigger, and Wagner was able to recognize individual trees that had shot up to a great height. Then they plunged into the green, and it was dark again. The road ran like a tunnel through the forest. In the headlights Wagner saw leaves, tree trunks, creepers. It was surprisingly silent, except for the flapping wind from the car. Now and then some birds fluttered into the air. Wagner would gladly have got out of the car, simply to stand quietly in the forest for a moment. He hooted and flashed, at which Bredow increased speed, hooting to show he understood, and a tearing drive began through the primeval forest. Wagner drove, his foot hard on the accelerator and staring at the road. The roots ran like veins under the asphalt that had broken apart in many places and been driven into potholes. Suddenly Bredow braked. Wagner saw the three lorries with drums of concrete. The lorries were on the right at the edge of the road, the wheels churning in the soft ground. Wagner drove behind Bredow past the lorries, on which the concrete drums were slowly revolving. On the first lorry the concrete shute was not properly closed, concrete fell in heaps onto the road. This was when Wagner noticed the snake, an emerald green snake gliding across the road in front of him. He tried to swerve, but almost got into the deep tyre tracks on the shoulder, so drove on and braked by the driver's cabin of the first lorry. He tried to draw the attention of the driver, a youngish man with Indian features, to the fact that the drum was losing concrete. The man didn't understand, didn't even listen to Wagner, He stared at the road. Wagner got out and pointed to the trail of concrete. Only then did he see the snake. He had driven over it more or less in the middle and thoroughly plastered it onto the asphalt. As the head of the snake jerked and tried to drag the flattened body forward, the tail curled. Wagner wondered whether he ought to stamp on the animal and kill it, but even the thought of touching the animal with his heel revolted him. He again tried to indicate the trail of concrete to the driver, but he was staring as if spellbound at the writhing snake. Wagner got back in and slowly drove on. In the rear mirror he saw the other two drivers get out and go to the snake. What was so unusual? Surely they drove over several snakes daily. Soon he had caught up with Bredow and after ten minutes the forest opened to a large clearing. The stumps of felled trees rose from the ground. The area had been burned, only an occasional charred palm still stood. Shoots were already thrusting out of the grey ash. They drove to the site on which stood four cranes. A two-storeyed concrete building was finished. It was the future office wing, now being used as the site office, as Wagner knew from the building plans. Next to it was a second, small building, the generator that provided the site with electricity and that later, when the overland cables had been laid, would be converted into a transformer. Around both buildings a barbed wire fence at least three metres high had been erected. Bredow drove through the open gate in the fence, past a guard in khaki. The man wore a heavy revolver, the sort Wagner knew from westerns. Bredow pulled up at the entrance to the office wing. Wagner got out and went over to Bredow who was still sitting in the car, pulling on yellow rubber boots.

'Why did you stop?'

'The concrete shute on one of the lorries wasn't properly closed.'

Bredow laughed: 'They've laid a concrete trail through the forest.'

They went into the office wing. A man came towards them on the steps. Mid-fifties, Wagner reckoned, blondish grey thinning hair, a puffy but suntanned face, a khaki shirt stretched over a mighty stomach.

'This is Mr Steinhorst, deputizing manager.' (Bredow had not said: Deputizing for you.) 'Mr Steinhorst has been taking care of things in the meantime.'

'Taking care's a nice way of putting it,' Steinhorst said, 'I'm glad,' and he pressed Wagner's hand, 'you're here.' No doubt he wanted to let Wagner know he had no aspirations at all to the job of manager. He looked out of sky-blue eyes at Wagner; they were damp, the lids shimmered, inflamed red. Steinhorst led Bredow and Wagner into a largish room, the canteen, in which about twenty men were gathered – the engineers, technicians and site foremen. Among the dark-haired brown faced men Wagner immediately noticed the third engineer on the site, Hartmann, a youngish man, short nosed and with a bald freckled head. A head that reminded Wagner of Darwin.

Bredow was talking to the people in Spanish. As a student Wagner had once been on a Spanish course, but he understood nothing Bredow was saying. An older dark-skinned man with grey curly hair brought in paper cups on a plastic tray and handed them out. 'Follow him, did you?', a big Indian asked Wagner. He wore his bluish black hair tied in a pony tail that hung over his jeans jacket. Wagner was so astonished at the regional accent and idiom coming from this Indian mouth that he said 'yes.'

'If you want to know something I'll translate it. I'm Juan.' Wagner wanted to ask Juan where he had learned to speak the language with that regional accent, but they all raised their paper cups and glasses, and Bredow said; 'To success.'

They drank to Wagner. He drank, choked, it was not champagne as he had supposed. He coughed, the Indian patted him on the back, and when Wagner looked up he saw friendly grinning faces. For a moment all the unfamiliarity disappeared.

'That's cider,' Juan said.

A siren wailed for the work to start and the men left the room. Steinhorst fetched a yellow plastic helmet and brought one for Wagner as well.

'Isn't that a little dramatic?', Wagner said.

'Not at all, or you'll soon have sunstroke.'

'Are you coming too?' Steinhorst asked Bredow.

'No, I've an appointment, anyway I don't know the first thing about this building. You can manage without me.' He slapped Wagner on the shoulder, called 'Adios' and left in his gleaming yellow boots.

Steinhorst led Wagner over the site. Wagner had carefully studied the plans at home. Here were the three large factories in which the paper was to be produced. The foundation for factory A had already been laid and the beams and supporting walls were in the process of being poured. Then they went to an excavation in which three caterpillar trucks were scooping earth.

'Factory B will be built here. And factory C goes there,' Steinhorst said and pointed to an area marked by red and white posts. 'The two warehouses go here and the workshop there, next to the canteen.'

A little to the side were Nissen huts, round, with roofs of corrugated iron.

'The workers live there,' Steinhorst said.

Wagner saw two quite large cooking areas, a stove, an oven. Under the corrugated iron which rested on posts were several homemade tables and chairs. Pigs lay in the shade, a few mangey chickens pecked at the red earth. A man in rags and with long black hair was chopping wood.

'Are they Indians?'

'Bolivian, but many are Indian.'

'Why Bolivian?'

'They're cheaper and work harder,' Steinhorst said. 'They have to, or they're out.'

'Are there any problems with them?'

'None at all, or they're deported.'

'Are there political problems?'

'You mean guerillas? Hardly any left. The military did a thorough clean-up after the coup. When we began here things were still hot. A bomb went off almost every night in the city. And there was always shooting. We had acts of sabotage here. An arson attack on a crane, slashed tyres, stolen sparking plugs. They still get stolen, but no longer for political reasons. They steal like magpies here.'

They had returned to the site of factory A. Wagner watched the wooden frames being made for the pillars.

'We'd begun the excavation for factory A when Ehmke was kidnapped. You've heard about that, I'm sure.' Steinhorst stared over to the edge of the forest as if he could see him being kidnapped there.

'Was he kidnapped there?' Wagner asked.

'No. They took him from his house on the hill where you're living now. It was night. His wife and children were already asleep. Ehmke was sitting on the veranda smoking and having another beer. In the morning his wife found his burned-out pipe and half-finished glass of beer. No one had noticed a thing. They came over the garden wall, threatened Ehmke with revolvers, tied him, gagged him, pushed him into a waiting car and drove to the city, where they held him in a small room for three weeks. But even later the police never found the flat. Ehmke said that he could see under the door into the kitchen. Under a kitchen cupboard he saw two pomegranates. There was something cheering about that. And he did say later he never thought they would shoot him.'

'But why was he kidnapped then?'

'The guerilleros kidnapped him to put pressure on the Junta to make a statement on television. A statement directed against the military, but also against our company, even against this project.'

'And why?'

Steinhorst took the plastic helmet from his head and wiped his forehead with his shirt sleeve.

'At any rate not in order to protect the forest. It had to do with shabby dealing, bribery, land sales, I wouldn't know. You can't get to the bottom of it. You'll see for yourself.'

'And how did Ehmke get free?'

'That was simple. One day he was back, with a thick beard. They dropped him off on a street in the city. He wasn't a big enough fish. The military took no notice of the ultimatum. If they'd done away with Ehmke, as far as the company was concerned it would have been nothing more than an industrial accident. In this job you have to live with that risk these days.'

Steinhorst started to laugh. 'Mrs Ehmke should have been happy. In the first place she would have got rid of her nagging spouse, and as well as a pension she could have cashed in a fat life insurance policy. He was highly insured of course. I hope you are too.'

Wagner had to laugh.

'You know,' Steinhorst said, 'I think they weren't even after Ehmke. They took him for someone else. It's Bredow they wanted, that would make sense.'

'What sort of sense?'

Steinhorst shook his head and grinned, then he patted his stomach and said: 'About time I had a drink. The desert calls.'

When Wagner came to his room Juan was sitting on his chair. He had put his legs on his desk and was reading a comic. Juan only looked up briefly.

'The needeth me?'

'No,' Wagner said, 'but it would be nice if you took your feet off the building plans.'

Juan took his feet off the desk and slowly got up. But he glanced at the comic, he probably wanted to remember the page.

'Where'd you learn the language? In Hamburg?'

'Ne, in hous,' Juan said, 'in Gran Chaco.'

Wagner laughed: 'Sounds like Indian esperanto.'

'Ne, forsothli, mine foulk speken Mennhonite, muchen Mennonite in Gran Chaco they comen dwellen.'

'Can we have a quiet talk?'

As he was leaving he asked Wagner, was it true Wagner had killed a snake.

'Killed,' Wagner laughed, 'that sounds very dramatic, at least when not in dialect. Who said so?'

'The workers. Was it emerald green?'

'Yes. Why?'

'That's the Acaray snake. You're not allowed to kill it,' Juan said without resorting to dialect, and now it sounded grave.

'Ok,' Wagner said, 'ok, I'll be more careful next time, but now I need to work.'

Juan left. Wagner sat down at his desk, overhead a fan stirred the hot air. He tried to put his thoughts in order, but there was a constant ringing in his head.

Four

 Sophie had served the evening meal to constant grumbling and later with the same grumbling cleared the table. Wagner had heard her say something about worshippers of idols, a sickle and a roaring fountain. He had wanted to ask, what sort of roaring fountain, but then she had stayed in the kitchen. So he had gone onto the terrace and sat on one of the glossy white benches, put his beer on the ground and lit a cigarette.

The sun was sinking into a streak of orange mist and for a last moment everything seemed to recover a clear and sharp outline, the smooth green leaves of the orange tree, the parapet of the wall, a white garden table tipped on its side, to fade a little later into vagueness, into the dark. He sat in pleasant weariness and listened to the shrill scraping of the cicadas that had grown louder with the onset of dusk. Already before the meal he had booked a call to Hamburg. He wanted to talk to Susann who would now, it was five hours earlier, soon be going to bed. Probably she was just setting the table for tomorrow's breakfast. A few days ago, at home for the first time on a working day in a long while, he had watched her. Susann had come into the house, taken off her yellow raincoat, there was still chalk on her skirt, and gone straight to the kitchen. Sascha had to wash his hands and then set the table in the kitchen, not in the dining room where they always ate at weekends. Susann ran backwards and forwards in the kitchen and Wagner suddenly had the feeling that in this daily course of events there was no room for him. When he sat down at the kitchen table Susann pushed the plate laid for him to the end of the table and said, 'We'll disturb you less here.' In fact, he was the one who disturbed. He listened to her and Sascha, and mostly knew nothing about what they discussed, to do with friends and homework and recorder lessons, and tidying a box of toys, problems that normally only reached Wagner at weekends as reports that conveyed a mood. Sascha disappeared into his room. He had to do homework. Susann sat down at her desk to prepare an English lesson. Wagner roamed through the house they had built three years ago (the design was by an architect friend). Somehow it had turned out too full of right angles and too big. Though they had wanted three more children when they planned the house, they had stopped talking about that even before they moved in. Susann went every two years to the doctor to have her coil changed. He had only found out later and more by chance. Wagner would have liked to have another child but he never talked about it to Susann because he saw what demands the school made on her (and she allowed the school to make these demands, as until now she had always refused to take leave or reduce her hours), also how she took everything to heart, her students' problems, and most of all Sascha's problems. He was a vulnerable, rather timid child who began to cry for no apparent reason. If asked why, it turned out he couldn't find a shoe or had forgotten an exercise book at school. And Sascha was still unable to go to the lavatory anywhere except at home. So Susann padded his underpants with a sanitary towel and cotton wool. Susann racked her brains for reasons, her thoughts forever revolving round what she was doing wrong, after all the boy should do well, he should be all right, he should be happy. Wagner always felt uncomfortable when they talked about Sascha, because he believed they should ignore Sascha's timidity. The boy'll be all right, he'd say, and Susann would look at him, silent and reproachful. Apparently he was the one who made excessive demands of the boy. He put Sascha on the bike and said, off you go, cycle. And Sascha cycled. Susann came to watch and said, now take care, and Sascha instantly fell and hurt his knee. Sometimes they quarrelled about the best way to help Sascha. Wagner always thought it would be good, particularly for the boy, if he were at home again. And yet, without hesitating even for a moment, he had taken this job. When he thought of Sascha he felt he had abandoned him, when he thought of Susann it was as if he had been pushed aside. That day, telling her, for a moment he suspected she had another man. But there were really no grounds for the thought, not because it was inconceivable exactly, but because Susann would have told him. On the Friday, while they were together with Berthold and Renate, he had watched her carefully. But all that struck him was that she talked much more humourously (she was very good at imitating the way people spoke) and in greater detail about her school experiences, than earlier alone with him. Yes, he had noticed before that she regularly saved the more interesting stories. While earlier she had only told him about the tiresome everyday problems, the minor irritation with the headmaster or some student or other. They had slept together and as always it had been as if she were letting him have his way. Which strangely enough took nothing from his pleasure, it was as if he had to wrestle with her for her pleasure, until the first little sigh.

Sophie came and asked if there was anything else Wagner wanted.

'No, thank you.'

She shuffled in her bright pink plastic slippers into the house. He wanted to get up, but remained seated so he wouldn't meet her again in the house. Later he went into the living room, listened, there was silence in the kitchen. He got a can of beer from the refrigerator, turned the television on in the living room. A thriller. It was evidently set in New York. Then suddenly the advertisements came, a brand of whisky, a baby lotion, a perfume, then trees toppled to right and left, a colossal bulldozer pushed aside a small hill, a mountain flew into the air, in slow motion lumps of rock were driven into the earth, a tar machine crossed the landscape behind a bulldozer, beyond it on the horizon cars raced on the completed motorway into the oval logo of the company to the accompaniment of Beethoven's 'Joy, from heaven to earth come down'. So this was the way into the future.

Then, after reverting briefly to the previous scene, the thriller continued. A killer enters a small bar. Night outside. The killer orders something and while the barman is busy at the espresso machine takes a revolver from the holster under his arm, without hurrying screws a silencer onto the barrel. He looks out of the window, there is no one in sight. He shoots the barman in the back. The man falls, raises himself on his arms, then sinks to the ground.

Wagner suddenly remembers the snake, the green snake stuck fast to the asphalt. The violent dogged attempt to crawl forward into the protective vegetation.

Wagner gets up and turns off the television. He sees the unfamiliar room, the furniture which he would never have chosen for himself, the low ceiling, the wallpaper the colour of a vanilla pudding. He notices the door to the veranda is open. He wants to lock it but hears a noise outside, a sound as if from an animal, a snarling, then a distant but loud argument. He goes cautiously into the lit garden. He can find nothing. He goes to the wall that separates his garden from the plain: a wall built of breeze block with a round coping intended to prevent anyone on the other side holding on and pulling himself up. In front of the wall, but at least two metres lower than the garden, is the plain, bare, sandy, with countless channels formed by the rain. At least two hundred metres away are several huts, between them some wooden poles from which lamps are suspended. There is an open fire by which figures crouch and a little to the side of the bluish flickering of a television standing outdoors, in front of it children and adults huddled together. Suddenly shots are fired. Wagner starts, though immediately tells himself they were fired in the thriller. He goes back into the house, locks the door, lowers the steel roller blind. He goes to the bathroom and cleans his teeth. His right eye is strangely inflamed. He turns on the air conditioner. As he lies down when a dog begins barking in the neighbouring garden, a savage frenzied bark, other dogs join in, it spreads from garden to garden as if accompanying someone running up the hill, a ferocious barking that slowly recedes and becomes less noisy. Wagner wonders whether he should get up and go into the garden again, when suddenly the barking stops. Then there is silence. He listens. He can hear the quiet hum of the air conditioner. The curtain moves softly in the breeze.

He is walking through a garden. It is the garden in front of his house in Hamburg. The fence has been trampled down. He goes out. Outside grow huge plants he has never seen before with curled leaves that lie on the ground like tongues and next to them strange reddish brown lumps. They look like melted parts of a machine. He picks up a piece. It turns out to be iron and he can still recognize a part of a cogwheel. This is the excrement of the plants. In one plant he recognizes a woman's arm. The arm is slowly being swallowed by the plant, the hand reaches into the air as if to find a hold. He approaches and recognizes his wedding ring on the hand. Then he becomes aware of something touching his leg, reaching under his trouser leg, something warm, soft, like a tongue. He looks down and discovers one of the plants has taken hold of him with a leaf and is drawing him to itself. Berthold calls to him, he must sing with all his might, it makes the plants ill and they let go of their prey. He tries to take a deep breath, but is unable to get out any sound.

Wagner was woken by the phone ringing. He leaped out of bed and staggered through the dark room, looking for the light switch, the door. He bumped his arm, his hip, finally found the phone in the hall. A woman's voice said: 'Alemania'. Then he heard Susann's voice, hoarse and drowsy, but clear and very close, Sascha calling in the background, Susann saying, 'Sascha's awake.'

'No,' Wagner called, 'don't hang up.'

Then again Susann's voice and in between, Sascha's. 'Hello,' Wagner called 'do you know what, yesterday I saw a snake, a big green snake.'

'And Indians?'

'I've got one, he's my interpreter, an Indian tribe in Gran Chaco.'

But then Susann's voice was back on the phone: 'How are you?'

'Fine. It's hot, unbelievably hot.'

'It's raining here, really gloomy weather. And the people?'

'They're all right.' He told her about the enormous size of the bungalow and said, 'I'd like to have you here, both of you,' and wanted to say, I'd like to hold you in my arms, Susann. Sascha was sure to be sitting on her lap. still warm from bed. But then Susann's voice went and Wagner heard humming, the strange humming of many thousands of voices, now and then a voice stood out briefly and he thought he could understand a word, a sentence; it was as if at that moment he were hearing every telephone owner on the earth talking about his business affairs, his dreams and his fears. He heard it as if from an icy distance. Years ago on television he had seen the earth for the first time, a sphere, or rather an ellipsoid, wreathed in a wonderful blue. This is the blue we breathe, the commentator had said. The voice of the operator said: 'Ohla, ohla, quién habla?'

Wagner said: 'I've been cut off.'

The operator said something in Spanish which he didn't understand. He hung up.

Five

The Egmont Bar was on Plaza 25 de Mayo, a half-concreted square with shaggy palms in the centre of which stood the equestrian statue of San Martin. Egmont in blue neon lettering shone into the night on the facade of the three-storeyed house. Two caryatids with heavy stone breasts flanked the entrance. On the swing door with brass handles hung a chipped porcelain plaque: Salón de Té.

The bar, a large high room, was filled with old cast iron café tables. A counter stretched the length of the room. Foreigners sat and stood there, the engineers and technicians of Swiss, Belgian, German and North American companies. Among them a few girls in tight dresses and short skirts. Wagner caught sight of Steinhorst, whom he had arranged to meet here, at the bar. The Abbas boomed from the loudspeakers. When he saw Wagner Steinhorst slid from the bar stool, for a moment had to hold on to the bar, he swayed that badly, but insisted Wagner take the stool.

The astonishing thing was that Steinhorst could still speak clearly. Wagner sat on the stool and deeply repelled felt the warmth from Steinhorst's backside on the plastic cushion. Steinhorst stood close, but well below him. Wagner saw the big drops of sweat on Steinhorst's forehead.

'Whisky?'

'No,' Wagner said, 'a beer.'

'Good German beer. The only place you get it.' Above Steinhorst a large wooden fan stirred the smoke-filled air.

'Why Egmont, of all names to call a bar?'

'The owner's Belgian,' Steinhorst said, and with a movement of his head indicated the cash desk near the entrance. There a small dapper man was entering bills and in a high-pitched voice calling out orders to the waiters.

'He's called Durell,' Steinhorst said, 'but people say that's not his real name. He was in the Belgian army, with the paratroops. He was in the Congo and then with Tshombi's mercenaries, and after they were driven out he formed his own private army; they were called the white giants, although he's very small himself, as small as Napoleon, as he always stresses.'

Durell, who wore his thick grey hair cropped short, waved across to Steinhorst.

'The type women are mad for. Seems he came here six years ago, straight from Africa, from Rhodesia, I believe, which had become independent. It got too hot for him there. Opened the bar here, a gold mine, but doesn't drink himself, apparently because he once had hepatitis, but in actual fact doubtless because of his past. He doesn't want to let anything out when he's drunk. Not that anybody here doesn't know. He even shot an actual minister, in the Congo, that's to say he stuck a hand grenade inside the waist-band of a black whose hands were tied behind his back. But perhaps that's just one of those stories,' Steinhorst said, downed the whisky and with a raised thumb ordered another. A dark-haired girl standing next to Steinhorst raised her glass to Wagner. Her dress, slit at the side, had slipped – or been pulled – so high it revealed the dull brown skin of her thigh through her silver silk stocking. Next to the girl stood a stocky man with bulging blue eyes. He was talking in Swiss German to the girl who nodded from time to time, as if she understood, while smiling at Wagner. When Steinhorst noticed the looks she was giving, he grinned. 'You can take her home without worrying. You won't have any problems. The girls here like blonde men. Put them under a shower first, apart from that they're ok. The only one with a dose is the Vietnamese over there. You need a condom for her.'

Wagner ordered himself a third bottle of beer.

'And the project? Any inside information?'

'A disaster, like every project in this country. Just about everything's gone wrong.'

'What exactly?'

'Everything. The concrete, the workers, the calibre of the reinforcements, even the location, nothing's right.'

'Why not?'

'The factory should actually be built at least 500 metres further west. Oh well, you'll see. These are the little surprises that make life so thrilling. Otherwise one would die of boredom.'

The grey-haired Belgian came over, greeted Steinhorst and shook Wagner's hand, saying he hoped Wagner would soon feel at home, if he had any requests to let him know.

Wagner saw the gold fillings in Durell's mouth. The moustache, in contrast to the icy grey hair, was still dark blonde.

'Do you play tennis?' Durrell asked.

'Yes.'

'Then we should play doubles against the Bredows. Perhaps in a couple of days, once you're acclimatized. No team so far has been able to beat the Bredows. Christi's an exceptionally good player.'

Durell was called back to the cash desk. Wagner watched as he went, small, upright, head held high.

'His German's very good.'

'Yes', Steinhorst said, 'also his Spanish, a linguistically gifted man.' Steinhorst again pointed to his empty whisky glass and raised a thumb.

Wagner wanted to enquire in more detail about the shifting of the site, but then through a quite irrelevant question – how Steinhorst felt here – opened a floodgate through which private problems, anecdotes and opinions on god and the world poured never endingly. Why it was that Steinhorst had to give up his chair at a technical college, why he had then gone to Africa where he'd converted church taxes into concrete cathedrals, cathedrals that, solidly built, were overgrown two years after completion and four years later had been swallowed by the jungle, sites for future archeologists to discover. But above all he talked about his private catastrophe – the reason why he had left the technical college for Africa – a catastrophe that had destroyed his family, his happiness, from the day he had come home and found a letter from his wife on the hall table, consisting of only one sentence: I am leaving. A sentence that at first he had not understood, only that night, towards morning, when for the first time in their twenty-four year marriage she was still not back, did it dawn on him that she had left him, without any warning, six months before their silver wedding. There had been no quarrel, nothing unusual had happened, she had simply moved in with someone else, taken all her papers with her, not her make-up though, probably had a second set lying around at the other place. Because – and this was totally beyond comprehnsion – she had been having an affair with the other man for eight years already, the headmaster of the school where she taught, the very man who in her evening accounts figured as a stickler for red-tape, with this man of all people she had spent something like two hundred dirty weekends, calculating exactly, two hundred and twenty-three, because from a certain point in time she had set out every Saturday afternoon on lengthy walks that she always wanted to take alone. After all wasn't she constantly with people all week long, she wanted to be alone, she only took the dog, Dojahn, a wire-haired terrier. He was allowed to watch, Steinhorst laughed, but his laughter was more like weeping. He emptied his glass. With the back of his hand he wiped the sweat from his eyebrows, then patted his stomach over which his shirt had burst open, and said: 'I'm fit as a fiddle, this is all liver.'

'And what's all this about the land?'

Steinhorst began talking incoherently, suddenly and almost without transition he was so drunk no further conversation was possible. Steinhorst said, slurring the words: 'I'm not giving anything else away.'

Wagner drove in his car over to the hill. He had drunk a strong coffee, nevertheless everything he saw and heard seemed blurred. The street was empty and dark, but the hill, the streets, houses and gardens, were lit. While Steinhorst was talking about his wife Wagner had thought about Renate and Berthold. Susann and he had been friends with them both for seven years and he already knew Berthold, if only slightly, from their student days. In the last three years, being almost neighbours, they had seen each other every week, mostly on Friday evenings, but as the children were friends also on Saturdays and sometimes Sundays. Berthold and Renate had two sons, one of them, Peter, was the same age as Sascha. Berthold was a head shorter than Wagner, but broader and sturdier. Berthold went sailing and as well as his BMW drove a Mercedes sports car of 1928 vintage at the weekend. On Saturdays he was mostly to be found leaning over the engine of his car. He could always talk about two things: sailing and cars. Susann and Wagner knew most of the stories, had often heard them two or three times, and yet Berthold always succeeded in getting their attention. In fact, Berthold told them in a way that made it impossible not to listen, loudly and with great gestures, sometimes leaping to his feet to demonstrate something by pacing up and down, yes, or perhaps to demonstrate his Finn Dinghy capsizing would sit on the arm of the sofa, there show how he was riding the boat when the squall struck as he turned, the sail caught, the boat capsized, and Berthold would let himself drop onto the carpet.

Above all with Berthold you could have a really good laugh. Berthold's laugh, a deep, uninhibited and loud laugh could silence every other conversation in the room and make people join in who didn't even know why they were laughing. For two years, since completing the airport at Jeddah, Berthold had been head salesman with a steel-girder construction company. He sold steel structures for industrial buildings and had increased the turnover by fifteen per cent, which didn't surprise Wagner. Anyone who became involved with Berthold would have difficulty escaping his beserk charm. Renate had been married to Berthold for ten years. Since Wagner had known her she had dyed her hair with henna. She maintained that the natural colour of her hair was a dreary brown. Her hair colour made her look brash. She had interrupted her literary studies when she had had her first child, but two years ago begun to write for radio. At the beginning of September she had paid Wagner a surprise visit in Lüdenscheid. He had just returned from the site when the bell rang and it was Renate.

'My God, what a way to live! How can you bear it?'

'I only sleep here.'

'But these bare walls, that terrible wallpaper.'

'Yes,' he said, 'you have to look away.'

They had gone to the Italian where he often ate in the evening. Renate had told him about the feature on which she was working. She was interviewing workers who had taken over a bankrupt company and now ran it as a cooperative. Then they had gone back to Wagner's flat because he was expecting a phone call from Susann. He got a bottle of Frascati from the refrigerator and they sat by the open balcony window, it being a quite unusually hot September day and still warm even now, at night. They drank and smoked, touched glasses. Renate told him about another feature in which she was making a study of young people's slang, she'd say it was somewhere between bestial randy and full of shit. Suddenly she said Wagner's place was nice, even the wallpaper had lost some of its infinite dreariness. Wagner said it had to do with the open balcony and the street noises they heard. How silent, lifelessly silent the Hamburg suburbs are. 'It's nice you know how to listen. Listening is an art greater even than talking. No, I don't want to be compared to Moltke. You're the one who's hesitating,' she said, put her arm round his neck and kissed him, first on the cheek, then on the mouth. They undressed and went to bed. Afterwards they lay a long time together. Renate told him about Berthold, he really frightened her because he was so rough when they made love, even brutal. Aggression that had increased over the years, she was only waiting for the day he would strangle her.

Wagner was so surprised that at first he thought she was exaggerating. He said he could hardly associate that with the Berthold he knew, there was always something so good-naturedly oafish about him.

'I can't understand it either,' she said, and began to cry. From the bed Wagner looked over at the roof of the house opposite, where the light was on in the attic.

Renate had quickly recovered without him having to comfort her; what could he have said? For a year she had been considering whether they should separate, but it wasn't that easy, above all because of the children who adored Berthold. And he was especially loving and nice to the children. But she couldn't breathe the moment he entered the room. Even physically, and then he took everything upon himself, whatever had to be bought, every decision. She really regressed in his presence.

'One doesn't notice it when you're together.' 'Exactly,' she said, 'but it takes a great effort.' And then, after a short pause in which they lay silently side by side she said it was terrible, this feeling that would sometimes suddenly come over her, as if everything had stopped. The telephone rang. It was the call Wagner had been expecting, but he didn't answer. He lay beside Renate and listened to it ring, he would have liked to switch it off, and thought of Susann at home now sitting at the table, the phone in front of her. He knew she was smoking and had poured herself a glass of wine. At last there was silence. Renate got up, gathered her clothes from the floor and went to the bathroom. Wagner had got up and gone to the open window. Renate returned dressed and said: 'Don't tell Susann anything. Forget it.' She kissed him lightly and left. He heard the lift going down, she had gone – and he was grateful to her for it – to the hotel.

The next morning he found her lipstick on the ledge by the bath. He put it in the bathroom cupboard because he thought she might ask for it. But she didn't. They met almost every Friday evening when he came back from Lüdenscheid, either at his place or at Renate and Berthold's. They told each other about the events of the past week, and it always slightly irritated Wagner that in comparison to Berthold, who really got around a lot, so little had happened to him. Susann and Renate talked about some recent literary event, a film or radio program, while Berthold got under the table to show Wagner how narrow the cabin was on an Arab dhow. They drank and laughed. But occasionally Renate looked at him. And Wagner wondered whether she was sorry she had so exposed herself to him. Sometimes he was convinced she could go on talking, that he would hear from her again and that one day she would be outside his door at Lüdenscheid.

A few weeks ago as he was clearing out the flat (there were only a few things there anyway) he had found the lipstick. He pulled off the golden lid and unscrewed it. Half had been used, it was smoothly round and a wonderful colour, a dark cherry red he liked very much. He smelled the lipstick. A mild, faint smell of cherries. Then he threw it into the rubbish bin.

Wagner had turned on the car radio. The hill was already before him when suddenly he saw two figures in the headlights. They were walking at the side of the road and one of them had taken the other's arm as if to support him, as if he were drunk or injured. Wagner took his foot off the accelerator, was about to stop, then thought of what Bredow would have said, and drove on. He looked into the rear mirror, but it was dark.

Six

He was woken in the morning by the noise of a low flying helicopter. Sophie was busy in the kitchen.

She mumbled something that sounded like good morning.

She was spreading mayonnaise on slices of limp white bread. Standing, Wagner drank the coffee she had already put on the table for him. As she began piling the sandwiches into a red ice box he asked her, 'What religion won't allow you to run over snakes?'

'That is superstition', she said quickly 'the whoremongers are outside, the murderers and idolaters, and those who lie.'

'Who,' Wagner asked, 'who?'

'The Lord hath said the snake is of the devil and those also that do its work.'

Wagner put down his coffee cup, took the ice box and briefcase and left the kitchen. He heard Sophie come shuffling after him. He wondered whether it might not be better to find another housekeeper, better one that spoke no German than one that pestered him with crazy religious nonsense.

He turned off the alarm and unbolted the door. He plunged into a dark, sticky heat. The door fell shut behind him, locked and bolted from the inside. Moths reeled in the light of the headlamps. Wagner got into his car and drove down to the

49

barrier that was lit by two floodlights. A soldier with a submachine gun slung over his shoulder came from the guardhouse and greeted him.

The country road to the north was almost empty. He passed a few lorries driving in the other direction and a military jeep with headlights turned full on. A little later he came to a road block. Two military trucks had been positioned across the road. A military policeman in a white helmet signalled him to the roadside with a lit disc, to where the lorry was standing. Leaning against it, legs wide apart, stood the driver. A soldier was running his hands over the trouser legs. Scattered on the ground, in the headlights of a jeep, lay a few possessions, a pocket knife, a packet of cigarettes. A soldier had asked for Wagner's passport and driving licence, and when he saw it was a foreign passport handed everything on to an officer. The officer leafed helplessly through the passport and Wagner gave him the company's work permit. The officer saw the company's logo and let Wagner through.

In the headlights he saw fluttering and whirling. He thought of the snake. The fierce thrashing of the head and tail, the desperate attempt to pull the flattened body from the road. Wagner paid no attention to the road. He drove with indifference over whatever ran or crawled across it. From time to time creepers struck the windscreen or large insects, from which a jelly-like mass oozed. When he came to the clearing, into the sudden light of the rising sun, he saw the butterfly wings glued in front of him and shining yellow, dark blue and carmine red, the wonderful patterns of colour tattered at the edges.

He pulled up at the iron-barred gate to the office building. None of the engineers were there yet. He hooted. After a while a watchman came running. He had strapped a heavy revolver over his pyjamas. The man was barefoot. He had to fiddle a long time with the padlock before he could open the gate. In the office Wagner put on rubber boots and went over to excavation B. He stood at the edge of the huge excavation and stared into it. The three bulldozers were standing in mud. Water had gathered overnight in the caterpillar tracks. There could be no doubt, the water level was higher than it should have been according to the ground survey. Wagner went to site A. Plants had forced their way up through the grey ash. The shoots were small, delicate and a transparent light green, but darker and larger leaves that swallowed the light were already visible, lush and heavy. Wagner heard the siren from the office building. The workers came over from the Nissen huts and spread to different sites. Wagner kept going, following a narrow path through tall, proliferating plants, accompanied by a constant fear that he might step onto a snake. Steinhorst had said the land needed to be cleared by fire every three months. Not until trees for making paper had been felled over a wide area would the forest yield, and with it the rampant undergrowth. What would remain would be a red brown, hilly eroded plain.

Three lorries on which big concrete drums slowly rotated stopped at site A. One of the cranes swung the first bucket of concrete across. Nobody took any notice of Wagner. They didn't know who he was. It had been calculated that the site could bear the weight. He had already turned and gone a few steps in the direction of the office building when he stopped. Something he had seen had irritated him, without him knowing exactly what. He went back. In the excavation a supporting beam was being poured. Wagner could see that the supporting rods were missing. He suddenly heard himself yell, without self control and inarticulate. The workers in the excavation stared at him. Naturally they didn't understand him as he shouted: 'The rods are missing.' They turned off the electric concrete vibrator. The bucket of concrete hung from the crane, tilted over their heads, and swayed gently backwards and forwards. They were small, graceful men who looked up at him, Indians. Some of the men were barefoot, others wore sandals. Their shirts and trousers were in rags. They looked at him with passive composure. It suddenly struck him he was comical, standing here like this, perspiring, his face probably red with rage and sweat and with the sunburn he felt on his forehead. Wagner gesticulated and yelled and knew at the same time that what he was doing was wrong. He knew everything depended on how he introduced himself to the engineers and workers because the image they now formed of him would be decisive for the next few months. Others see us as we wish to be seen, that had been a rule to memorize on the company's management courses. He had resolved to be calm, precise and friendly, but no excessive familiarity, not even with the other engineers, brief clear instructions, think first, then decide but firmly, no undue excitement. Shrieking, leaping about soon wears thin and looks ridiculous in a manager. Wagner knew this and in Germany had always kept to it. He asked for the foreman. As he didn't know what that was in Spanish he tried a few words he was convinced were internationally understood: boss, kapo, chief. The man looked at him silently, neither friendly nor unfriendly, perhaps a little curious. Wagner realized all these words could equally well apply to himself and the men below might now think he wanted to indicate his role. It was ridiculous. The entire situation was ridiculous. Wagner was forced to retreat. He couldn't even send one of them for the interpreter but had to go himself, while they very likely continued to pour concrete into the mould.

He would have preferred to run, but to arrive running was obviously out of the question. Nevertheless he rushed into the canteen, drenched in sweat and breathless. The local engineers were standing about drinking coffee. They had, as Wagner realized, only just arrived. They stood holding small paper cups as if at a cocktail party. They stared at Wagner in alarm.

Wagner yelled: 'Juan'. He had only meant to say the name loudly and clearly but, out of breath, had shouted incomprehensibly. He had to call the name again. Now the Indian came. Wagner told him to interpret for the engineers that they were to meet here in the canteen in an hour, if, that is, they were no longer preoccupied drinking coffee. A mistake, Wagner thought immediately, another mistake. Playing the slave driver is wrong and petty. But to ask Juan not to translate the comment about drinking coffee would be a worse mistake. Juan most probably would have told the engineers later. Wagner asked where Steinhorst was.

'Not here yet,' Juan said.

'Then Hartmann should come.'

Wagner went with Hartmann and Juan to site A. The workers were standing just as he had left them, holding spades and concrete vibrators, the tilted bucket of concrete dangled over their heads. Wagner had Juan ask for the foreman. One of the men stepped forward and took the frayed straw hat off his head. Three parallel scars ran diagonally across his face from his forehead to his mouth. The right eyebrow was split in two places and had grown back not quite aligned. The man said something and Juan translated that the man had stayed at home today. The foreman, as Wagner discovered on enquiring, had not been on the site for three days. No, he wasn't ill, he was helping his brother-in-law build a house. They had started pouring the beams yesterday. They had used supporting rods in some, not in others. They had used rods until they ran out.

The man with the torn face pointed to the beams and then each time said 'Si' and 'No'.

Wagner gave the order to tear the wooden mould away from the beam that had just been poured. The men knocked down the pieces of wood. Some concrete slid out, exactly the half load from the bucket that still hung in the air. The base remained, it had obviously been poured yesterday.

'A monument to careless and sloppy work', Wagner said to Hartmann, who was the opposite of his name: shy, a smile as if perpetually apologizing on his face. As Juan began translating Wagner's comment, Wagner waved to him not to. The reproach applied to the men below least of all.

They returned to the site office. Hartmann said most foremen had to increase their pay with work on the side. Really one couldn't even complain, it was the general practice here.

'It's a practice we'll have to change', Wagner said.

In his office Wagner stood by the window and thought over what he wanted to say to the engineers. He looked out over the site, as seen from above, an area of confused and unplanned activity: bulldozers, cranes, tipper lorries, concrete lorries, around them people. Bustling activity, the sight of it bewildered Wagner. He simply could not succeed in concentrating on a detail, in visually isolating it. In the foreground a heavy lorry loaded with concrete pipes crossed the view, nearer still men shovelled something from one place to another, concrete slabs swung past. He tried to concentrate but could only hear a roaring in his head, the blood no doubt, but he had never known it so loud. The door was flung open. Steinhorst came into the room. He looked as if he had just fallen, his face was scratched and bloated, the eyelids inflamed and the tear ducts swollen, as if he had spent the night crying. Wagner smelled the exhalation of alcohol and stale cigarette smoke. His shirt and trousers were dirty. 'What's going on,' Steinhorst asked, 'they're all excited outside.'

'Such shoddy work, I've never seen anything like it. It beats everything.'

Agitated, it annoyed him that he had let Steinhorst lead him onto this subject instead of asking him where he had rested his battered head all this time. Steinhorst obviously had the drinker's knack, if ever one should want to refer to their weakness, of changing the subject.

'Yes,' Steinhorst said, 'incompetence and shoddy work, they're criteria better left in central Europe.' He drank greedily from a bottle of mineral water. He put it down and wiped his mouth with the back of his hand. 'Three weeks ago two multi-storeyed buildings collapsed in the capital. One still under construction, the other had been lived in for a few weeks. Twenty dead. He took a swallow from the bottle. It was twenty-five, yes, I think it was twenty-five. Wagner stared at Steinhorst. The uncontrolled thirst as he poured water into himself repelled him, as did Steinhorst's delight in disaster and the excessive sweating, Wagner had never seen sweating like this before. It ran from his pores as if he were instantly sweating out the water he poured into himself.

Wagner turned away and went back to the window. He looked across at the excavation in which the three bulldozers were at work. 'It's nothing but a swamp,' he said quietly. 'Yes,' he heard Steinhorst behind him, 'shortly after completion the factory will sink into the mud, but that's still better than collapsing.'

At last Wagner could yell, he yelled a second time. But now he couldn't bring down the volume: 'Nothing is going to collapse here, and the incompetence has to stop, I don't build ruins, we're not in Africa.' He turned to see Steinhorst calmly drain the bottle of mineral water and belch.

In the afternoon Wagner went with Steinhorst and Hartmann over to the excavation in which the bulldozers were at work. But only two were in use, one stood idle. Wagner had Juan ask why the bulldozer wasn't working.

'The sparking plugs are missing.'

'Why?'

'They've been taken,' Juan translated.

'They take everything: cement, the wood for the moulds, sparking plugs, screws, spades.'

'Who's they,' Wagner asked Hartmann, 'the Bolivians?'

'They're the least likely, they can't do anything with the

stuff, they all live here in the huts. But it could be anyone, including the engineers.'

'Then we'll check the cars before they leave the site. That also applies to engineers.'

'That'll create bad feelings.'

That morning Wagner had told the engineers and technicians assembled in the canteen that whoever was absent, as from now, would need to give a reason and with it a medical certificate. Wagner had threatened instant dismissal and with Steinhorst in mind, though not putting it directly into words, recall.

Wagner stood with Steinhorst and Hartmann at the edge of the excavation. If one of the two working bulldozers stopped for an instant, water immediately gathered between the tracks. The third bulldozer seemed already drowned in mud.

'No panic on the Titanic,' Steinhorst said.

Wagner wondered whether he ought to make the men stop work immediately. But first he wanted to talk to Bredow.

The siren wailed, two short bursts, one long.

'That's for you,' Hartmann said to Wagner. 'You must go to the office right away.'

Wagner started to run. After a few metres he was already breathless. The sweat poured down his face. He was exhausted, tired, he found it hard to think clearly: It's this crazy heat, he said to himself, the change of climate, the time difference, this weird talk of whoremongers and idolaters. The water in the excavation, the flattened snake, the bad luck it's supposed to bring, the supporting beams without the supporting rods. He was convinced a new disaster awaited him in the office, news of collapsed walls, snapped crane cables, overturned lorries, people wounded, perhaps dead. He rushed into the office, but there a technician simply held the phone out to him.

'Wagner,' he gasped into the receiver.

And then he heard Renate's voice. Across thousands of kilometres he heard that she would have liked to see him alone again before saying goodbye. She wanted to talk to him. She wanted to tell him she had good, really beautiful memories. Could she write to him? She'd like to write about her work, in fact about herself. He heard her and at the same time a woman's voice speaking Spanish, overlaid by sobbing. She's crying, he thought, but then he heard her talking again, then another voice that spoke English, and then another, incomprehensible, in a language he had never heard before, and then sobbing again. He listened to this far away babble of languages.

'Can you hear me?' Renate's voice called. 'Yes', he said, 'yes, but not clearly.' He stared at his notes, he had made them at the meeting that morning, had also noted the engineers' complaints, even the concrete came not mixed according to the proper ratio. Too much sand had been added. We're building on sand, Wagner thought, on a swamp. Then Renate's voice grew clear again, close. 'I want to leave Berthold,' she said, 'I can't bear it any longer.' For a moment he was afraid she would say being with him, that night, had finally made her see the light, but then she said that was quite independent of anything that had happened that time, and her voice again sank into the babble of languages. 'I can't hear you,' he shouted into the phone, 'I'm sorry'. What an idiotic thing to say, he thought and hung up. He hoped she had not been able to hear him properly, just as he had been unable to hear her. But he had to admit to himself that he would have liked to meet her again. Not to sleep with her again, but to talk, because bodily proximity had achieved one thing: openness. Suddenly one could talk about one's secret fears. He had wanted to ask her what this feeling was that she had described as everything coming to a halt. He had wanted to ask her at the time, but they had been interrupted by the phone, and later he no longer wanted to ask her when she had first become aware of the feeling. Was it comparable to the feeling that had come over him one day, a year ago at least, and returned with ever increasing frequency, a shortage of breath – he could only call it that – that he had first experienced cycling with Susann and Sascha in Jenisch Park, in other words in the open air, a feeling of being raw inside, of not being able to breathe properly, an anxiety that could be felt physically; but at the same time it was something more, as if he were letting go of everything, as if people and things had become separate from him in a dull indifference, as he had from himself, so that he saw himself sitting on the bike and his feet stupidly turning, and had to keep breathing out, breathing in, out and in. They rode through the park on the gravel path, other cyclists came towards them, their feet too were turning. What always disturbed him was that he had to cycle so slowly, not only because of Sascha, Susann also cycled slowly. It was a perfectly ordinary Sunday morning.

The attacks increased. But they only came at weekends, at home, in Hamburg, not in the Sauerland on his building site, not in Lüdenscheid, though he couldn't stand the dump. But then, three weeks ago at least, he had an attack there too, in the morning, surprisingly as he was going down in the lift, that small, cheerless lift covered in formica tiles, that dull tugging again, not in any way painful, but a tugging that came from inside and slowly crawled to his throat. For a moment he had had to hold onto the walls of the lift, then the door had opened at the bottom, and he was able to breathe again. It had never occurred to him to talk about it to Susann. Why not? It was the fear of questioning something taken totally for granted and decreed: their togetherness. And yet the feeling that for a long time something was missing had become deeply rooted, without him being able to say exactly what.

He stared at his notes. How would he get all this under control? But this was what he had wanted, had hoped for, gratifying problems. But where should he begin? He found it hard to prevent his mind from wandering. He wanted to make a list and then write down item after item, and number them according to urgency. He took the ballpoint pen and wrote 1, then got up again and looked out. In the middle of the site where the vegetation was coming up through the ash two lorries were unloading bricks. Why just there, in the middle of the clearing? They simply tipped the bricks anywhere. He wanted to run down, but told himself not to waste his energy. He had already lost himself in all kinds of petty detail. First he would have to clarify whether factory B did in fact belong where the excavation was being dug; in other words whether the ground survey corresponded to the present location, and if so, whether the plans for construction would need to be altered as otherwise the factory with its heavy machinery would sink, and the same would happen to the factory that was situated only two hundred metres away. Then he wanted to see the concrete about which one of the young local engineers had complained. (Juan had translated: 'It's muck'.) Wagner felt the sweat burn his forehead. In the lavatory he looked at himself in the mirror. Although he had been out only briefly yesterday without covering his head, his forehead was badly sunburned. His blonde hair hung sweat soaked from his head. He wanted to take a few steps in the open air. He put on the plastic helmet and went out into the fierce light. He stood for a moment and considered where to go. He thought it might be good for a change to take a look at the workers' accommodation. He went over to the nissen huts. He counted twelve of these corrugated iron huts, at least fifty metres long. There was no one in sight. For a moment he wondered if it was right to go there, now while the men were at the sites. But then he went. Because he had seen a pig. It lay in the shade of a hut, a big, dark brown, long haired pig. As he approached to look more closely it briefly raised its head, then went on dozing. But it seemed to him as if it had bared its teeth, unusually large and pointed fangs. He walked between the huts. The undergrowth had been trodden down. A few chickens scratched in the red sand. Ragged shirts and trousers hung drying on stretched lines. In a water-filled, dented tar barrel a dead animal floated, similar to a mole, it had long claws for digging on its front legs. There was a pair of rubber boots with holes, a hide stretched out to dry and nailed to a board, skin side up, a large fireplace made of brick, an oven for baking, a dog that got up as Wagner approached and went through a doorway hung with red plastic strips.

Wagner hesitated, then went to the door himself, hesitated again, then stepped over the threshold and was enveloped in an oppressive heat and an unbearable stench. He waited a moment until his eyes had become accustomed to the dark. Some cracks in the corrugated iron threw sharp streaks of light onto the beds carpentered from rough wood that filled the hut. The beds were two and three-tiered bunks on which lay sacks of straw. In front of the beds were boxes with a few possessions on them, knives, tinned food, pipes and tin cups. Wagner wanted to get out into the fresh air because he felt he was going to be sick when he heard panting, groaning, gasping. He strained to hear in the darkness of the hut, it came from the back, there somewhere, between the beds. Then the gasps were interrupted by coughing and he went cautiously further into the hut past the connected bunks until he saw the figure lying on one of the wooden beds. He stopped again because he thought something had moved at the back. But all he heard was the panting breath. The stench was unbearable. Cautiously he leaned over the figure, a small slightly built body covered, despite the heat, by a wool blanket full of holes. A youngish man whose eyelids rested heavily in their sockets. His breathing was a violent struggle for air. At the same time he could hear a buzzing. Next to the bed stood a clay jug with water. Wagner hesitated a moment, then with the hollow of his hand scooped a little water from the jug, hesitated, he was not sure it was good to let the man drink. He moistened the man's lips. He looked at the man's hand that lay open and as if relaxed on the blanket. Only then, through a hole in the wool blanket, did he see the blood soaked bandage on the chest and the yellow-green vomit by the straw sack, greasily gleaming, flies swarming on it. Wagner held his breath and ran out. He vomited before he got to the door. And outside he continued to retch, although he only brought up phlegm. He took a deep breath and with his heel tried to scrape sand over his vomit. Only then did he notice that someone was watching him. It was the man with the scars on his face. The man was standing in the narrow passage between two Nissen huts and had watched as he scraped sand over his vomit like an animal. It was humiliatingly ridiculous. Wagner turned abruptly and went back to the site office.

He went to the bathroom, took off the sweat-soaked khaki shirt and washed his face and the top half of his body. He drank some of the lemon tea Sophie had put in the ice box. Then he called Juan and asked him to ask the engineers gathered for the midday break, if anyone had been injured in the last few days, had there been an accident at work.

No one knew anything about anyone injured.

'In one of the Nissen huts there's somebody badly injured,' Wagner said and ordered an ambulance to be called from the city. Hartman wiped his freckled bald head and said: 'Accidents at work are always dealt with by the men themselves.'

'As they have their medicine men at hand,' Steinhorst explained.

'The man is badly injured', Wagner replied, 'perhaps dying. Call an ambulance.'

'It's better if they sort this out amongst themselves,' Steinhorst said, 'they let you know if they can't cope.'

'I simply don't understand how no one could have noticed, it's not just a scratch.'

'With a site this size? Nobody notices anything unless they

want us to. And that's their only protection. Otherwise they're instantly deported. Only a few of them have a work permit. Better leave them alone, they've their own way of doing things, one shouldn't meddle.'

'Call an ambulance', Wagner again ordered and went to his room. He saw them all staring at him as he went, the engineers and technicians eating their salads and sandwiches. They looked helpless and unsure. They had followed the argument, but understood nothing. But one of them looked at him and smiled a little. It was the same young engineer who had complained about the concrete. They must be thinking: a new broom sweeps clean, if there's such a saying in Spanish. He decided to ask Juan.

Wagner went to the window and watched the men coming from the site and going over to their huts. Some washed their face in the water barrels. Most went into the huts. Wagner kept his eye on the hut which he thought was the one in which he had found the injured man. Several men had gone in. Of those that came out again after a while to draw water or go with their tin plates to the cooking area, there was nothing that struck Wagner as unusual.

Then he sat down and began to study the ground survey and compare it to the building plan. The entire site had been shifted at least 500 metres to the west. And in fact a ground survey had been made for the new site, moreover by a state-owned firm. A good gravel base had been established for the location of factory B, which had also been shifted at least 500 metres from its original site.

In the late afternoon Steinhorst came in without first knocking. In one hand he had a bottle of bourbon, in the other two glasses. He pressed the door shut with his elbow on the door handle.

He put the glasses on Wagner's table, poured, said: 'We've

no more ice, but the whisky's been cooled. Drink,' he held a glass out to Wagner.

'A bit steep for you, all this,' Steinhorst said and refilled.

'Thank you,' Wagner held his hand over the glass, 'or I won't be able to drive.'

'Never mind,' Steinhorst said, 'apart from snakes there's nothing to run over.'

'Has the ambulance been?'

'No,' Steinhorst said, 'not yet, but Juan has phoned. If I can give you some advice, don't go to the huts. None of us do. And they don't come to us. The two worlds are neatly separate, and that's all to the good. If you want anything from them you'll have to deal with their spokesmen. Each hut has its elected spokesman. You've already spoken to one, that's the jaguar man.'

'Why jaguar man?'

'The man with the scars on his face. They say he fought a jaguar with his bare hands. Not on this site, on another, where the Bolivians were earlier. Apparently he was attacked by the animal and strangled it with his bare hands.' Steinhorst looked at his bare hands, as if to check whether they were capable of doing the same. He shook his head. 'Perhaps it's just one of those stories, it doesn't matter, the man enjoys a great reputation, even with the local engineers. Would you like some coffee?' Without waiting for an answer Steinhorst clapped his hands and when the little black man with grey frizzy hair came in, called out: 'Dos café!'

The sun was low in the west and shone in faint rays through the blind. The building plans with the brown imprint of coffee cups lay on the table, on top of them the empty glasses, the ashtray filled with stubs. I have to clear this table first, Wagner thought, this is still Steinhorst's table. Pedro came in. He was balancing two coffee cups on the large tray. He was unsteady, clearly he was drunk. Steinhorst said something in Portuguese to the man, who grinned, looked at Wagner, and poked his lips with his finger.

'What does that mean?' Wagner asked.

'Pedro says you'll like the coffee. He's the only black around here.'

Wagner drank the black, strongly sweetened coffee that slowly freed him of his listlessness. They sat in silence. Wagner had put his feet up on the table, something or other broke, but he didn't care. Steinhorst sat on the chair, arms resting on his legs, empty paper cup in his hand. He'll be thinking about his wife, her meetings with that man, the headmaster, about the dog and about the letter, Wagner thought, but didn't want to ask. He was afraid his question would release a flood of words that would drown his sympathy.

'If I can give you some advice,' Steinhorst said, 'let things take their course. Don't meddle. Do your job, but nothing extra. You can change nothing here. You'll only cause confusion. I'm going,' he said and stood up, 'perhaps you can give Juan and Hartmann a lift today. I'm not going straight to the city.'

Wagner went through the empty office building. He again looked out at the Nissen huts. In the cooking area, sheltered only by the corrugated iron roof, fires were already lit. The shadows at the edge of the clearing had lengthened.

Hartmann and Juan were standing down by the gate. Wagner had not imagined Indians so tall. Juan towered over Hartmann by almost a head. On the other hand the Bolivians – and they were Indians too – were small and slightly built.

Below the last lorry was leaving the area. Workers were standing on it crowded together. Some hung onto the door and stood with one leg on the running board. A man ran beside the slowly moving lorry looking for a place on the running board, but the lorry accelerated. The man gave up, stopped, then visibly exhausted went to a tree stump and sat down, his face buried in his hands as if he had lost everything. No sooner had the noise of the lorry faded into the distance than the forest could be heard, a babble of calls that increased by the minute, a singing, croaking, gurgling and snarling that slowly filled the clearing. Wagner got into his car. Hartmann sat in front, Juan at the back.

'Where are they going?'

'To the city,' Hartmann said, 'the Bolivians that have a work permit go to the city once a week. It's an important trip, they buy mainly tobacco and, of course, maté.'

Wagner stopped by the man on the tree trunk.

'Come on, tell him to get in,' he said to Juan.

Juan spoke to the man from the lowered window. The man only looked up briefly (he was still panting from running), shook his head and said something.

'What did he say?'

'He doesn't want to.'

Wagner drove into the forest.

'Why didn't the man want to come?'

'Don't know,' Juan said, 'but perhaps because of the snake.'

'What about the snake?'

'No one really knows,' Hartmann said, 'the snake has a special significance for some of the Bolivians. It's supposed to be the Inca snake. It's a kind of life symbol. Anyone who deliberately kills it dies, at any rate that's what the technicians here say, and they've only heard it from someone else.'

'Dies?'

'Yes, drowns, apparently.'

Wagner laughed. 'It's an accurate prophecy, if I look at the excavation. The entire factory is going to sink.'

'Are there any problems with the Bolivians?'

'No, none at all. They're quiet and quite unaggressive.'

'When's the ambulance coming?' Wagner asked Juan.

'De har to don. But soon, come soon.'

Wagner had to laugh again. 'How did the Mannonites get to be in the Gran Chaco?'

'Coomin' out a Roshyia.'

'Then say it in Russian please, because I don't understand your dialect,' Hartmann said.

'I'm sorry,' Juan said and dropped the dialect. 'Well, the Mennonites came to Paraguay fifty years ago, in fact from Russia where they'd emigrated two hundred years ago. They originally came from Fresia. After the revolution they came to the Gran Chaco where my tribe lives and settled there. So we became labourers on their land and learned Mennonite from them. I was the first they sent to a missionary school, in Basel. I would have learned Swiss dialect there if a woman making documentaries hadn't made a film about me. I left the missionary school and went with her to Berlin. I lived and studies there for three years,' Juan laughed. 'Ethnology'.

'And why did you come here?'

'It's now happen what happen, ok happen different.'

Hartmann had fallen asleep. His head hung heavily on his chest and jolted at every bump.

'And don't you want to go back to your people?'

'No can, me yes, general say no.'

'And here?'

'Dictators are the same in every country, but they like to set the left at each other's throats.' Juan laughed. 'That's national pride.'

It was dark when they reached the city. Lights were on everywhere and people sat out on the street, the men in clean, ironed pyjamas. Juan pointed to the block of flats where he wanted Wagner to stop. Hartmann started and said he must have dozed off for a moment.

Wagner asked Juan if he knew anyone who could give him Spanish lessons.

'I look see.'

66

Wagner was going to shake hands with Juan, but he quickly reached past the outstretched hand and grabbed Wagner's wrist, like someone grabbing a drowning man to hold onto him. Now I've found someone, Wagner thought, to whom I can talk without the others understanding. Of all people, an Indian who speaks a dialect I understand. Wagner had to laugh.

Seven

The next morning Wagner was again the first outside the site office. On the first day he had thought the high fence had been put up against predatory animals. This turned out to be a rather exotic idea, as Steinhorst had explained to him that the fence had been erected because of the workers, in case they ever came over, and saying it had pointed to the Nissen huts.

Wagner went to his office and from his window watched the sun rise over the forest.

Sometimes on a Saturday morning when the rattling of lawn-mowers in neighbouring gardens woke him, Susann next to him, head buried in the pillow and blowing little bubbles as she breathed quietly, able to sleep despite the noise, he felt a desire, the more urgent for being vague, for things to be different. But how?

Below buses were now pulling up outside the building. Two jeeps came from the forest, in each jeep three soldiers. They were military police, as the soldiers wore white steel helmets. The jeeps stopped in front of the building. Two soldiers came over to the entrance. They were wearing shining white gaiters.

A little later there was a knock at the door. Juan came in and said a captain wanted to speak to Wagner.

A slightly built young man came in behind Juan, his white steel helmet under his arm. The captain saluted and explained in clumsy German how much he admired the Germans, then switched to Spanish, and Juan translated: The captain would like to know in which hut Wagner had seen the injured man.

Wagner only now again remembered the man.

'What's been done about him?'

'The ambulance came last night. But they didn't find any injured man. The workers say they don't have anyone that's been injured.

'Nonsense,' Wagner said.

'The captain asks if you would please show him where the injured man was.'

Wagner went with Juan and the captain over to the Nissen huts. A few paces behind them the two military policemen, the safety catch released on their submachine guns, as Wagner noticed. What a performance, he thought. There were workers in front of the huts, some washing themselves, others crouching at the entrance and drinking maté. Now and then one of them would come from a hut, bleary-eyed, black hair tangled and flattened.

Wagner went to the hut in which he thought he had been yesterday. The jaguar man stood at the entrance. He held the straw hat in his hands, the scars on his face glowed red. His eyebrows, grown together crooked, gave him an arrogant look. Several men still lay on the bunk beds, others sat on boxes in the gangways, others stood and talked. They fell silent when Wagner, and behind him the captain and Juan, entered. The jaguar man followed them.

But where yesterday a two-tiered bunk had stood, now stood a three-tiered bunk. Things seemed to have been moved around. There was a stool where yesterday he had seen a box with pipes. The captain's helmet glowed white. It had obviously been painted with luminous paint. A good target, the thought flashed through Wagner's head.

'Have you found the place?' Juan asked.

'It's not quite as a I remember it. Perhaps that's because yesterday the huts were empty.'

The captain, without waiting for Juan's translation, had given an order to the two soldiers. They went into the hut and shouted instructions. A moment later the men crowded into the open. Wagner was astonished that there were so many men in the hut. It was as if they had gone round the hut and climbed in at the back in order to come out again at the front. When no one else came out Wagner went back into the hut and along the bunks that were randomly placed, and the more he looked the more he began to doubt. Had he not perhaps after all been in another hut? He came out and went into the next hut and then the next, the same scene everywhere: bunks confusingly arranged, and men in rags lying or sitting on the beds. He went back to the hut he had been in first. In the meantime Steinhorst had arrived and stood grinning. It was a grin of undisguised malicious satisfaction. Wagner went through the hut again. Overhead the siren wailed the call to work. He flinched, the sound was so loud and shrill here. He went to a bunk in which he thought the man might have lain yesterday. He leaned over the straw sack. But he could not smell anything, at least not the stench of blood and vomit. The captain turned on a torch and ran the light over the straw sack. There were no blood stains to be seen.

The captain wanted to know, had what Wagner had seen been dried blood or fresh. Was the man ill or had he been injured?

'Naturally I didn't see the wound, but I did see a blood stained bandage.' Wagner forced his way past the jaguar man and the captain with his white glowing helmet and went out. He needed to take a deep breath. Outside the men had gone to their places of work. Only one stood next to the sergeant, an Indian wearing threadbare army trousers, much too big for him.

The captain said: 'Gracias'.

'They want to take him,' Juan said to Wagner.

'Who?'

'The man, the Bolivian. They say he doesn't have a residence permit.'

'Just a minute,' Wagner said, 'he can't just take one of the men away. What do they want with him?'

Juan and also Steinhorst spoke to the captain. Wagner heard Steinhorst's strong German accent.

'What's going on? What's he saying?'

'He says he doesn't have a passport, and no residence permit.'

'Tell him we need the man. I shall complain.'

The captain, who had understood, said, heavily rolling the r: 'Terribly sorry, regulations. Goodbye.'

They went over to the two jeeps. A soldier with a submachine gun sat by the Bolivian. Both jeeps left through the gate in the direction of the forest.

'You must phone Bredow immediately, if he backs us we'll get the man back,' Steinhorst said.

'What will they do with him?'

Steinhorst shrugged: 'Deport him. They'll put him on a group transport and send him across the border. Hopefully.' The scratch on Steinhorst's forehead had become inflamed and glowed a swollen blue-red.

An engineer was waiting at the site office. He was talking to Juan, his face red with excitement. Wagner had already noticed the man at the meeting when he had complained about the concrete.

Steinhorst said: 'This is engineer Esposito. He's complaining about the concrete again. He's an idealist of the enthusiastic variety. He's been pestering me for weeks. Says we're squandering the country's wealth. A man who'll repeat to you over and over, no bungling, no corruption.'

'What does he want?'

'He says the concrete's even worse than usual today.'

'Good, I'll see to it.'

Wagner went to his room. He sat down and thought, the concrete supplier wants to see how much he can get away with, with me. 'Not much,' Wagner said and realized he was talking aloud to himself. He turned on the table fan. I can't have been that mistaken, he thought, and why have they arranged the beds in that chaotic way.

He phoned Bredow's office. A Mrs Klein answered the phone and said she would be so pleased if he were to call at the city office, then she could meet him. Mr von Bredow had already enthused about him.

Wagner promised to drop in within the next few days and asked for Bredow. He wasn't there and wasn't expected back until tomorrow. Could she help in any way?

'A Bolivian was arrested today.'

'Oh dear, oh dear. But only Mr von Bredow himself can help you there.' Wagner pulled the fan closer and cooled his face, which dripped sweat. He read the notes he had made for himself yesterday and which stated the problems under headings: theft, water level, absence without leave, Susann, ground survey. He had actually included Susann. His handwriting suddenly seemed unfamiliar, as if written by someone else.

Eight

On the Sunday morning as Wagner walked to his car the shadows were still long and cool. He threw a tennis racket and bag onto the back seat. And as he had the time, he drove slowly up the hill. A maid was washing a Chevrolet and spraying some children who ran away shrieking. In one garden a family were at breakfast, the woman in a white blouse, the man and the children in white shirts.

Bredow had told him the English had come here at the turn of the century and – in the middle of the primeval forest – built a saw mill. The quebracho trees, being exceptionally hard wood, had been felled, cut into railway sleepers and shipped to England. Then in the thirties the sawmill had been abandoned. The rain forest had been cut down, except on this hill where the English directors and engineers had their houses. 'You'll see,' Bredow had said, 'at the bottom of the hill you can still find some of the old rain forest vegetation, while at the top there are exotic trees such as oak and scots pine.' At the top of the hill the houses did in fact look as if they were in Cornwall or Devon. And wealthy local families inhabited them, those Bredow had called rancid because they had been here so long. Wagner drove down the road again past villas, cube-shaped, plastered white, iron tube railing on the verandas and balconies, in fact built in pure Bauhaus style. Here lived the Jewish doctors and lawyers who had fled Germany in 1933. In their midst rose the first typically German gabled roofs of the fifties. Here, as Bredow had said, lived the nazis who had come to the country in 1945. Wagner drove slowly past the plots of land. There were blue spruce in the gardens and, Wagner was convinced no one at home would believe this, garden gnomes holding spades and pick axes. A grey-haired man in short trousers, sandals on his feet, was standing hosing a lawn. He looked with curiosity at Wagner. One house was like a prison, surrounded by a wall at least two metres high. Then came the dreary bungalows in which the managers and engineers, local and foreign, lived; dreary bungalows such as one also found in Hamburg, but in the gardens there were palms, bottle trees and quebracho trees. Then came the wall that surrounded the hill. Beyond it the plain began.

Wagner drove past the guard to the western edge of the city. The tennis courts covered a large area, already visible from the hill. The trees, still tied to stakes, had clearly only been recently planted, and in places one could still make out the squares of lawn that had been laid: fine lines in the deep green that appeared artificial against the surrounding dusty red. Around the club grounds there was a high wire fence with barbed wire coiled at the top. Wagner slowly drove the length of the fence looking for a place to park the car in the shade. To the left of the road were shacks and huts with big dented water tanks on the roofs. He parked the car close to a whitewashed wall. On the wall three letters had been painted in red and black, not in a hurry but carefully, the black bordered by the red: PIR.

On the footpath, sitting right by the fence, was a soldier. In front of the soldier was something bulky, dark. A few steps away stood a dog. Now, approaching, Wagner saw it was a man that lay on the ground. On his stomach, left arm stretched out, leg slightly pulled up, the face half turned, a face still young, cheek in the dust as if asleep, carefully dressed, light blue shirt, beige trousers, black casual shoes, dusty except where the trousers had rubbed them in running and the polished leather gleamed. Next to him on the sand was a dark, damp patch. The soldier was sitting on a can and smoking, the submachine gun by him on the ground. He looked at Wagner from under his helmet with a brief, shy smile. He was very young, almost a boy. Suddenly he stamped with his heavy paratrooper's boots to chase away the dog, a mangey cur that had slunk to the damp patch, sniffing greedily. The dog ran away with tail tucked in, but not far, and then stopped. Wagner walked on. He wanted to turn, but refused to let himself. Only when he reached the entrance – a concrete oval in the shape of a tennis racket – did he look back. The soldier had got up and was throwing stones at the dog. An attendant in a black uniform opened the door. Wagner went to the club building. Gardeners were watering the poplars and shrubs. Others were crawling between the flower beds with garden shears.

Bredow, Christi and Durell were on the court already, warming up.

Wagner was unable to concentrate on the game and so he and Durell narrowly lost. After the game, when they met under one of the straw umbrellas in the garden restaurant, Durell said: 'Once we've got into our stride we'll break the supremacy of the Bredow family.'

Wagner watched the ring of bubbles that had formed round the slice of lemon floating in his glass of coke.

'I've just seen a dead man on the street.'

'A dead man?' Christi looked alarmed at Wagner.

Bredow wiped his face with a white towel.

Durell drank his Cuba Libre.

'Where did you see the dead man?' Durell asked.

'Outside by the fence.'

'And where did you park?'

'Over there, by the houses.'

'You should drive onto the club grounds,' Bredow said, 'the entrance is over there. Members and friends can leave their cars here.'

'The man was lying on the street. Shot. There was a soldier by him sitting on a can. And a dog.'

'A dog?'

'Yes, the dog was trying to get at the blood of the man that had been shot.'

'Horrible,' Christi said, 'it's dreadful.'

'Yes,' Bredow said, 'these are bad times.'

There was something on the wall opposite: PIR.

'That's the guerillas,' Durell said. 'There's a war on, a dirty war. But the military will pull it off. They've been well trained, and at least the officers are well motivated.'

'Yes,' Bredow said, 'it's all a bit hard to understand for those that are new here. From over there it all looks quite simple. A military dictatorship, withdrawal of human rights. But for those here who lived through it and what went on before, and who really know the circumstances, everything is much more complex. You should have been here then, the raids, the kidnappings, the attempts on people's lives. The military had to intervene. Instead we now have a normal situation, even if terrible things still happen.'

'The situation is never normal here,' Durell said. 'At any rate I always have a case packed for flight, small, handy, documents, some money, dollars naturally, some gold, but not too heavy to carry so one can cover a fair distance on foot.'

'Light luggage packed for flight won't help you either,' Christi said. 'The international airport will be closed long before you get there.'

'Naturally, if you intend to drive there on the state highway. One has to go by another route. And always the shortest that takes you to the frontier. Airports, and this is experience gained in Africa, are always the first to be taken by rebels, airports and TV stations.'

'Well yes,' Bredow said, 'but we haven't come to that yet. But we'll give you a return match.' He got up.

'When?' Durell asked.

'Tomorrow morning.'

'Can't manage that, I have to be at the site early,' Wagner said and thought, how can I talk in that self important way as if getting up early and having to go to work were something to brag about. 'For the time being it's important I'm there early.'

But Bredow only laughed and slapped him on the shoulder. 'That's what they pay you for.'

'Were you able to do anything about the Bolivian?'

'No,' Bredow said, 'unfortunately. It was the weekend, the offices are all closed. And one can't go to the administrator with small problems like that.'

'All the same, he's one of our workers. What will they do with him?'

'He doesn't have a passport, a work permit. They'll put him over the border.'

'I have to go,' Durell said, 'see you soon.'

'We really must still discuss a few things, the concrete and the water level in the excavation.'

'Fine,' Bredow said, 'come home with us. First we'll take you in our car over to yours.'

When they came to the fence the body had disappeared. And the soldier. But the dog was still there licking the dark, damp patch on the sand.

Nine

At about noon Wagner drove home, still in his tennis clothes, sweaty, tired and – although he had only drunk two martinis at Bredow's – dazed. To the question about the location of the factory Bredow had replied that it had in fact been shifted, but in accordance with regulations they had asked for a detailed survey from a local firm. The siting of the building was in any case a matter for the state authorities. And then Wagner said the entire factory would sink into the mud in five years, if it hadn't already floated away during the first long rains, Bredow had replied that the same prophecy had been made about the cement factory five years ago. But it was still standing. 'Five years isn't exactly a long time,' Wagner said and suggested building a basement for factory B. Factory A's foundations would have to be put on an even keel by adding supports. Possibly rebuilding, but this time with a basement, would be more economical.

Bredow looked at Wagner as if he had gone mad. 'Listen,' he said, 'I don't understand the technical side at all, but I do know a thing or two about business. This is all quite impossible. The calculations for this project are extremely tight and we were only given a supplement after considerable sums of money had been paid in bribes, which actually used up the last of our reserve funds. There simply isn't more here.' Bredow, who was sitting on the veranda in his swimming trunks, laughed, 'try reaching into the pocket of a naked man.'

'We're building the Tower of Babel,' Wagner said.

Bredow had laughed again. 'One can and one must quite simply go on building.'

'And the wretched concrete? And then the stealing, even the sparking plugs from the bulldozers.'

'Something can be done about that, I'll put in a couple of extra watchmen.'

What had annoyed Wagner most about this discussion was that often Bredow had not even listened properly. With his obliging smile he had looked past Wagner at a television behind Wagner. A football match was on. Once, when a goal was scored, Bredow had actually leaped up. Bredow tried to explain the positions in the national leagues. He named names, clubs, cities, players that meant nothing to Wagner. In the end, while talking about ratios for mixing concrete and groundwater pressure, Wagner also began turning round more and more. In the bungalow Wagner went into the kitchen. He was hungry and craved an apple. Sophie was busy at the stove. He asked her for a coffee and, as there were no apples, took a mango. Sophie peeled it for him and muttered that someone was waiting for him in the garden. The whore of Babylon.

Wagner went, eating the mango, into the garden. On the veranda Juan was sitting at the white table with a girl, slight build, dark hair, who got up as Wagner came to the table.

'This is Luisa.'

Wagner wondered if she was Juan's daughter. Not that she had the distinctive Indian features, but she had the same blue-black hair, black eyes and unusually long, straight lashes, and beneath them the eyes lay in shadow. The girl was perhaps sixteen, she had delicate limbs as if still in the process of growing and small upright breasts under her white cotton dress.

Juan wanted a coffee, the girl water.

Wagner called Sophie.

She arrived muttering and snorting through her large nostrils. For some reason she disapproved of this visit.

'Luisa is a Spanish teacher,' Juan said.

She had sat down again and pulled her cotton dress over her brown thighs to her knees. She sat like a schoolgirl expecting at any moment to be asked a question.

'Is this supposed to be a joke,' Wagner said.

'Why?' Juan asked.

Sophie brought coffee, fruit juice and water. Without being asked she had even brought a plate of biscuits.

'You must be trying to pull my leg, the girl's still at school.'

The girl went red and said something to Juan. She got up, prepared to leave, Juan also got up and said something to her.

'Does she understand German,' Wagner asked.

'No, French, she misunderstood. She thought, well, you know.'

'Tell her, all I want is to learn Spanish. But she's very young.'

'She's nineteen, but she's a teacher. You can teach in primary school as soon as you've finished secondary school. But they let her go after three months.'

'Why?'

Juan briefly raised a hand – 'who knows?'

The looks Wagner had been giving her had not escaped the girl. As if deliberately she changed her position and put her legs together, a touching attempt, Wagner thought, to give a respectable impression. She had small feet, a child's feet, inside high heeled shoes. The shoes were neatly polished, but the leather on the heels was scuffed.

'Good,' Wagner said, 'we can give it a try.' He was convinced Juan wanted to help this girl. They'd probably thrown her out at the school or she'd run away from home.

Sophie came with a tray. She had put a blue checked apron

over her white overall and carefully put her grey hair up in a pony tail. She handed out plates, knives and forks and put a tray of sandwiches in the middle of the table. With a gesture Wagner invited the girl to take something. And she immediately took a sandwich and holding it wrapped in a paper napkin ate it quickly, although she made an effort to seem relaxed. She was hungry.

'Where are the lessons to be?'

'Here would be the best place,' Juan said. 'As you've a housekeeper Luisa can come here. But you must provide her with a letter so she can get past the guard down there.'

'Good,' Wagner said. She could not have known Juan too well as he had to repeatedly ask her for information, her address, how she had come here. On foot or by bus.

'How much?'

Wagner interrupted Juan and said the company would pay. She would get a good wage. Did she want to be paid by the hour or by the week?

'By the week.'

'When could she begin?'

Wagner looked at the girl, she was eating the third sandwich. 'Now, if she wants, as she's here. But I'd like to change and have a swim first.'

Juan and Luisa whispered quietly together.

'Luisa wants to stay,' Juan said, but he would have to go now.

'Shall I call for you tomorrow?'

'No thanks, I'll take the company bus.'

He accompanied Juan to the door.

Luisa sat leaning back in the chair. Wagner noticed that she must have put at least two sandwiches in her straw bag.

'Voulez vous nager?'

'Merci, non. J'attends, je lirai quelque chose.'

She spoke French the way the driver had spoken German.

From time to time he looked at her as he swam. She was reading a book and had put on large blue sunglasses.

He watched her put her finger to her mouth – a gesture both childish and erotic – and then turn the page. When he was dressed and came to her she took off the sunglasses and looked at him, not in the least unsure, but as if quietly assessing him. He indicated the book she held open in her lap: he read, *El siglo de las luces*. She had small narrow hands, the fingers were deep brown, pale pink on the palm side, the finger nails carefully painted red in strange contrast to her face that was without make-up. Wagner, who had leaned over her to read the book's title, felt her hair softly brush against him. It was like a small shock, and he had a sudden wild desire to touch her, her neck, the soft skin in which the collar bones were lightly delineated. She put her sunglasses back on and said in an emphatically businesslike way: 'Il faut travailler'.

She reached into her straw bag, in a way that prevented Wagner from seeing inside, and took out a tattered Spanish text book and put it in front of her on the table.

He sat down at the garden table the way a schoolboy sits opposite a teacher.

'Yo mo llamo Luisa,' she said and with her index finger with its red nail tapped her chest. She took off her sunglasses, got up and walked up and down in front of Wagner like a mannequin on a catwalk, upright, with legs straight and short energetic steps, pelvis slightly pushed forward, right hand on her hip: 'Yo camino,' she said and waved to Wagner to get up: 'Usted camina!' She moved her hand as if conducting.

He got up and walked up and down, tense and awkward because he was concentrating entirely on how he moved.

She watched him closely as if, in order to learn Spanish properly, he would first have to learn to move.

'Usted habla: Yo camino.'

'Yo camino,' he said.

'Bravo,' she cried.
Wagner had to laugh at her delight.

Ten

In the afternoon a messenger had come and delivered an envelope from the Vosswinkel family: on heavy deckle-edged, hand-made paper, an invitation to an evening reception. Addressed to F.L. Wagner B.Sc. Eng. In sloping old-fashioned handwriting: Dear Mr Wagner, only now do I learn of your esteemed presence on our hill. May I therefore invite you, at short notice but no less eagerly for that, to our reception this evening. Sincerely, Vosswinkel. Wagner had phoned Bredow and asked him who this was. 'You absolutely must go,' Bredow had said, 'it's your professional duty, as it were. The entire German colony meets there.'

The invitation requested a black tie and so Wagner wore his dark blue double-breasted suit. After dusk had set in he drove up the hill. The house was almost at the top, immediately below the English country houses. At the open wrought iron gate two torches burned. A butler in grey livery directed Wagner to the parking area, at the centre of which stood a huge palm tree. The way to the villa was lit by small oil lamps. Wagner walked over the crunching gravel to the building, the base of which was of large square blocks of stone. The narrow high windows were of coloured glass and the facade was topped with battlements and two corner towers. The house, probably built after the turn of the century, resembled a castle in rural Tuscany. White marble steps led to an entrance hall supported by columns, from the ceiling of which hung a massive wrought iron chandelier fitted with neon lights. A tapestry with faded parrots and birds of paradise made waves against the wall. It smelled of mould and mothballs, a smell that grew stronger as the host, Mr Vosswinkel, approached and greeted Wagner. Vosswinkel was wearing an anthracite coloured wool suit with immense turn-ups on the trousers. Vosswinkel was as tall as Wagner, at least one ninety, but more massive and with a box-shaped head from which his eyebrows hung like heavy grey brushes.

'Welcome,' Vosswinkel said, 'so you've come to build our paper factory for us. Do you know what it was that caused the tepidarium of the Baths of Caracalla to collapse?'

But before the giant could offer an explanation his niece, who looked considerably older than he did, arrived. An old woman in a sleeveless dress that Wagner at first took for an overall. 'Come,' she said, 'I want to introduce you to the Intendente.'

This was a youngish man in a narrow fitting white uniform with thick silver epaulettes. He stood at the centre of the entrance hall. All attention seemed to be direct towards him. He greeted, nodded and exchanged a few words with those queuing to meet him, when their turn came. Miss Vosswinkel led Wagner past this queue of waiting people straight to the officer.

'Colonel,' she said, 'may I introduce the new manager of the paper factory, Mr Wagner.'

The Intendente shook hands with Wagner and Wagner was startled. He felt something lifeless and dry. The man was wearing white gloves.

'Most welcome,' the colonel said in accent-free German. When he heard Wagner was from Hamburg he praised the opera and the view of the Elbe. He had lived three years in Hamburg and been a guest at the Federal Military Academy.

With strangely lustreless dark brown eyes he gave Wagner a scrutinizing look.

'I know what you're thinking,' he said, 'but believe me, we would all be very happy if we could return to our barracks.'

With a slow movement the fan standing in a corner pressed the silk dresses of the women between their legs.

'What I most admire in the Germans is the reconstruction after the war. I've seen photographs of the destroyed cities. It's almost unbelievable, the way this destroyed country was rebuilt in fifteen years. We should have a little of that energy, that application and sense of duty in this country of ours. And the country's rich, you know, and the people are fundamentally well-disposed.'

A waiter in a white musical comedy uniform brought wine glasses on a silver tray.

'I can recommend the white, a local wine, not a Rhein wine naturally, but not at all bad.' He handed Wagner a glass and took one for himself from the tray. 'To success.' He savoured the wine as if at a wine tasting, nodded to Wagner and asked if there were any problems. 'Well, problems,' Wagner said and wondered if he should talk about his problems to this colonel in a white uniform who smelled so pungently of aftershave. 'They send us wretched concrete, the water level's too high, the sparking plugs disappear from the bulldozers and what's more, the factory's not actually where it should be.'

The colonel laughed: 'Yes, this is all shocking to a newcomer.' The laugh disappeared. 'That's the problem in this country: this incompetence, this lack of any sense of duty. We want to modernize, but lack the simplest prerequisites. People come when they feel like it and they take what they want because they believe it belongs to them. To say nothing of superstition. Instead of relying on engineering they bury dead

86

dogs in the concrete because they believe that keeps up the bridge.'

'Dead dogs?'

'Yes, or cockerels. It's quite unbelievable. You're sure to experience it yourself. Only the army functions according to European standards. That's why we had to take over the country's regeneration. Don't imagine we were desperate for the job. But the country would have sunk into chaos. We would have had a civil war here, by contrast what we have now is a trifling affair. They should have seen it before we took over the government. And that's what the know-all critics in your country forget.'

In the city Wagner had seen the poster with the head of the Junta here and there, a general with a heavy black walrus moustache. The face was already familiar from the papers in Germany. While the adminstrator was talking Wagner had noticed something small and round in the breast pocket of the uniform jacket that left an impression on the thin material, then he realized it might be a contraceptive and immediately remembered – for the first time in years – what they used to call it: assault equipment.

'I hope,' the colonel said, 'we shall meet at a less formal occasion. I'm curious to hear your views on the country and the people.' He gave Wagner his gloved right hand. Wagner walked through the large room, on one side of which a buffet had been set up. Bredow was standing there, he waved and came over.

'You've already had a chat with the city's strong man,' he said.

'Who's that?'

'Colonel Kramer. Son of German immigrants, as you can tell from the name and good German. After the coup, though still very young, they made him the city's military governor. The mayor disappeared. Colonel Kramer, as you can well imagine, is extremely important to our project. Without him nothing's possible here, with him everything.'

Wagner saw the colonel being led to the buffet by Miss Vosswinkel and then fork some crab out of the vegetable stock. He had taken off his gloves and put them in the side pocket of his uniform jacket.

'Well,' Bredow said, 'the buffet's open, the Intendente's eating, we can start. I can recommend the river crab. The meat dishes are mostly tough because Vosswinkel has his oldest cattle slaughtered for the occasion.'

They stood with their plates by a wall on which hung an enormous oil painting of guachos lassoing a cow. An old man was making his way through the groups of people, concentrating completely on the plate he was carrying on the palm of his hand like a tray. The man had shoulder-length grey hair.

'This is Mr Bley,' Bredow said.

As if he had heard, the man looked up. He greeted Bredow, asked after Christi and the children and held out a small narrow hand to Wagner.

'Mr Bley is the best confectioner in the entire country,' Bredow said. Bley looked at Wagner with a distracted smile.

'It's not hard to be a good confectioner in this country. The heat makes people oversweeten everything, sweetness stimulates sweating, one always forgets the bitter is complimentary to the sweet and the appeal is in discovering the taste of the one in the other.'

Bley had an Austrian accent.

'Had he learned confectionary in Vienna?' Wagner asked.

'No, Bley said. I'm an autodidact.' He took off his narrow gold-rimmed glasses and polished the lenses. 'I was a singing coach in Graz until 1938. Then I came here with my wife, a singer, and as one couldn't make a living by music we opened a confectionery. Neither my wife nor I had ever baked even a simple cake before, to say nothing of fancy cakes. And in its texture our first Sachertorte bore a certain resemblence to liquid asphalt. Also in taste, my wife maintained.' He laughed and spilled mayonnaise down himself. He put the plate down on a table and began to wipe the lapel with a napkin.

'Mr Bley's chocolates are the best I've ever tasted,' Bredow said. 'They're covered in bitter chocolate and have the most incredible centres, for instance date jelly with arrak. They're little works of art, even the shapes, symmeterical and asymmetrical and covered with little coloured pearls of sugar. Black Diadem, that's the name of one gift box. If you take them home in the summer, that's to say at Christmas, without putting them in an ice box, they melt into unsightly black-brown lumps that strangely enough lose nothing of their taste. And that's how the quite unique seasonal custom of melting Bley's chocolates came about. On New Year's Eve, often the hottest time of the year, people buy Bley's chocolates, but they don't put them in the ice compartment immediately. Just after midnight they're taken out. And the entire German colony then tries to read the future in the wierdly set shapes: Siamese twins that one devours with relish.'

Wagner laughed and said, 'It's a beautiful nutritious custom.'

'Do you know,' Bley said, 'the secret of enjoyment lies in the taste buds, those narrow, longish sensory cells that have begun to decrease by the age of twenty and that in old age are reduced by a third. Those with the richest palate are precisely those who can't afford its delights, or are forbidden them, children.'

Wagner noticed a strange, gradually increasing uneasiness in Bley, repeatedly and at ever shorter intervals he tapped the gold bridge of his glasses, tugged at the knot of his silver tie as if it were choking him, brushed back his grey hair, all the while looking past Wagner. Wagner turned and saw a tall gaunt man with a deeply suntanned face, his thinning grey hair carefully parted. He looked like an old tennis coach or ski instructor and approached, slowly making his way along the buffet, holding an overfilled plate. His dinner jacket bulged on the left side as if with a heavy wallet.

'There are even animals,' Bley said, staring at the man, 'that can taste with their feet. So for instance the ends of a butterfly's legs are a thousand times more sensitive when it comes to tasting sugar than the tongue of a human being.' Bley turned abruptly and left.

Before Wagner could ask the reason for Bley's uneasiness, Bredow said, 'this is Mr von Klages.'

Klages had come up to Bredow.

'What was your name?' Klages asked, after Bredow had introduced Wagner. Klages stood leaning forward a little to be sure of catching the name.

'Wagner,' he repeated, his face set in thoughtful distrust. Where did Wagner live in Germany? And had Wagner's father also been an engineer?

'No,' Wagner said, 'manager of a factory that made batteries.'

'And was Wagner's father the Colonel Wagner on the General Staff?'

'No,' in the war his father had been in the navy. This information for some reason seemed to calm Mr Klages. He changed the subject, praised the buffet, made a joke about Mr Vosswinkel who every evening searched the sky for extraterrestrial flying objects with his telescope, and said, after looking briefly into Wagner's eyes, he was sure Wagner would succeed with the factory even if building conditions were chaotic. Wagner was the right man. 'I can tell,' Mr Klages said, 'the stress threshold of people.' Surely Wagner knew the story of the German entrepreneur who had had a heart attack and been ordered by the doctor to take things quietly for five weeks. As far away as possible so as to be out of reach of the phone. So the man goes to Brazil to the upper reaches of the Amazon to a small, very remote Indian village. For two days he stands on the river bank and fishes. On the third day he employs an Indian to keep an eye on the line. On the fourth day he employs two more Indians to look for worms. On the fifth day he employs three more Indians to bait the hooks. When he leaves three weeks later there's a fish factory in the Indian village. Klages, who laughed loudest, watched Wagner as he laughed. Then he moved on.

'He's without a doubt the biggest swine in the room,' Bredow said. 'But he can tell jokes.'

'What does he do?'

'Nothing. He was an SS standard-bearer with some task force in Russia. He came to the country via the Vatican in 1945. He had nothing with him except a small case. A case, people said, out of the Arabian Nights, because he can take limitless supplies of money from it. He built himself a house on the hill with a high concrete wall, well, you saw it the other day. Behind the wall there's a trench for dogs. Klages keeps twenty-three Alsatians. Anyone that climbs over the wall turns himself into dog food. A German couple, members of some strange sect, keep house for him. Apart from them no one's seen the inside of the house. Naturally people tell the wildest stories about this house. Sometimes at night you can hear the dogs barking. People in the neighbourhood originally complained, now they're quite happy with it. They're animals with a keen nose. The bulge in his dinner jacket isn't a wallet, but a gun. He's afraid the Israelis will kidnap him. No doubt that's not his real name, and he has the strange habit, as you'll have noticed, of asking anyone to whom he's introduced to repeat his name, as if he were waiting for a message or for someone he only knows by name.

'Come on, I still have to introduce you to Dr Hansen. He's a surgeon and five years ago opened a clinic here where he removes three metres of small intestine from those gluttons that can't be restrained, with what's left they can eat as much as they please without getting fat. It's the only thing that's international in this place, his patients even come here from Brazil. Incidentally Hansen's a good doctor, should you ever need one.'

Hansen, a man in his fifties with a narrow face deeply marked by wrinkles, immediately asked Wagner how the factory was progressing, after all he had been obliged to treat all the managers, the first, after the guerilleros had set him free, and the second after his nervous breakdown.

'Nervous breakdown, what does that mean exactly?'

Hansen laughed: 'Well, that sort of thing does happen. An overreaction, actually very healthy, the body simply no longer participates, it switches off, the climate, the problems, suddenly the man was standing on the building site screaming, screaming until he collapsed. After that he stopped responding. One needs to be thick-skinned here. Do you know,' Hansen said and turned to Bredow, 'three days ago they sprayed a slogan on the wall of my clinic: *Times will change for you too. And what will you do then with only four metres of intestine?*' Hansen gave a tired laugh. 'It's almost bad for business,' he said. He drank from the wine glass. 'Frightful, this, local wine. If I can be of any help, let me know.' He gave Wagner his card.

'Now you can have three metres of intestine cut out free.'

Miss Vosswinkel approached in her overall dress. She waved to Wagner and Bredow. 'Come,' she said, 'Mrs Krüger is just telling about the robbery.' Miss Vosswinkel in her sturdy leather, low heeled shoes and socks rolled down over her ankles led the way to a large group, at the centre of which stood a young woman in a black dress, next to her a blonde-haired man, white shirt under black jacket. He was the only one in the company that was dressed so casually, because as he approached Wagner saw that he was wearing faded jeans. 'This is Mr and Mrs Krüger,' Miss Vosswinkel said and again introduced Wagner by saying he was a senior engineer. Mrs Krüger put an arm round Bredow.

'You must tell the story from the beginning again for our young friend from Germany,' Mr Vosswinkel said.

'All right,' Mrs Krüger said, 'we were robbed, you see, here on the hill three days ago.'

'It's already the fourth robbery in the last two months,' Miss Vosswinkel said. 'It's hardly surprising, that mob from the city that comes to us here. There was a time, only ten years ago, when one could leave doors open.'

'Let her tell her story, Tinchen,' Vosswinkel interrupted his niece.

'Well,' Mrs Krüger said, 'three days ago my husband and I came back from a party. We'd put the car in the garage, which I'd recommend incidentally, and I'd gone back because I'd lost an earring. When I came to the house two men were standing there. Nylon stockings over their faces, but you could see they were cabecitas negras, probably half castes. They pulled the jacket over Ewald's head, you could hear the seams crack. That beautiful jacket, I thought,' and she laughed. 'The things that go through one's head at a time like that, I hope it won't tear.' Mr Krüger also laughed, and they all stared at his jacket as if the tears were still there. 'The gangsters said: "Open". I thought, there's no point in screaming. The neighbours wouldn't hear. So I unlocked the door. They shut Ewald in the bathroom and instantly started rooting through the drawers. One of them knocked over a fruit bowl. It shattered. They were both quite shocked, they apologized and began picking up the pieces off the floor, that's when I realized they were novices. I sat on the sofa and the first thing I did was push my rings and bracelets between the cushions. They were both searching. They were looking for money and jewellery. After a while I said I had to have a drink. They said I was to stay put. I said I had to have a drink, I was pregnant.' She laughed, and so did her husband. The other listeners grinned and the colonel, who was among the listeners, nodded to Wagner, a gesture Wagner was unable to interpret.

'I got up, went into the bedroom and took the jewellery box out of the safe, went into the kitchen and put the box into the freezer. Then got a glass of water and a vitamin pill and went back into the living room. Meanwhile they'd discovered the safe in the bedroom, and as they'd not found anything yet they wanted Ewald to open the safe. They brought Ewald from the bathroom, pressed the barrel of the gun to his throat' (she held her outstretched finger to her husband's throat). 'He should tell them the number. Ewald naturally wanted to play the hero and said: "You won't get the number from me".

' "The number", they said, "or we'll blow your head off". Ewald said: "No".'

'Well,' the man in the jeans said, 'it wasn't quite as dramatic as that.'

'It was,' his wife said, 'you stood there, hands on your back, and you said: "No". Now those two gangsters were in a tight spot. They looked at each other, then at me, but as if they wanted me to intervene. I simply told them the number. That made them happy. They went into the bedroom, opened the safe and found files and documents. They returned and slammed the door. I said, "quietly please, the children are asleep upstairs". They apologized and said unfortunately they would have to lock us in the bathroom. They even wished me good luck and good health when they left.' Mrs Krüger laughed, and everyone else with her. But it was not pleasant laughter, as Wagner realized, but malicious, venomous even.

'After two hours our faithful Anna arrived, she had been visiting relatives, and let us out. Then we had a whisky, the deep frozen money on the table in front of us.' Again they all laughed, Miss Vosswinkel even applauded, the colonel raised his wine glass and said: 'To brave women with presence of mind.'

The circle of listeners dissolved into small groups, Wagner heard fragments of conversation, the topics were dogs trained to attack, electrified fences and electronic security systems.

Wagner asked Bredow what Krüger did for a living.

'He has an agency for scent.'

'Scent?'

'Yes. He's the richest man on the hill. He imports various essences from the USA. The essences are the basis of the country's perfume industry. You'll smell it soon enough, the consumption of perfume is vast here. Krüger imports the essences in tiny bottles. They can be carried in a suitcase or a bag and are worth more than their weight in gold. The man has a nose for business and naturally also good friends at the customs. The gangsters knew why they were paying him a visit. But of course they hadn't reckoned with the woman.'

Mrs Krüger had stayed to chat to the colonel who put his hand on her arm every time they laughed – and there was a lot to laugh about – and then come over to Wagner and Bredow.

'My name's Angela,' she said to Wagner, 'how do you like it here?'

'I don't know yet. I'm not yet even familiar with my site.'

She laughed. 'Pay us a visit soon.'

Suddenly the barking of many dogs could be heard very near. The conversations, the laughter, the whispering faded to silence, all stood for a moment as if paralysed, then, hesitantly, as the barking slowly diminished the conversations began again, but a little later the first guests said goodbye, and Bredow too said, 'It's time to go.'

Eleven

Wagner arrived home shortly before midnight. He had unlocked the front door and was about to turn on the light in the hall when he saw a strip of light under Sophie's door, which went out a moment later. Wagner went to the room he had chosen for his study. A desk, a chair, a couch and a long bookshelf, in one section of it were a few books left behind by his predecessor. Non-fiction, travel books, some detective novels in English and German, and among them as if by mistake something by Joseph Conrad: *An Outpost of Progress*. Wagner didn't know this story. He had read all Conrad's other books, already as a student, and one even several times: *Heart of Darkness*. He was as pleased as if the battered copy of *Outpost of Progress* had been a present because the book Renate had bought him, the new work of a highly praised author, had rested heavy as lead in his hands as he read it, and after fifteen pages he had wearily let it fall.

Susann could start up from a book she was reading and say, 'that's right, that's exactly right.' If he asked her what was right, what she meant, she always said she couldn't explain, he would have to read the book. There was a time when he did read many of these books, novels, German, American, Faulkner, Steinbeck, Thoreau, and English, Lawrence and Doris

Lessing. He read the books and looked for the passages that had reduced her to these sudden outbursts. And so kept track of her by reading. But at some point he had given up. He could keep up neither one way nor another. And once he had taken on the management of his first major building project there had no longer been the time. Only on holidays did he still have the opportunity to read some book or other. If he then wanted to talk about it to Susann, for her it was only a distant memory. When she read she was unreachable. If she smoked while reading he always had the feeling she was about to burn her fingers.

Wagner saw the building plans, the structural analyses, the ground surveys lying on the desk, just as he had left them that afternoon. He began to shiver, his head felt heavy, signs perhaps of the onset of flu. He thought of Susann who would now be asleep and soon would need to get up, and of Sascha. The time difference, the distance in their lives was a fact as banal as it was hard to grasp. In three hours Sascha would be going to the school he hated so much, sometimes with clenched fists, he hated the school and he hated the teacher, a woman whose face displayed a sullen bitterness.

On Sunday mornings Wagner sometimes went for a walk with Sascha along the Elbe, just where the beach began, a filthy grey-brown beach permeated with lumps of oil. But it was sand you felt under your feet. As a child Wagner had gone there to watch the arriving, but even more, the departing ships. The smell of water, tar and oil, the spot where the harbour pilot left the ship and the river pilot boarded, all this was protection against the dreariness of Sunday afternoons. The water surged past, dark with an iridescent film of oil. On the beach was driftwood, the grain worn smooth by water and sand. On the bank some willow bushes, hanging from them were tattered plastic bags from the last tide.

Wagner had undressed and lay on the bed. For a while he

tried to read *Outposts of Progress*, but was too tired after all. Just as he was falling asleep he heard footsteps. He started up. The footsteps had stopped outside the door to his room. For a moment he waited for someone to knock. But everything was quiet. He listened. He heard nothing but the quiet humming of the air conditioner. He got up, quickly went to the door and flung it open. There was nobody there. He went out. In the corridor and the entrance hall it was dark. Far away he could see the strip of light under Sophie's door. For a moment he stood helpless and dazed. Then he went into the living room, turned on the light and placed a call to Hamburg. He wanted to talk to Susann. He wanted to tell her about these strange Germans, about his Spanish teacher who looked sixteen, and perhaps even the names of things to which she pointed, to then either nod in approval or with a small shake of the head indicate that he had mispronounced the words: silla, mesa, arbol, she tapped her neck with her finger, cuello. She did this with charm and without the least affectation and he often hadn't paid attention because he had been looking at her hair, at the small ear behind which she constantly pushed her silky black hair. Once when she caught him staring into her low-cut dress he thought he had blushed, at any rate he had felt the blood rise to his face and had instantly stumbled in repeating a word. His behaviour was idiotic. His initial high spirits had soon turned into the attentive, serious demeanour of a schoolboy. He kept being reminded of his schooldays, and in particular of a girl in the parallel class with whom they had produced Thornton Wilder's *Our Town*. Actually the girl had directed, she had slowly taken over as a matter of course from the teacher in charge and the man, whether pleased or resigned could not be established, had stepped down. The girl had the singular name of Columbus. At rehearsals she tugged at Wagner, pushed him backwards and forwards, showed him how to say his lines. At the time he had fallen in love with the girl in a devious, sleep destroying way, without ever attempting to show her his feelings.

The phone rang, it was the operator: 'A call to Germany will take more than five hours.' Wagner cancelled the call. He didn't want to receive a call tomorrow at the site. Tomorrow he wanted to take firm action. Tomorrow he wanted to decide the matter of the building's foundation. And he was secretly glad the call hadn't got through. The thought of Luisa had pushed aside the desire to speak to Susann. At the same time the longing to be close to Luisa had taken hold of him, the desire to touch her was making itself physically felt. He shivered. He pulled up the blind and opened the veranda door. Outside it was swelteringly hot. The moon appeared as if behind frosted glass. Wagner went into the garden. The sweat rose on his forehead. He could hear a deep croaking, a snarling from the top of the hill, the barking of dogs far away. He went to the garden wall and stepped onto the stone plinth. Shots whipped through the air. He ducked instinctively. Then he heard voices and the neighing of horses. He looked over the wall. In front of one of the huts a blue light flickered. He saw figures crouching in front of the television. A burned-down fire glowed. There was a smell in the air as if of potatos baking. He could see nothing unusual, but the huts seemed to be much closer than they had been three days ago.

Twelve

 He was woken by a scream. Even in waking he had noticed that the singing of the night birds had stopped. There was a lifeless stillness to which he listened. He froze, soaked in sweat. His skin had retracted in icy shock. Then suddenly the singing began again and overlaid the frenzied barking in the distance. He had fled to the cellar because of a tremendous explosion, the cellar of his house in Osdorf. After the blast which had torn the roof from the house with a roar, a storm had come that had sucked the air and every sound out of the cellar. He was in a soundproof room and only his scream brought him release. Probably his scream had woken him. He got up and went to the window. But he could see nothing outside. When he turned he saw that under the door there was a light in the hall. He went out. In the corridor and the entrance hall the light was on. It was still dark outside. He heard a strange hissing from the kitchen. He went in and saw the water over the flaming gas. The water must have been boiling a while because it only spurted now and then from the spout of the kettle into the hissing yellow flames. A small pool had already formed on the stove. He turned off the gas and went into the living room. The veranda door was open. Had he forgotten to shut it last night? He went out into the garden. It had not got any cooler. He saw a figure standing by the wall. He called: 'Sophie'. She came over. She held her hands in front of her so that the tips of her fingers touched. She went silently past him into the house. For a moment Wagner hesitated, then he went over to the wall. Opposite everything was dark. In front of one of the huts a fire still glowed. Everything was quiet, only in the distance up on the hill in the kennels of Mr von Klages the dogs still raged. As Wagner returned to the house he noticed a thick red carpet of flowers floating on the surface of the pool. The bottle tree had lost all its flowers as if it had been struck. So there had been an explosion after all. Wagner dressed, put the building plans into the briefcase and went into the kitchen. Sophie poured him coffee. He drank the coffee standing and asked what the explosion had been about.

She shrugged her shoulders, then came close to him and whispered: 'The time has come that was prophesied; as it says in the bible, woe, woe unto that great city where all have grown rich that had ships at sea, of the goods therein. For in but an hour that city shall be laid waste. Armageddon is at hand.'

'What do you mean?'

'Look outside, into the night, brother kills brother. One month ago they came, the swarm of the evil one, the locusts. For decades no sign of them but then the sky grew dark, they fell upon the fields and all was devoured and out of the wells came black water, and those who drank it died, and those who dwell in ignorance and in vanity, they shall fall. In our community we pray, we pray and so must you, to be spared when that day comes and fire falls from the sky. For the dogs and the whores and murderers are outside – Will you have your tea with sugar? But only unsweetened lemon tea quenches a thirst.'

'That's fine,' Wagner said, 'whatever you think. I have to go now.' Once on the subject of the end of the world a torrent of words burst from this mumbling taciturn woman, to the accompaniment of graceful movements of hands that otherwise hung limply. Where did the strength of her convictions come from? Surely not simply from bible quotations. For her the present held omens of the imminent end of the world. But he didn't want to ask her because he was afraid that a discussion would then await him every evening. Through an innocent question he had literally opened the door to two Jehovah's Witnesses who had stood outside his door in Lüdenscheid one evening. The two had slowly, but tenaciously worked their way into his flat, until they were sitting on the sofa comparing the building of a power station to a sparrow's nest. Everything lies in God's hands, they had declared as they said goodbye and left behind several booklets about the resurrection.

Driving to the site Wagner again considered ways of giving the factories a foundation that would bear the weight.

Yesterday he had made a rough estimate; it showed the best thing would be to build a basement for factory B that would prevent it from subsiding. High density concrete would be required and even more reinforcement rods, which again would make it more expensive. He didn't want to make any decision at present regarding factory A, already completed at its base. He would write a report for the central office in Düsseldorf and they could decide what to do. Because what was required – and he would write this – was redevelopment of the factory that was in the process of being built. Conceivably, but at considerable additional expense, several beams could be sunk until they reached firm ground. Why Steinhorst had allowed building to continue, while he was temporarily in charge, was completely incomprehensible to Wagner.

As he drove up to the site office and after hooting several times the guard appeared again in his pyjama trousers. In the car's headlights Wagner saw that this time the guard was holding a revolver. He's probably afraid I shall come earlier every day. Wagner smiled at the man who only nodded, half asleep.

Wagner turned on the light in his room and immediately began the sketches and calculations for the basement.

After an hour's work he heard the first cars and buses drive up, bringing the engineers and technicians from the city. He went to the window. The clearing was now bathed in a purple light. How did this colouration, which he had never seen before, come about? The workers stood in front of the Nissen huts. More and still more came out of the huts. Slowly they went towards the rising sun, then, their faces turned to the sun, stood still as if worshipping this blood red light. He wondered what ritual lay concealed behind this gathering, then noticed the jerking movement some of them made with their bodies. The first men turned round and did their trousers up again. They had been pissing.

Wagner went back to his table and decided to have a latrine built. Again he remembered the scream and the explosion. But perhaps it had been his own scream. There really had been an explosion, the flowers from the bottle tree floating in the water were proof of that. With inconceivable speed he must have dreamed a reason for the explosion.

Wagner called for Juan and told him when work began, when the siren went off, he should call all the engineers, technicians and foremen together to the canteen. Anyone absent would then have his name put down. Wagner went to the window. The light had not lost any of its red. From the workers' kitchen a tall column of blue-black smoke now rose into the air. He saw the men sit at the long wooden tables that were covered only by corrugated iron on wooden posts. Further away, but still within the area of cleared land, several vultures were circling.

'Outside are the dogs, the sorcerers and the whores and the murderers.'

The siren wailed and Wagner immediately went over to the canteen where everyone had already gathered. Juan gave him a piece of paper with the names of those that had not yet arrived. Steinhorst sat at a table in front, on it a bottle of mineral water. Wagner began talking, Juan translated. 'Anyone absent without leave is out. Until a time clock is installed the time of beginning and ending work is to be entered on the list of those present.' As Juan translated, his face imperturbable, Wagner noticed the uneasiness among those sitting there; suddenly there was whispering (at least they were only whispering), only a few turned round and put their heads together. Wagner allowed himself a short pause, he suspected the next point he had noted would produce far greater agitation: 'On leaving the site as from now all cars and briefcases will be checked. Anyone with a good conscience will accept this as a voluntary control.' Wagner looked at them, but nobody said anything, they all sat as if they were holding their breath. 'Naturally no one is under suspicion, but we have to get this daily stealing under control.' Steinhorst belched. 'Increased control of working hours and material is necessary. And in the general interest a latrine must be built for the workers. Organizational problems must be named, analysed, and then removed. We're badly behind in our schedule, what matters is to catch up.' Wagner heard Juan translate his sentences. He would have liked to add: This sloppy attitude has to stop, but then he saw Steinhorst sitting there, bloated, the mark still on his head but now turned lilac-blue, and so only said: 'To work and good luck.' Now Steinhorst suddenly got up, went over to Wagner, reached into his trouser pocket and put something on the floor in front of Wagner, a perfectly ordinary glass ball with a blue curved fragment, a child's marble. Everyone stared at the marble. What's all this about, Wagner was about to say, when the marble began to roll, slowly, then getting faster, it rolled in the direction of the window side. Steinhorst got up from his crouching position. He quietly wheezed and grinned at Wagner.

'We're already listing. The ship is sinking on the starboard side.' When Juan had translated, after a moment's pause, laughter broke out. An aggressive laughter that, Wagner thought, was directed solely against himself.

Thirteen

In the afternoon Wagner drove to the tennis club. He had arranged to meet Bredow there. He found him in the changing room. Bredow was just stepping out of his suit trousers and then with a quick tug pulled the tie from his shirt collar. Wagner asked if Bredow had found out anything about the arrested worker.

'No,' Bredow said, 'I tried, but the man has probably already been deported to Bolivia.' He was afraid there was nothing more one could do. Wagner told him about the instructions he had given. Bredow stood still for a moment with one leg in his tennis shorts. 'It'll cause bad feeling,' he said finally, 'checking briefcases is absolutely not done here. Least of all with the engineers. One can do that in Africa perhaps, but not here. People's pride here is very sensitive. It really will cause bad feeling.' 'Could be,' Wagner said, 'but we can't miss deadlines just because people steal sparking plugs from the bulldozers and lorries. To say nothing of reinforcement rods and wooden frames.'

'Then you'll have to search the workers' huts more often.'

'What would the Bolivians do with sparking plugs and reinforcement rods? I'm not sure it's the Bolivians, but the local people.'

106

'It's very close, it'll rain soon,' Bredow said as they went over to the tennis courts. 'You wait, you've not seen rain like this before, you'll think the world's going under.'

'Yes, that's right, the rain. I'm working on the draft for the basement. But there has to be an immediate improvement in the concrete, it's sand. You absolutely must complain at the factory and insist on better quality.'

'It won't be easy.'

'Why? Threaten that we'll not accept any more concrete of the present quality.'

Bredow laughed. He pulled the racket from its case and hit the ball of his left thumb with the strings. It made a clear singing sound. 'It's not that easy, you know. It's the only concrete factory within a radius of three hundred kilometres.'

Christi and Durell were already warming up on the court. Durell served Christi volleys and she smashed them back.

'Perhaps we'll win today,' Durell said, 'we're *en pleine forme*.'

Durell and Wagner did in fact win. Bredow played without concentration. On several occasions he got the score wrong in his and Christi's favour so that Christi kept having to correct him and assured them, that usually when his mind was not on the game he got the score wrong to his disadvantage. This egotism of his was something new.

The game had attracted spectators who even applauded certain strokes (Wagner's slams, Christi's returns). Wagner fought grimly as if he were battling for the Wimbledon Cup. Every bend, sprint, serve demanded an enormous burst of energy against the oppresive heat. After the game he could feel his own heaviness. Durell said goodbye, he had to open the bar for all the thirsty technicians and engineers.

'There was one good customer from the site at least,' Wagner said and laughed.

'That's a professional secret,' Durell said.

Bredow and Wagner sat down at a table near the swimming pool. Christi came out of the changing cabins. She was wearing a scantily cut, black bathing suit that left her thighs bare to the waist and was cut low in front. She climbed the five metre diving tower, positioned herself on the diving board, quickly drew herself up and dived a neat somersault. At a table nearby there was applause. Six Americans with crew cuts were sitting there, they wore T-shirts, shorts, trainers (not tennis shoes) and tennis socks. The six looked as if they were members of a football team. In the distance the muted clatter could be heard of mechanized mowers on which the gardeners drove seated over the meadows.

The layout of tennis courts and swimming pool had been completed barely six months ago. The previous grounds had been too small and in the meantime had been developed by a Swiss food combine. Bredow's stories were confused, Wagner could see he was thinking of something else. The Americans were laughing again. One of them was telling in a broad Texan accent about a man who, for reasons Wagner was unable to understand, had not come in through the door but made his way in by the window, and a cigarette had something to do with this. The Americans roared with laughter. Christi had got out of the pool and come over. Her high round breasts gave a softness, a fullness to her muscular body. The Americans called out something to her. She laughed. 'No, I'm always an alligator and I won't see you later.' She sat down, ran her hand over her red-blonde hair and looked in her linen bag for cigarettes and matches. She couldn't find the matches. Christi went over to the Americans. They made eyes. But none of them seemed to smoke. Christi was already on her way to the restaurant when one of the Americans leaped up, ran searching for something on the ground, picked up a small piece of wood and a stick which he examined carefully and then scratched with his thumb nail, then, as everyone watched, crouched before Christi on the ground, with his thumb nail peeled the bark from the stick, rubbed the wood lying on the ground with the stick in the way Wagner knew from books on Indians, rubbing faster and faster, then at tremendous speed, then threw away the stick he had held to the wood that now really did send up a thin puff of smoke, then the paper caught fire, Christi had sat down on the lawn beside him, he got up and with the spill gave her a light.

Christi thanked him and, showing the Americans her half-bare buttocks, came over.

She'd never been given a light in such a complicated fashion. At least the man could always say yes if he was asked for a light.

'Yes,' Bredow said, 'but it takes time, and then the man's exhausted.' She lay down on the deck chair and smoked with eyes shut.

Her nipples under the thin black material stood out like little corks. Wagner went to the changing cabin and put on his swimming trunks.

The water was warm. He swam a few lengths. Suddenly there was wild spray about him, as if sharks were in the pool. The six Americans passed him doing the butterfly stroke and forced him right against the edge of the pool.

When he came back to the table Christi and Bredow were about to leave.

'Who are those Americans,' Wagner asked, 'a swimming team?'

'Don't think so. Probably something to do with the military.' Wagner asked Bredow to try again to do something for the arrested worker.

He embraced Christi and felt her warm skin that smelled of sun oil and her wet hair on his face.

The Americans had got out of the water and were tussling, their muscular bodies in top form. The table with its glasses and half empty plates fell over. A boy in a starched blue uniform came running from the restaurant. He picked up the glasses and remains of the salad from the lawn. One of the Americans had been looking for music on a transistor, a Latin-American hit, and was now clapping in rhythm.

Wagner had read a while ago about an Indian tribe somewhere in the upper reaches of the Amazon that, if he remembered correctly, had come into contact with white men for the first time twenty years ago and had then resolved to die out. Since then no children had been conceived.

The Americans were romping in the pool again. Wagner got up, went to the club building, put on jeans and a polo shirt, took his tennis bag and strolled across to his car which this time he had parked on the club grounds. Putting the tennis bag into the boot he discovered the sign. It had been carefully scratched into the paint on the boot door. A snake rising in coils from a cup, if it was a cup. Not hurriedly scratched into the paint, but carefully, in exact detail with strokes to shade and indicate the curve of the cup. Wagner turned as if he might still catch the artist, perhaps watching Wagner from a distance. But all he could see were two gardeners cutting the edges of the lawn with gardening shears. He told himself the snake had probably not been scratched onto the car here, but on the site. He remembered the snake he had run over on his first journey. And he thought of the prophesy of which the Indians spoke, that whoever kills the snake drowns.

He took the roads that led to the Green Hill. Coming towards him on the other side were overcrowded buses and hundreds of pedestrians. Only one figure was going in the direction of the hill. As he approached he recognized Luisa. He braked and drove up to the kerb. She walked past the car without looking in his direction. Only when he called did she look up. He got out, went round the car and held the door open. He said: 'Get in.' From the other side of the street someone shouted something. Several men had stopped. Luisa hesitated a moment, then got in. The men jeered and laughed. Wagner realized, as he sat down again at the wheel, that he had done her no favour. Probably she had only got into the car not to hurt his feelings. She sat next to him and stared out of the side window, her face bright red.

He said to her in French that he hadn't understood the situation in time, he was sorry. She said nothing, but turned up the window a little because her hair was blowing in her face. Then she said something in French that he didn't understand, he had to ask her to repeat: 'Ça changera ici, si on peut jouer tennis après le travail.'

Outside the bungalow he showed her the scratched snake. He asked her what the sign meant. She didn't know. Sophie met them at the door. She was wearing a white blouse and a brown skirt. On her feet white shoes that made her feet seem even bigger. In her hand she held a handbag.

She had made roast beef, the meal was ready. She had left it in the refrigerator.

Wagner asked if she was going to her people.

Yes, to her community.

As she left she pulled white cotton gloves over her red fleshy hands.

Wagner brought food on to the veranda where Luisa had already put the tattered book on the table. They ate in silence. Sometimes, as she drank, she smiled briefly at him. They carried the dishes into the kitchen together and when he came back, first getting himself another can of beer from the refrigerator, she was already bent over a sheet of paper writing out the conjugation of trabajar for him. Again she made him repeat words after her, pointed to things, gave their names, and Wagner had to repeat them: arbol, the bush: arbusto, the chair: silla, her brown arm: brazzo, she tapped with her fingers under her left breast, the red lacquered nail indicated the white cotton blouse, there where the heart is: corazon. And burst out laughing as Wagner, distracted, repeated the word. He looked at her, for a moment saw inside her mouth, the rosy gums. It was a childlike, quite uncontrolled laughter that had broken through the seriousness she normally displayed. He had obviously mispronounced the word and given it some other meaning unknown to him.

After exactly two hours (he had turned on the veranda light and put a candle on the table) she put the text book into her straw bag, got up and said: 'Hasta mañana.'

He offered to drive her home.

'Ça n'est pas necessaire.'

But as it was already dark he simply went ahead to the car, held the door open and let her get in. When they came to the barrier on the road the guard peered into the car, grinned and raised the barrier.

They drove to the city that lay brightly lit before them. She sat next to him and looked out of the side window, but there was nothing to see in the dark glass. In the city she directed him through the streets with brief gestures, until they came to the old town. In this district the streets were straight, the blocks of houses set out like a chessboard. Suddenly she raised her hand. Wagner stopped in front of an old dilapidated house on which the pompous plaster rosettes above the windows had crumbled. The house had two floors.

'Merci,' she said, and got out without giving him her hand. He had already pressed down the door handle, then stopped. If he followed and invited her for a drink, faced with the people sitting outside she could only say no. He drove slowly through streets that all looked alike until he came to the Plaza. He couldn't go home now to that huge empty bungalow. He went into the bar. All the tables were occupied. Men and whores were crowded at the bar. Wagner noticed the six Americans from the tennis club. They were standing round a girl, black,

112

wearing a blonde wig. Wagner ordered a beer and watched Durell who sat at the cash desk taking bills and money from the waiters and handing out change. He did this concentrating and without looking up. And only looked up once, in the direction of the Americans who suddenly yelled and clapped. The girl had pulled down one of the straps of her dress and showed a breast, the nipple painted silver. Wagner drank another beer and listened to the incomprehensible babble of languages around him. He paid and left. He went through the dark streets, apparently aimless, and yet without admitting it to himself he was looking for the street on which Luisa's house stood. From the open windows he heard voices from a television film, sometimes he saw the glaring, coloured images, there was a smell of roast meat and garlic. An old man sat on a chair outside a doorway and hummed to himself. He was wearing dark glasses. Black dogs slunk cowering across the street.

He roamed the streets almost an hour like this without finding the house. Quite suddenly an oppressive tiredness came over him. He sat down where he was, on the kerb. He sat there in the heat of the night and for the first time since coming to this country thought how everything was just as he had always imagined it, the sweltering heat, the shrieking of the night birds, the fragrance of certain flowers, the strange incomprehensible people, his exhaustion. Even thinking about Susann and Sascha had nothing unsettling about it any more. He was sure since his departure hardly anything in their lives had changed. They would miss him at the weekends, above all Sascha, but even without him everything would continue as before.

A military jeep stopped in front of Wagner. A sergeant in a helmet that glowed white got out, a heavy-calibre revolver in his quick-draw holster. In the back seat sat a second military policeman, holding a submachine gun. The barrel pointed at Wagner. The sergeant asked Wagner for his passport.

Wagner said: 'No.' He pointed to his shirt to indicate he had no pocket for a passport, and gave the name of his company. The sergeant's manner eased, he asked Wagner: 'Where is your car?'

'Plaza 25 de Mayo.'

'Please, step in,' the sergeant said and pointed to the empty seat in the jeep, next to the soldier with the submachine gun.

Wagner got in, the sergeant sat in front next to the driver and the car started with a jolt. Wagner tried to make out the soldier's face beneath the helmet. He was still young and for a moment Wagner thought he was the one who had sat by the dead man. He had his finger on the trigger of the submachine gun, the safety catch was released. It was on F. Wagner tapped the safety catch with his finger. The street was full of potholes. The soldier only nodded and grinned. So Wagner pushed the barrel carefully forward. If the gun went off, now the sergeant would get it in the back. The soldier grinned again, and this time Wagner was convinced it was the same man. He tried, in English and in German, to ask if yesterday he had been sitting on a container outside the tennis club.

But the man didn't understand him. Wagner again tried to draw his attention to the submachine gun with its safety catch off. Now the sergeant turned and said:

'That's all right. We are still in a war.' Then he said he had been at a training camp in Panama, later he'd met a girl, an American nurse he had wanted to marry, but unfortunately his pay was very low. That's why he'd joined the military police. It's dangerous but better paid. In the distance Wagner could already see his Ford under a street lamp, but it stood at a slant as if it were listing. Wagner and the sergeant walked round the car. Both tyres were flat. The sergeant examined the tyres. Then he pointed to the holes. The tyres had been slashed. Wagner was frightened. Because the slashed tyres were in fact a sign that he was being watched and Wagner was being given to understand that his means of flight could be taken from him at any time. The sergeant offered to have his driver change the tyres. But Wagner only had one spare tyre. He'd have the company do it for him tomorrow. Wagner wanted a taxi, but the sergeant insisted on driving him home. They drove over to the brightly lit hill. The soldier next to Wagner had fallen asleep. He had slumped against Wagner. Several times the hand in his lap twitched in a dream. He gave off a smell of sweat and of leather dried in the sun, a smell Wagner knew from the barracks when they returned from field exercises on summer evenings.

The guards at the barrier were amazed when they saw Wagner sitting in the jeep. They greeted him military style and raised the barrier. The jeep stopped outside the bungalow. The young soldier next to Wagner had woken with a start. He groped for the submachine gun he had put between his legs. The sergeant said goodbye. He waited until Wagner had unlocked the door. The alarm wailed briefly. Wagner shut the door behind him and heard the jeep drive off.

He stood in the hall and listened. The house was silent. He went to Sophie's room, knocked and not hearing anything pressed down the handle and switched on the light. Apart from a garish picture of Christ, the walls were bare. A bed, a table, a chair, a wardrobe, on a small chest of drawers a large old-fashioned radio. A model on which one could also pick up distant stations. Somehow he had imagined the room as more mysterious. The furniture reminded him more of an office. Only the insipid picture of Christ disturbed this impression.

He got himself some roast beef from the refrigerator and took it onto the veranda. He ate and listened to the melodious song from the bottle tree, a song that always ended with a croak. He looked into the darkness. He felt his tiredness as a steady pulling at the back of his neck, the heaviness of his eyelids, but he still didn't want to get up and go to bed. In front of him on the white garden table was the plate, smeared with mayonnaise, next to it the crumpled tinfoil. On Saturday mornings Wagner would often begin clearing the plates and cups while Susann still sat at the breakfast table drinking her coffee. These plates smeared with jam and butter gave him a feeling of physical revulsion. He would then roam through kitchen and living room and pick up scattered pieces of Lego, school books and lipsticks. Susann would watch him and at some point say: 'Let me at least have breakfast in peace.'

Then he would say, 'let me,' and that would mean it didn't disturb him that Susann was still having her breakfast, but from this *let me* of theirs quarrels would develop, the course of which they both very well knew, but nevertheless were unable to stop. It was like a compulsion: why can't things that are left lying around be left lying around, why can't things that are lying around be picked up. That exactly was the question, thoroughly ridiculous but none the less important, because it was the question of why one was the person one was, and not someone else. Even in their disorder things had an order that was hers. Sometimes Wagner would plan to clear out and rearrange the rooms, especially their bedroom. But he did nothing because he knew nothing would change, and neither would he.

In the distance he heard explosions. He got up and went to the wall. The television outside the huts was still on, though it was now past midnight. Two figures sat in front of it. He had the impression the huts on the right had crept forward. Perhaps his tiredness deceived him, or this sticky heat, or perhaps yesterday he hadn't looked carefully and noticed the distance. He also thought he could see the figures in front of the television more clearly, and also the figures on the television. The set stood on a box. He clearly saw the logo of his company light up the screen. It was obviously the same television slot he had seen three days ago. Then Wagner heard the bleeping of a space station approaching a planet. He heard several galactic explosions and in a flare of light saw what seemed to be a shadow beneath him, a suspicion only, a reflex, and as he leaned over further saw a figure at the bottom of the wall. He drew back sharply and had to force himself to look over the wall again. He saw a man run crouching the length of the wall and disappear into the darkness.

When Wagner returned to the house he checked that all the windows and doors were locked. He checked to see the alarm was on, and then went into the bedroom. He listened. He remembered he had left the plate and a bottle of beer outside. He wondered whether to go out again, but then lowered the iron roller blind in front of the veranda door and picture window. He phoned Hartmann and asked if he could have a lift tomorrow on the company bus. They had slashed two of his tyres.

'All right.' Hartmann said and asked if everything else was all right.

'Yes. See you tomorrow.'

Wagner turned the air conditioner to cold. There was something soothing about its steady hum. He undressed and lay naked on the bed. A shiver ran through him. Quietly the curtain moved in the breeze from the air conditioner.

Fourteen

In the morning Wagner woke soaked in sweat and for a moment lay as if drugged. He had dreamed that a human being, but with a pig's snout, had chased him to eat him. It had snapped at him, but then said he was too lean, leaped into a fire and roasted itself.

Sophie had not come yet. He went into the kitchen, made himself coffee and buttered some bread. He enjoyed sitting there quietly without that pointed babbling in the background.

He hadn't yet finished his coffee when the doorbell rang. Hartmann and Juan were outside in the Volkswagen bus. As he got in he saw Sophie come up the street. He waved to her as they drove past. She stopped, surprised and without waving back. Wagner saw her look at her wrist watch. Strange, Wagner thought, that someone who expects the end of the world should wear a watch.

'Are there only the two of you?' he asked Hartmann.

'No, usually three local engineers come too.'

'And where are they?'

'They're going in someone's car today.'

That they were not on the bus today obviously had something to do with him. He would have liked to know why, but didn't ask. He told them about the slashed tyres. 'Does that often happen?'

'No,' Hartmann said, 'not with private cars,' no, he hadn't heard of it before. Military vehicles, yes, if they were left unattended the tyres were slashed.

Juan took a thermos flask from his bag and offered Hartmann and Wagner some of his cold lemon tea. The tea was strongly sweetened. Wagner told them about his dream and said since he had been here he was dreaming more than usual.

Hartmann said it was exactly the same with him. He supposed it was a result of the change of climate.

'No,' Juan said, 'it's the earth.'

'Yes, perhaps,' Hartmann said and ran a hand over his bald head, 'perhaps the earth is trying to tell us something.'

'What?' Wagner said, 'I don't understand.'

Hartmann looked out. The landscape lay in the first delicate rosy light. 'This is what we leave behind us.' Hartmann said, 'this wasteland, this moon landscape, that's what haunts us, this desert.'

Wagner thought of Ernst, whom he knew from his student days. One fine day he had discontinued his research (solids) in order to grow kiwi fruit in Corsica. Ernst had caused a lot of laughter among Wagner's friends. But Wagner had always defended him. He admired the courage and determination with which Ernst had again so radically changed his life. But to run into a similar pair here of all places, Steinhorst, an alcoholic and cynic, and this young Darwin with bald head framed by red-blonde hair, a professional sceptic. Wagner's reply came out more aggressively than he intended: 'Would you like to withhold industry and technology from the people here? Are they only supposed to supply wood?'

'No, but surely they don't have to repeat the same mistakes.'

'What do you mean, mistakes?' Wagner said, 'I like going to England, I like the countryside, the green of the meadows and here and there an oak. There used to be oak forests, they've vanished, they were turned into timber for ships, pit props and charcoal. Oak forests bore me. There's no view.'

Hartmann laughed, 'Well, that follows. But the countryside here isn't green, but it's red, dust, no grass, an immense red moonscape.'

'I always wanted to go to the moon, even when I was a child. Imagine it: a red moon.'

Hartmann looked searchingly at Wagner for a moment, as if to make sure it was a joke: 'Good. Best of luck to you on this trip.'

'You should wish us all good luck.'

'No,' Hartmann said, 'I'm going home in two weeks. I've handed in my notice.'

Wagner was so surprised that all he could manage was a rather helpless 'Oh'. He asked why he was only learning about Hartmann's decision now, and in his question lurked the suspicion that the decision might have something to do with him.

He had written a letter yesterday to Bredow and now he was informing him, Wagner, who therefore would be the first to learn it. The time that remained was so short because so much leave had accumulated, well over two months.

'And why are you going?'

'My time here's finished. I would have had to extend my contract. I don't want to.'

'We'll miss you,' Wagner said and wondered if he should ask Hartmann his reason for leaving. But didn't think it advisable in front of Juan. 'We'll miss you because one can't always count on Steinhorst.'

'Leave Steinhorst alone. During the time he managed the site not a single Bolivian was deported. Before that, with both your predecessors, there were always raids because of theft and workers were always being deported, quite arbitrarily.'

'You think it's my fault the man was arrested on Saturday?'

'No. You weren't to know. The searches because of theft are the problem. How would you stop people removing things?'

'I don't know.'

'What would you do in my place?'

Hartmann looked at Wagner and smiled his gentle apologetic smile: 'But then I don't want to be in your place,' he said.

In the east a fiery red now lay over the hills and rain forest. For a while they all looked in silence out of the windows. Wagner, who was sitting behind Hartmann and Juan, looked at Juan's black hair which he had tied in a pony tail. The hair stood up strangely as if electrified. Wagner had almost fallen asleep when the driver called out something, Hartmann and Juan looked out of the window on the right. The driver braked and they drove at walking pace past three military lorries parked at the roadside. Wagner saw the soldiers crouching on the lorries, the submachine guns between their legs. Some had put blankets round themselves. But it was hot. That they felt cold was obviously due to not having slept for a long time. The lorries were parked on the side road leading to the site as if they wanted to block access.

'You should drive to San Isidor one weekend,' Hartmann said, 'in the middle of the primeval forest there's an immense monument that we've built to ourselves, a motorway bridge, a good 150 metres high. German and French loans financed it, and German and French firms built it and naturally did well out of it. The bridge was put there, a, because the former president was born near there, and b, because there was a tin mine near there that, by the time the bridge was ready, was no longer profitable and was closed. And as in the meantime the president had also been deposed by a coup the bridge stayed as it was, completed, but not connected to a motorway. There the bridge stands, six lanes and quite superfluous, but the country still pays the interest and the interest on the interest on the loans that built it.'

'You know,' Wagner said, 'we build bridges, but where they lead and how they're used isn't our business. It's not our job.'

'Yes it is.'

'What would you suggest?'

'One should know exactly what one's doing, and for whom.'

Juan suddenly turned and said: 'That's where my tribe lives, on the Rio Yacare, there's a missionary up river, and there's a missionary down river. Our cacique always says: it's two too many.'

'All right,' Wagner said, 'we're no missionaries.'

'But you are,' Juan said, 'you engineers are missionaries. And you're the more powerful ones. You accomplish the miracles about which the others only talk, you change everything from one day to the next.'

'No, we only carry out the work, and there's nothing miraculous about it either.'

'You know what the Bolivians call you?'

'No.'

'Big Foot.'

Wagner laughed too loudly. 'I know', he said, 'I move fast, I take giant strides.'

They entered the forest. The driver turned on the lights.

What a stupid comment, Wagner thought and was annoyed with himself for being annoyed at the nickname. But Big Foot was close to Big Mouth and that was annoying. It hurt him, though probably it was not meant that maliciously. But even as a child he had been hurt by remarks about his big feet, always interpreted by his mother as an indication of his future size. His classmates teased him and when he ran about in the ever larger shoes his mother bought he did indeed look like Charlie Chaplin, a nickname he was only able to bear with a degree of composure after he had become provincial junior

122

champion in the crawl, where his big feet helped him. This Big Foot obviously alluded to his visit to the Nissen huts and his instructions to call an ambulance to take care of the badly injured man. What had happened to the man? Or had he died and they had simply buried him somewhere on the clearing? Big Foot. How big-mouthed and clumsy he must seem to those Indians. More even than the name it was Juan who annoyed him, who had told him, although he told himself Juan had wanted to warn, not hurt, him. They arrived at the site. This time there were already many cars in the parking lot and the guard came in the prescribed khaki uniform and pulled open the sliding car door to let Wagner out.

Wagner phoned Bredow's office. Mrs Klein answered. Wagner asked her to phone a garage to put two new tyres on his Ford, which was on the Plaza. And then would Bredow please phone him as soon as he came to the office. It was impossible not to detect the triumph in Mrs Klein's voice as she said, 'Mr von Bredow is already in the office.'

A moment later he heard Bredow's voice. 'I was a bit slack at tennis yesterday, but you can have a return match today.'

'Have you done anything about the concrete yet?'

'Not yet. The director of the concrete factory doesn't come in until ten. Incidentally, you should look round for another Spanish teacher.'

'Why?'

'You know, it's not really my business. And I'm not really interested with whom you learn Spanish. It's friendly advice, that's all.'

'But why?'

'Things are quite simply different here. The people are deeply catholic. It would be better if you were to find yourself a male teacher. You have to remember that on the hill everybody knows everybody. They know who comes and goes. And there's a great deal of gossip.'

'I never was bothered by what people say. And in any case, it's quite unimportant.'

'Not always. The colonel for instance, he's well disposed towards you, he's received some information. It's been established there's a connection between the girl and the guerillas.'

For a moment only the interference on the line was audible. Then Bredow's voice was back: 'I'm sure you understand that to get involved here is dangerous, deadly dangerous.'

'What do you mean, get involved, I'm learning Spanish, that's all.'

'But it could be seen differently. Put yourself in the position of security for a moment.'

'I neither want to nor could.'

'Be careful! Come to the club today and remember to park on the club grounds.'

After this conversation Wagner phoned Juan and asked him if he knew Luisa well.

'No,' Juan said; he had heard from an acquaintance that she was looking for a job.

'Why has she stopped teaching?'

'I think the school gave her notice.'

'And why?'

'There are a thousand reasons for loosing a job. Here teachers are not civil servants.'

'Do you know anything about her politics?'

'No.'

When the siren wailed Wagner went through the canteen where the engineers were standing drinking their coffee. Probably this was their way of indicating they would be back at work in a minute. As he left they all followed him.

'The captain always goes first, except into the lifeboat,' Steinhorst said.

A stupid joke, and Wagner didn't even make an effort to laugh. He went over to site A. He had the clear impression that something had changed. There were no longer endlessly straggling columns, instead people went purposefully and in groups.

Five years ago his first job as manager had been on a school complex near Flensburg. The building was approximately half finished, but they were hopelessly behind for the completion date. It was a disastrous mess. His predecessor, an alcoholic, had been dismissed without notice for selling building material. There was fighting among the workmen. Whores stayed overnight in the building sheds, drunks fell from the scaffolding. It had taken him two weeks to put things right. He had thrown out four men, had had a building engineer removed and on one occasion had had a patrol car take away two pimps. He had had to thoroughly clean out the place, but had then been able to hand over the building on the agreed date. This had given him a reputation for putting a botched project back on its feet. And Steinhorst wasn't so wrong in comparing him to a captain, after all Steinhorst had also at some time or other been on one of those management courses the company regularly offered those engineers that were considered potential managers. 'Being in charge of a building is like being in charge of a ship,' the course instructor would say, 'one can't discuss the route, one can't debate decisions, but there's a logic to it. That's not capriciously authoritarian, it's a matter of necessity. And never forget: No one's going to ask you later what the mood was at work, but only whether you finished the job on time and built well.'

When they got to the site of factory A the concrete lorries had not yet arrived. The men stood around waiting, others were still working on the frames. Wagner didn't want to wait and said to Steinhorst he'd look over the site and check the building material lying around. He went over to site B. Two caterpillars were at work in the excavation. The third was still where the sparking plugs had been removed from it during the night. The caterpillar tracks were filled with water. Hartmann was at work behind a theodolite, determining the angles for building. Next to him a technician was taking down figures. Hartmann called out something in Spanish to the man with the surveyor's staff. Wagner decided to learn Spanish more intensively over the next few days. He would practise for two hours every day with Luisa and on his way to the site learn vocabulary by heart. From the excavation he went by a trodden path on a detour to factory A. He thought it was a matter of urgency to have plans ready for the basement, then it would require a licence. He didn't care what Bredow's estimates were, unless the central office expressly gave instructions to continue building on a shaky foundation. 'I don't want Skapa Flow,' Wagner heard himself say aloud.

Here the vegetation was already knee high again, large yellow flowers wound through it. From it a repeated bird call rang out, a clicking that ended in a thin fading sound. Sweat ran down his forehead and burning into his eyes. The lenses of his sunglasses were sticky. The path was now quite narrow and almost entirely overgrown. Wagner wondered if he ought to turn back as he'd come almost to the edge of the clearing where there were immense trees from which creepers hung. Then he saw the birds in front of him on the ground, fat gigantic creatures, bare-necked with big heads: vultures. He had never seen these creatures from so close and went on walking. The birds hopped sluggishly before him on the path. They were near enough to touch. The repulsive smell of rotting flesh hung in the air. Then he saw it, covered by leaves and vultures, an animal lying on the ground (or was it a body?), dark red-brown, ribs, bones, something stringy in the beak of one of the vultures. Wagner stopped and held his breath. The thought flashed through his mind that it might be the body of the wounded man (he assumed wounded) whom he had seen lying in the hut. He took two, three steps towards the body, but then had to quickly turn away in order not to vomit. He went back. He would make himself totally ridiculous if they saw him throwing up again. He wondered if he ought to send someone to see what exactly it was lying there. But then he thought of his nickname and the ridicule if it turned out to be only an animal; if he, insisting on punctuality, kept people from work with these boy scout errands.

When he got to site A, exhausted and thirsty after this short walk, they were already looking for him. Steinhorst was sitting on a cable drum, in his hand a bottle of mineral water, Pedro who had got it for him standing next to him in his grimy white jacket. All the workers were waiting, not one of them was working, nor the engineers, even the two crane drivers had got down from their cranes, and all were looking at Wagner.

Steinhorst said Wagner would have to decide whether the concrete that had just been delivered was to be used. Strictly speaking it was wet sand rather than concrete. Steinhorst pointed to the flow table on which the concrete had been tested. Wagner went over to the five concrete lorries on which the drums were slowly turning. The drivers were standing smoking in the shade of the trucks. He had the concrete tested a second time on the flow table. Steinhorst checked with a stop-watch. The concrete spread quickly, far too quickly. He made them put out a larger amount to test. He wanted to gain time. First of all he wanted to be able to think straight. He poked about in the concrete with his finger, took some between his fingers. Not that it was wet sand, that was an exaggeration, but the quality was wretched. He tested from every lorry. There must have been something magical for the workers about his movements and gestures. There was no overlooking the aggravation and problems that would arise if he sent back the four loads. But at the same time he told himself if he now let this pass and declared himself satisfied with the quality, wretched but just defensible, then all bungling and botching would be beyond criticism. Then he would have accepted the rules of the game. And all of them, watching him as he checked, knew this.

He slowly straightened. They looked at him. He said to Juan: 'They can have this muck back. We're not building on sand.' One of the engineers, the young man with the black moustache who had already complained about the quality, clapped and shouted: 'Bravo', even before Juan had translated.

Wagner went to his room and phoned Bredow. He said he had just sent back the morning delivery of concrete. for a moment Wagner thought Bredow had hung up, then he heard his voice: 'Come to the office now. We'll talk to the director of the concrete factory.' Steinhorst had come into the room while Wagner was on the phone. He hadn't knocked and had sat down on a chair. He put the plastic helmet on the table covered with building plans. 'Very brave', he said.

'No, not at all, it goes without saying.'

'Take care, they're hyenas.'

'Who?' Wagner wanted to know.

'All of them.'

Fifteen

At noon Wagner went home on the company bus. He showered, put on a white shirt and his beige summer suit. On the way he had wondered whether to drive straight to Bredow's office, sweaty and filthy as he was, but thought that when it came to paying – it was after all a question of money – an ironed shirt was more suitable than a khaki shirt with dried salt streaks under the arms.

Sophie had made him coffee as he changed. He asked her to order him a taxi.

'The name of the house is El Dorado,' Sophie said, 'they all call it that in the city. And it too will disappear.'

Had she enjoyed her day off? She had prayed in her community. She poured the coffee for him and asked if he had any request for the evening meal. She put the question in such a way that really he could only say no, though it was evidence she wanted to do him a favour.

'No, thank you.'

He wanted to eat in the city today. Perhaps he could even invite Luisa for a meal, if he succeeded in finding her house again.

A little later the taxi came, a rattling old Ford. The springs had worked their way through the upholstery. The driver had turned up the radio, some combo was playing. He drove like a lunatic. Wagner found this pace corresponded to his mood.

The office was in the building that dominated the city: sixteen stories high, covered in honey-coloured glass that reflected palms, surrounding houses and passing clouds. In the afternoon sun the building stood there like a huge block of gold. This building accommodated all the big foreign companies that had settled in the province, as well as some of the big national firms. Wagner's company was building three factories in the province, a fertilizer plant, a power station and the paper factory. Bredow was responsible for business management of all three projects.

Wagner wanted to go to the entrance vaulted by a copper roof when a military policeman who had been leaning against a jeep parked on the pavement approached him, and held out a white gloved hand: 'Documentos por favor!'

After the soldier had compared the photograph with Wagner's face, he said: 'Ok.' The glass door, made of thick bullet proof glass, was opened in front of him, by a doorman from the inside. A second doorman approached, his manner deferential, his blue trousers pressed with knife-sharp creases. Wagner gave the man his company card. The man went into the glassed reception and phoned. He handed Wagner the company card with a: 'Thank you, sirrrr.'

Wagner saw himself in the mirrored walls of the lift. He was suntanned, his hair bleached. Susann always said: 'I'd like to have your hair.' But he looked tired, there were deep rings under his eyes.

When he got out a young woman greeted him in Spanish and led the way to the office. Her bobbed hair fell like a black wave over her face. She was wearing a green silk dress, silver sling-back shoes with very high heels that forced her to take short steps with knees straight. At every step a metallic tap drew attention: slim heels in iridescent black silk stockings.

Mrs Klein, an older grey haired woman, greeted Wagner as if she had been waiting for him for weeks.

She'd settled the problem of the tyres right away. His car was where he had left it yesterday, ready for him, hopefully, she laughed roguishly.

One could have comfortably roller-skated in Bredow's office. On one side a corner sofa in light beige cotton, on the other side, a good ten metres away, a mahogany desk, immense but bare, except for one photo framed in silver that showed a laughing Christi with their two boys, a leather bound diary and a dark green phone. What was Bredow doing in all this space? Wagner thought of his site office.

Bredow had presumably noticed Wagner's astonishment as he immediately began justifying the size of his office. The space was naturally far too large, but necessary nevertheless. They set great store on presentation in this country. Projects of the size and order of the paper factory could only be sold in offices of over 100 square metres. He always felt very lost in this space. He laughed, slapped Wagner on the shoulder, did he want a drink, the person to talk to, the director of the concrete factory, was already waiting. He kept running his finger tips over the back of his head, as if he wanted to check that his hair, combed straight back, lay flat, a gesture Wagner hadn't seen in Bredow before. Mrs Klein brought a file and winked at Wagner as if to say, there'll be trouble. Bredow again ran the tips of his fingers over his hair. 'Well, let's go.'

They crossed a corridor carpeted in dove-blue to the offices on the opposite side of the building. On an oval brass plate were the words: Betonera Santa Clara.

'Now that's practical,' Wagner said, 'you can literally break down his door if the concrete's no good.'

But Bredow had not even listened. They entered an office of the same size and divided in the same way as Bredow's reception. A secretary took them to the director, a young man in his late twenties, slim, in a narrow fitting dark blue silk suit. He squeezed Wagner's hand, a handshake bordering on pain. Bredow gave the name: Carillo. Carillo wore a pilot's watch on his wrist. His striking suntanned face became curiously crooked when he laughed. He kept his lips together as if he had to hide his teeth. But his teeth were regular and shining white, as could be seen when he spoke. This crooked smiling mouth, especially the lips when a little apart, reminded Wagner of a flat fish.

Carillo had returned only that morning from the capital. He had flown into turbulence in his Cessna and lost his way, as he explained in good English. The secretary brought in Martini and mineral water. Suddenly Wagner was annoyed that he had changed for this conversation. Bredow and Carillo exchanged their experiences of the three or four gourmet restaurants in the capital. Then Carillo turned to Wagner. He regretted that it had come to this misunderstanding. Had he been in his office at the time, he would have immediately phoned Wagner. He grinned crookedly. Wagner sat back in his chair and inwardly relaxed. He had not expected the discussion to be this free of problems.

He had asked an independent, state licensed expert for an opinion. He handed Wagner a paper marked with two official stamps over the table. The report was written in Spanish. Wagner looked up helplessly. Bredow dabbed his hair with his fingers.

'It's ok,' Carillo said and grinned crookedly. 'The expert has established that the quality of the concrete is faultless.'

For a moment Wagner wondered if he should strike the fragile glass table with his fist, but then only threw down the paper.

Would he please not take him for a fool, he was not new to the work, the concrete was wretched. It would be absolutely totally irresponsible to use it as then, in the not too distant

132

future, the ceiling would fall onto the workers' heads. Wagner got up, pushed the glass table slightly to the side, took two steps towards Carillo who sat sunk in his chair. He would write to company management, he would write to the building authorities, because with concrete like this one could build sand castles, but not factories.

Carillo had looked at him, first puzzled, then thoroughly frightened. He no longer grinned, only his mouth was still crooked in his face. Bredow again ran a hand over his hair and said: 'Hold it.' And to Carillo: 'Just a moment'. Then began talking to Carillo in Spanish, interjecting: 'Sorry, but this can really only be said in Spanish.'

Wagner was cut short in his stride. He had to sit down because to have remained standing, silent, the stupidity of incomprehension on his face, would have been ridiculous. Throughout Bredow spoke not as if the need were to stress that the concrete was wretched, but rather than on the whole it was quite good.

The conversation had turned, not Carillo but Bredow was offering an explanation. Carillo remained silent and looked morose, only after a while pulling a crooked mouth a few times. Then, quite unexpectedly, Bredow said in German: 'We've found a solution. There's been a misunderstanding.'

'And the expert's report?'

Bredow said: 'Well, tomorrow we'll get concrete of the old quality.'

Carillo squeezed Wagner's hand.

In his office Bredow let himself fall into a chair. He laughed. Suddenly he was so excited he clapped his hands, called: 'Ma petite, bring us a scotch and ice.' He made no attempt to hide his relief. He said, if Carillo hadn't gone along with it we would have had to shut up shop. Mrs Klein came and brought whisky.

'Cheers.'

'And what happens to this morning's damp sand, is it going to be used somewhere else now?'

'That's not our problem.'

Wagner would have liked to ask Bredow what had actually been agreed. But Bredow should have told him of his own accord.

'Did you ask Carillo if he can deliver concrete with a greater density for the basement?'

'Yes, he could deliver it now, but how do we get our hands on the money for this basement? Have you ever considered what huge sums are involved?'

Wagner handed him the note with the rough estimate. Bredow saw the figures and said: 'Dios mio. Who'll pay? Who has all this money?'

'Don't you still have some in reserve?'

'No, really not, I'd tell you if I had. We've past the completion dates, we're limping four weeks behind. Change of managers, this whole to and fro. And Steinhorst hasn't exactly driven the men to work in the last three weeks.' He stared at the note. 'I'll have to do some calculating. If you promise me you can make up at least two weeks, then I could go along with the basement. Probably he'll have a go at me now for factory C,' he laughed: 'Cheers. What about factory A?'

'I don't know, company management will have to decide. It'll have to be rebuilt. We'll have to put in supports. That'll cost even more.'

'Everything depends on not losing more time. You should know we don't have Carillo in the palm of our hand, the other way round, he has us in a stranglehold. If he turns off the flow of concrete it's a disaster for us. We have Santa-Clara-Concrete, or none. You understand? Let's drink to the basement, cheers. We'll get it somehow or other. This is all a bit much for you, they fly you in and you discover a crisis. You should go out. Let Consuelo introduce you to the city's gastronomic delights.'

Wagner only slowly realized that by Consuelo he meant the receptionist.

'Well, not the refinement of Paris, but easily digestible,' Bredow grinned.

'What are you getting at?'

'Oh well, there's only one meeting place for gourmets, that's the Hotel San Martin. A Swiss does the cooking. You can practise conversation with Consuelo and grammar with a teacher whose phone number I'll write down for you, he's a good man and he also speaks English well.'

Wagner got up. 'Instead of a new Spanish teacher I'd like a new housekeeper. No religious fanatic who persecutes me with her Day of Judgement.'

Bredow also got up. 'Keep your hands off the girl, believe me, it only creates problems, for you and possibly also for her. And Sophie is a good housekeeper, better one that talks about the Day of Judgement than one who steals from you. Well', he said, 'it's too late for tennis, whisky in this climate and I'm too tired to run.' Bredow accompanied Wagner out, past Mrs Klein who gave Wagner a maternally warm handshake, past the girl with the silver stilleto heels. 'Shall I ask her?'

Wagner laughed and shook his head.

In the lift he was suddenly sorry he had declined the offer and would have liked to go back up. But the thought of Bredow's understanding grin drove him out of the building. He wanted to walk to his car on the Plaza. Then he heard a strange tapping and saw a boy go past the railings to the garden in front, running a small stick against the bars. The boy held his head far back, as if he were following the clouds in the distant sky. His eyeballs were white, without pupils. The boy was wearing trousers much too wide and rolled up on his legs and a shirt full of holes that exposed his bony ribcage. In his right hand he held a small dented tin plate. Behind the boy ran a scrawny dog. Wagner reached into his pocket and took out a note, it was a new note and for a large sum. He tried to press it into the boy's right hand. For a moment he felt a hard, coarse hand. The boy had stopped instantly at the touch, felt the note after tucking his stick under his arm, and let it fall. He continued walking, followed by the dog that briefly sniffed Wagner's trousers and growled quietly.

Wagner stood looking at the boy go, then at the soldiers in the jeep who had observed everything. He hesitated, wondering whether to pick up the note. It was the equivalent of almost ten dollars. Finally he did pick it up, but held it in his hand as if he had just found it, instead of putting it in his pocket. He couldn't understand why the boy had thrown away the money with what seemed a gesture of contempt. Then he told himself the boy probably hadn't recognized the new note as money, never having had anything like it in his hand before.

Sixteen

On the Plaza Wagner found his car where he had left it yesterday. Two new tyres had been put on. No other damage had been done to the car. He saw the scratched symbol of the snake and in astonishment discovered that in the meantime someone had worked on it. The cup from which the snake coiled had been decorated with an intricate lozenge pattern. Wagner even discovered some paint shavings on the ground. While Wagner studied this strange symbol several people gathered round him in curiosity, watching him and then getting into an excited discussion. Wagner had the impression they assumed he had scratched the symbol into the paint. They kept drawing closer and more and more people stopped. He was overcome by uneasiness, forced his way through the inquisitive crowd and ran into one of the streets now filled with people because it was late afternoon and the shops were open again. Wares were on display outside small stores, fruit of an unusual size, apples, papayas and mangos, in baskets next to them sweet potatoes like beets and enormous pumpkins. In the butcher's window there was skinned calf's head, the eyes scraped out. A man came out of the shop carrying a small tin bowl in which something violet slithered. Next to the butcher's a café, three tables on the street, at one of the tables two women in pompous hats, in pink. Wagner walked in the half shade of the plane trees. A man squatting by a house wall, on seeing Wagner, tipped forward and skidded towards Wagner on his knees, supporting himself like a monkey on the knuckles of his left hand and in his right hand holding high two cigarette lighters. Wagner continued walking but the man slid after him shouting something in a treble. The people on the street turned. It was as if he had hit the man or robbed him. He quickened his pace, the shouting got louder and the shuffling faster. Wagner stopped. He saw that the man had strips of old tyre bound to his knees. The legs below the knee and the feet were crippled. The man held out two gas lighters. His wrists and knuckles were covered in thick callouses. Wagner took the iridescent blue lighter and gave the man a note, then hurried on. The man stayed behind, but continued shouting something at Wagner. Wagner turned into the next side street. The houses were decayed, the turn of the century stucco had crumbled, a smell of rot and cooking filled the air. Shrubs grew from the roofs of some of the houses and small trees twisted their way to the light from top windows. It was as if the forest were returning to the city over the roofs. The roots had already burst through the walls, while on the ground floor people still sat in rooms watching television or cleaning vegetables. But here and there was a completely abandoned house with giant ferns and thick-fleshed leaves growing rampant through the open doorway. Coming from this spilling vegetation Wagner heard a strange cackling, a croaking and even once, he thought, snarling as if from a large cat. At last he found the house outside which he had left Luisa. In front of the door an old woman sat knitting, with one knitting needle held under her arm like a spear. Wagner looked at her for a moment, but the thought of anything in wool in this heat made him shudder.

He asked the woman: 'Luisa vive aqui?'

But the woman shook her head as if not understanding. He

went past her into a dark, damply musty hall. The door to the flat on the ground floor was shut. Narrow, steep wooden steps led to the top floor. He cautiously felt his way up. The higher he got, the hotter it got. On the door at the top there was neither a bell, nor a name. He knocked. He heard hurried steps inside, drawing near, then away, then near again. A to and fro as if someone were quickly tidying. Wagner knocked again and decided to speak English, if someone other than Luisa should open the door. The door opened a fraction and Wagner saw Luisa's face, anxiously tense. The tension eased as soon as she recognized him.

She laughed and held out her hand: 'Buenos dias.'

She seemed to be relieved he had come. She went ahead of him barefoot, in jeans and a loose t-shirt.

A narrow corridor led to the kitchen. Light fell through the slats of the closed wooden shutters, the sun was already low. A kitchen table in the middle, three kitchen chairs, the white paint scuffed, a kitchen cupboard. Dirty white oil paint flaked from the walls. Rising mains led to the ceiling from which a large boiler hung, rusted and fastened with heavy bolts. Against one wall a cooker and a sink. A pomegranate lay on a table covered with a bright yellow plastic cloth.

Luisa pointed to another door and said: 'Adelante!'

'Vous voulez du café ou du jus de fruit?'

'Jus de fruit, por favor,' he said and crossed the corridor to a room where two wide open doors led to a roof terrace. Torn, grey-green wallpaper with a lozenge pattern, a ceiling lamp that looked like a marble bowl. In the corner there was a brass bed. On it lay a suitcase into which clothes had been heaped. Wagner had the impression the case had only just been packed. Was she going away? But surely she would have told him, above all she would have asked to be paid. He stepped onto the terrace that lay in the shade of an immense bottle tree. There was a wooden deck chair and two frayed cotton chairs. Wagner sat down. From below, from the yard, he heard laughter and tango music. He was about to get up and look over the balustrade when Luisa came out with a basket of oranges, a knife and a small ceramic squeezer. It was one of those old-fashioned squeezers Wagner had seen at his grandmother's when he was a child: a small plate with a ribbed cone in the middle. Luisa cut the oranges and squeezed them on the cone with a forceful turning movement. Only once did she look over at Wagner and laughed, a relaxed unaffected laugh. She took a fresh orange from the basket, smelled it, and then handed it to Wagner. The fruit was warm, probably had lain in the sun, and gave off an intense perfume such as Wagner had never smelled before.

Luisa poured the squeezed juice into glasses.

A siren could be heard in the distance. For a moment she interrupted what she was doing and listened.

'Ambulance,' he said.

'Non, police.'

He watched as she fished the pips out of the glasses with the point of a knife.

'J'éspere que je ne vous gêne pas à cause de moi.' He wasn't sure if she had understood, but she answered: 'Non.'

'Allons dans un restaurant?'

She thought about it as if it were a complicated question, then she said: 'Si.'

'Il faut que je me change,' she tugged at her t-shirt and went into the room.

He expected her to take a dress from the open case (he had seen no clothes in the cupboard in the room), and thought it was sure to be a red dress. He got up because he couldn't bear to sit and wait any longer, and went to the balustrade.

There were three palms trees in the yard, he was able to reach and touch the branches of the bottle tree.

Down below a woman was hanging up washing. A young man was repairing a motor bike. The tango music was coming from several radios. A chicken hung with tied legs from a post. A thread of blood dripped from the neck. A small boy was running about with the severed chicken head in his hand and shouting: 'Cococo.'

How strange, Wagner thought, that animals should be imitated differently in different languages, as if there were Spanish, English and German chickens. He heard her footsteps, on high heels, and turned. She came towards him on the terrace, as during the language lessons, taking a few steps as if on a catwalk. She was wearing a white skirt and a black blouse with white dots. She had tied her blue-black hair into a pony tail. She seemed even younger but, though on closer inspection the material of the blouse was really plain, sophisticated.

'Vous êtes merveilleusement belle,' Wagner said.

She looked at him, not understanding. Wagner laughed at the face she was making and would have liked to take her in his arms.

Seventeen

The restaurant was on the top floor of the Hotel San Martin. Wagner asked the manager, a youngish man who came from Fribourg, to give him a table on the terrace. The fronds of the palms set out in large tubs rubbed against each other in the breeze with a scraping sound. From here there was a view far into the distance, beyond the old town where the square blocks of houses lay between right-angled streets. To the west, towards the hill, the streets became twisted and crooked, here were the houses and huts built in recent years. The sun was going down behind the hill. A slightly hilly plain fissured by dried-out water courses lay in faint rays of light. In this last light the red of the dusty earth glowed even more intensely.

Wagner and Luisa sat opposite each other at the table and watched the sun dip into the brown-violet haze behind the hill. In the northeast – now hardly visible – lay a distant dark green strip, the rain forest.

Wagner said in German: 'There's the factory.' Then he tried in French to tell her about the problems: the stealing, the slack attitude, the poor concrete.

The longer he spoke, the less attention she paid to his explanation, instead directing it, as he noticed, more and more at himself, his gestures, his mouth, his hair. When with the help of a glass and a beer mat he tried to make her understand the problem of the water level, she began laughing aloud. She laughed so loudly people at the other tables looked over and, after a moment's astonishment, he also laughed.

The manager came with the menu as if he wanted to dampen this overflowing merriment. He explained the various dishes to Wagner. Luisa wanted fish. The manager recommended a freshwater fish that came from a river not too far away that had been dammed. (Wagner remembered that the company had been involved in building a dam.) This fish, the manager said, was usually only to be found in the lower reaches of the Amazon. For some inexplicable reason, after the Parana had been dammed the fish had turned up here, although this river and the Amazon were not connected.

Wagner ordered a Franconian wine that was criminally expensive, not because he wanted to impress Luisa, but because he thought it was a day to celebrate and it was the wine he wanted. Anyway, it would do to celebrate a victory.

As their glasses touched, he said: 'Viva la fabrica.'

He was filled with almost unrestrainable high spirits. He would have liked to tell Luisa what he'd achieved today. The knowledge that they were no longer building on a swamp (or sand, if he thought of the concrete) would lead to a quite different attitude, to pleasure in work that was meaningful, not only for himself but also, he was sure of it, for most of the engineers and technicians. The wonderful logic that arises out of the malleability of things, a logic that brings thing into the open. The stone also thinks, a sentence by Diderot that had made him thoroughly uneasy in his student days: *One must assume that the stone thinks.* Darkness lay over the plain, only the crest of the hill still rested in a last brown light. The electric street lamps had come on in the city streets. Fires could be seen flaring here and there. Far to the north, presumably on the state motorway, the headlights of a car could be seen.

They sat and were silent, and there was trust in this silence. Now and then she drank the wine and Wagner saw that wine meant nothing to her. She drank little, only sipping, but without tasting. He saw her profile in the glow of the lantern. Her nose was a little short, the lips well rounded, a gentle but also forceful chin, a straight forehead that he noticed only now because her hair was tied back. He saw her throat and in the neckline of her blouse the delicate formation of the collar bones, the little hollows his mother used to call salt cellars.

He had always had girl friends older than himself. And Susann was four years older. And he was shy with younger girls. The thought of taking a girl's virginity had something distressing about it, for him it was associated with the idea of surgery.

And also the thought of having to protect turned his sexual urge instantly into fatherly detachment, and with that it disappeared. But what was special about Luisa was the contrast between her youthful appearance (she could in fact have been his daughter) and her astonishing self assurance. There was no embarrassment or artificiality in her reactions.

The first course arrived, avocado mousse with river crab. She chose the right fork from those in front of her and ate as if she came here every day, without making remarks about how good it was.

'Vous êtes marié?' she asked.

The thought flashed through his mind to simply say no. But he nodded. He would have liked to talk about Susann, he could have tried explaining to her (and to himself) how this stagnation had come about, this relationship that was taken for granted and was without any excitement, and was what after all bound them. But it would have been impossible to manage linguistically, he would have had to put everything into simple and

144

therefore distorting French. He could have said: Yes, I am married, there are problems. But that would somehow not have been right, and it would also have created the impression that he wanted to belittle his marriage or complain about Susann.

He ate and looked at her and thought of Bredow's warning. 'Pourquoi vous avez quitté l'ecole?'

She looked at him as if she were able to read the reason for his question, why had she left school, on his face.

'Des problems,' she said, 'pour des raisons politiques. Et pourquoi vous avez quitté chez vous?'

'Des problems,' he replied, 'pour des raisons personelles.'

The fish was served, beautifully filleted and with a yellow-brown maracuja sauce that tasted spicy. The flesh was delicate, white and tasted like sole. Night birds and bats shot past the lamps, insects gathered in their light. In the distance, over by the rain forest, sheet lightning lit banked clouds. Wagner thought of the excavation filled with groundwater. He decided to have the snake symbol scratched on his car sandpapered. The wind had increased, the scraping of the palm leaves had got louder. He wondered whether he ought not simply to ask her what sort of political problems hers had been. But that could lead to linguistic confusion and she might misunderstand his question as that he was afraid of running into problems because of her.

Suddenly she put a hand to her forehead as if something had hit her and a pained expression passed briefly over her face. Wagner asked if she had a headache, if he should ask them for a pill. But she only said: 'No, gracias.' She stared past him and when Wagner turned he saw that Colonel Kramer, his adjutant, two civilians and three women had arrived. They sat at a table not far behind Wagner. They heard harsh inconsiderate laughter that kept getting louder. Wagner had to force himself not to keep turning round, partly out of curiosity, partly in anger. Their shared silence had been disturbed because now they waited for the next outburst of laughter, and actually should have mentioned it. Wagner called for the bill. He had just paid when a hand came down on his shoulder, the colonel's hand, who said: 'Don't get up, please don't let me disturb you.' Again the colonel had on his white uniform jacket with decorations on the chest (where had the colonel won these medals?). Wagner introduced Luisa to the colonel and thought that if the colonel knew Luisa a reaction would show it, however slight. When the colonel kissed Luisa's hand she sat rigidly still. The colonel revealed nothing.

'A charming companion,' he said, 'is she new at your company office?'

Before Wagner could answer he had asked Luisa obviously the same question in Spanish. She only shook her head quickly and without saying anything and then looked out over the plain, where the sheet lightning had increased.

'Will there be a storm?' Wagner quickly asked the administrator.

'I don't think so. When it comes from the north, which doesn't often happen, it usually stays over there. How are things at the site?'

'We're making progress.'

'If I can do anything for you please let me know. Just phone me.'

He gave Wagner his hand: 'A pleasant evening.'

He made a slight bow to Luisa. As Wagner sat down again he noticed that at every table people were watching. It was probably an honour if the Intendente gave himself the pleasure of going over to a table to greet someone.

When Wagner and Luisa got up, for the first time Wagner noticed a slight lack of assurance in her, she stood hesitating as if to let Wagner go first. He carefully took her by the arm and gently led her. Wagner saw the adjutant whisper something to the colonel. When Wagner passed the table and loudly and clearly said 'good evening,' the colonel did not react. He was deep in conversation with the three women, while the two civilians stared in silence at Wagner and Luisa.

The manager accompanied them to the lift and said goodbye in Swiss German and expressed the hope that he would see Wagner very soon again. Going down in the lift Wagner asked Luisa if she knew the colonel.

'Oui, tout le monde le connaît.'

'Et il vous connaît?'

'Non, je ne crois pas.'

They walked through the night streets and the trees seemed to breathe. Now and then sticky droplets fell from the blossoms. Through the wide open windows they could hear fragments of a TV film. A rattling, brightly painted bus drove past.

When they came to the house where she lived Wagner stopped for a moment, but as she went in without turning he followed her into the musty smelling hallway. It was dark, everything was quiet. Luisa switched on the light, a bulb hanging from the ceiling. The door to the flat on the ground floor was open, but the flat was dark and seemed to be empty. Only that afternoon he had seen the old woman sitting at the entrance. Luisa climbed the steep wooden steps and he followed her. Before him, very close, he saw her legs, the narrow ankles, the two parallel hollows at the back of her knees. In the kitchen Luisa lit the gas with a lighter and put on a kettle of water. They were standing opposite each other, Wagner leaning against the table not an arm's length from her, and their silence emphasized every sound, in the distance a man coughing in the yard, a car starting, voices and shooting from a film on television, and very close the hissing of the gas flame. He listened and knew that she also heard all these sounds. A black moth fluttered clumsily around the lamp, a frill of blue glass had broken off it. Luisa was standing as if absorbed in watching the gas which burned with a strange green flame. Then she raised her head, looked at him and held out her hand to him. Carefully with the tips of his fingers he touched her neck and there felt the beating of her heart.

Eighteen

He woke up. She was lying on her stomach, her face under his arm, so deeply asleep that when he got up she didn't move. It was just after three o'clock. He wondered whether to wake her, but then looked for some paper, folded it into a ship and wrote on the bow: Luisa, and on the stern: Hasta mañana. Je t'aime. (How easy to write that in French.) Then he put the paper ship on the kitchen table. Then he dressed, put the tie in his jacket pocket and quietly shut the door behind him. As he couldn't find the switch he felt his way down the dark stairs. Except for a few street lamps everything was dark and quiet. He looked up into the night sky, the stars glittered bright and near, as if the sky were breathing.

He had gone a few steps when he saw a cigarette glow in a car on the other side of the street. Three figures sat like shadows in a Ford Falcon. Wagner went on walking without turning round. Was he being watched? But the thought struck him as so unfounded, he shook his head at himself for thinking it. At the next crossing there was an ambulance in which two men were sitting. It stood in the darkness beneath a tree. What were they waiting for? He wondered whether he ought to step into a doorway and watch the two cars. But it was obvious those sitting in the car had spotted him a while ago and were now watching him. Perhaps he was only seeing ghosts. On the right sleeve of his jacket where she had taken his arm as they walked home he could still smell her perfume, a fragrance that reminded him of his childhood, the smell of a flower or, he suspected, a cooking essence. He walked through the streets like this, the sleeve pressed to his mouth and nose.

He came to the Plaza and here too everything was dark and quiet except for the Egmont Bar, there was still light there. As he went past he heard voices and music. He was thirsty and would have liked to drink a beer, but forbade himself because he thought his memories, which still held something of her bodily presence – he smelled his hands – would lose their intensity in the atmosphere of the bar. So he went to his car.

He drove up to the hill that rose, brightly lit, from the plain.

In the entrance hall of his house he found a note written in an old-fashioned handwriting.

Police called. 3.06 o'clock. Food in refrigerator.

Wagner looked at his watch. It was 4.09. He wondered whether he should phone the police. But there was nothing about that on the note. What did they want from him in the middle of the night? Probably something had happened at the site. Possibly they had found the injured man. But that was surely no reason to phone him in the middle of the night. His meal was in the refrigerator, hygienically wrapped in tinfoil. Three bowls. He was annoyed at the obdurate stubborness with which Sophie, while knowing he wanted to eat in the city, had prepared the meal that now stood in the refrigerator like a reproach wrapped in silver paper. He took a can of beer, pulled the ring pull, and finished it on the way to his room. A small coloured card lay on the table next to his briefcase, a bad reproduction of some medieval woodcut that had been brightly coloured in: pitch rains from the sky, small flames rise from the houses, water rushes onto a collapsing tower, the sun has grown dark, people flee in wildly distorted movements. Under

150

the picture was written: And a mighty angel raised a great stone and threw it into the sea and said: Thus with a storm is the great city of Babylon overthrown and shall never rise again.

Wagner decided to look in the bible in the morning. His memories of the book from the days of his confirmation classes were not that sinister. He went through the huge house and thought of his house in Hamburg, that had also turned out too big. Now he would write to Susann and have to tell her everything. Why should this huge house stand empty, why shouldn't Luisa live here. Let us move in together, it was all so simple, so wonderfully simple. He had met someone with whom he wanted to be, had to be, right now, beginning today. He decided to write that same evening when he got back from the site. He would try to explain everything to her. The words 'midlife crisis' went through his head. And naturally it was exactly what she would think. But she would be wrong, it was something different, quite different. It was not anything he had sought but chance, pure chance; it was precisely that that made it so compelling. It was a need from which he could in no way retreat even if he had wanted to, even if he should be saying to himself that it wouldn't work, that you only had to take a step back and look to see that it was mindless, crazy. Don't make yourself ridiculous, Susann would say. No, not Susann, Renate could say it, a girl twenty years younger than he was, he couldn't even understand her properly; but there could be no doubting, it's simple and straightforward, a need bordering on pain. Wagner realized he had been talking aloud to himself and added, as if to conclude, so be it. He got himself a second beer from the refrigerator and went onto the veranda. He was tired, but had no desire to sleep. He slowly drank the beer that rested cold in his hand. He decided to drive to Luisa tomorrow as soon as work was over. She only had to shut the case that was already packed (what made him think the case was being packed, not unpacked?), he would carry it down and put it in the car, and then they would drive here. It was as simple as that. He would ask Sophie to go back to her people, and pay her two, or better three months' wages out of his own pocket. And that same evening he would sit down and write Susann the letter. It was as if he had entered into a new life and he very much hoped this mood would stay with him. Suddenly there was an unsuspected wealth of possibilities and that old tenacious wish to be able to begin all over again with a different life (even if one continued to carry the old life with one) seemed as if it would be granted after all.

The sheet lightning had increased. The wind had risen, but it was a pleasant warm wind that he felt on his skin. Wagner finished the beer. He thought of the phone call from the police. He was convinced it was something to do with the factory. One way or the other, there was time for it tomorrow. He wasn't even particularly curious. He'd get everything under control. He felt relaxed about it all. The basement would be built. And he was sure he could make up the wasted weeks.

He was so tired he lost track of his thoughts, only when he thought of Luisa everything became vivid and clear.

He went to the wall and looked over at the city. From here one could see lit streets.

The huts in front of the wall were in total darkness. There was nobody in sight. Then far away he saw the headlights of a car by the wall. Three figures ran backwards and forwards in the beams of light, they seemed to be digging and hacking as if they wanted to undermine the wall. The two men dragged something from the car to the wall. The headlights suddenly went out. Wagner stared into the darkness and wondered whether he ought to inform the police, but then he thought of the man in the hut whom it had been impossible to find the next day, and he told himself it was better to keep out of this. Then in the distance he saw the beam of a torch, it darted backwards and forward over the ground, and quick shadow-like movements. Possibly stolen property was being buried, weapons or — a body. But it was an abstruse thought. It was sure to be something quite ordinary and banal. Now the headlights came on again and drew away, rocking slowly up and down. He heard the noise of the motor in the distance. The car was going in the direction of the city. The headlights disappeared behind a low hill.

Wagner remained for a moment standing by the wall. Somewhere high on the hill a dog began to bark. There was nothing to see or hear. He went into the house and bolted the veranda door.

Nineteen

When Wagner got to the site in the morning, there were small columns of smoke everywhere over the clearing. There was a smell of burning wood and foliage, a smell that reminded Wagner of home in the autumn when the smell of potato fires drifted over the countryside. The clearing had been fired in the night. On site A concrete was being poured. Wagner could tell from the gluey jet that shot out of the mixer that the quality of the concrete was good. Hartmann tested it and stuck a thumb up in the air for approval. He went back to the site office. For the first time he thought he could feel the tilt of the building under his feet. Wagner sat at his table and worked on the estimate for the basement. There was a knock and Steinhorst entered, sweaty and bloated. He had had his surveyor's telescope repaired in the city. Wagner could have asked him what had gone wrong with it, but let it pass, at least Steinhorst had looked for an excuse for being late. Order was slowly being restored.

'We'll have to take ballast on board,' Wagner said.

'Ballast?' Steinhorst asked. There was sudden distrust in his face. He probably suspected the word ballast in some way referred to his condition.

'We'll put down gravel in the basement, on the side of course

154

that's rising into the sky. Surely it's obvious, without the live load the building's too light for this soil. To prevent the gravel slipping we'll build bulkheads with planks. Then we can add or shovel out gravel as required and correct our tilt, until a statistician has worked out the exact load for us.'

Steinhorst took glasses tinted almost black out of the breast pocket of his shirt: 'You don't seriously think you can level the tilt that way.'

'We'll know by the time the first cracks have appeared in the walls. It's still better than this constant slant. When I saw the storm yesterday I thought our little ship would float away. But we've got out of this scrap with only a black eye. I'll drive to the capital at the weekend and have another look there at the ground survey, the land registration, and also get a permit for the basement.'

'Oh,' Steinhorst said, 'but the captain's the last to leave the ship.'

He tipped his plastic helmet and left taking big rocking steps, as if to ride the swell. Wagner sat at the typewriter spattered with white Tipp-Ex and began typing the minutes of yesterday's meeting with the concrete manufacturer. He wanted one copy for Bredow, one to send to the central office in Germany. He wanted a record of what had been agreed. He thought of Luisa who probably had just got up. Was she having breakfast? Did she have a friend? Strangely enough he was convinced she didn't have a friend. But he knew almost nothing about her. He was familiar with her gestures, the way she pushed her hair behind her ears, how when thinking she held her right index finger to her mouth, as if asking for silence. He knew her in her intimate impulses, but apart from that not at all.

Having written the minutes he sat down again at the plans for the basement. He calculated the quantity of steel required for reinforcement. He again considered whether he ought to halt building on factory A. He had made a detailed list of the problems, also the possible solutions. What he could not understand was why, though he knew these new buildings would sink into the ground, Steinhorst had simply continued to build. It seemed less a case of indifference, more like an act of sabotage, not against the régime, that hardly mattered to Steinhorst, nor against the company, but aimed at the profession. In a destructive act of self-loathing he had also resolutely turned against the world outside. On the other hand Wagner could understand his predecessor who had had a nervous breakdown. The man had reacted very normally to the conditions and promptly gone mad. Wagner laughed aloud: 'Those words: "Enough to drive you mad".' In the morning Sophie had told him over breakfast about the police phone call during the night. Because his car had now been two nights on the Plaza they were asking where the owner was.

So they're worrying about me, Wagner thought, or looking at it differently, they're watching me.

At the weekend he would drive with Luisa to the capital. He forced himself not to think of Susann, or of Sascha. But he kept having to make himself concentrate on his calculations. Shortly before midday he was finished and asked Hartmann to go through them and check them again. Then a drawing had to be made of the basement extension that he could take with him at the weekend to the capital.

He went out to see if the workers had begun building the latrine. He went out into the fierce light over to the huts. It was just before the midday break. A good 200 metres from the huts two men were busy sharpening stakes with axes, two others were ramming the stakes into the ground with the aid of a large block of wood with four downward-pointing handles. Wagner was about to return to the site office when one of the workers ran towards the edge of the forest and threw himself onto something dark and fat. As he approached he recognized an armadillo that had dug itself into the earth to escape its pursuers. Wagner clearly saw the scaly armour on its back and the sparse wiry hair. The man tugged at the hind legs, but astonishingly the animal was able to dig deeper into the earth. In the meantime another worker had come running and now both pulled at the animal. In vain. It sat there as if anchored to the ground. Then one of the workers put his finger into the animal's anus and pulled it almost effortlessly out of the ground. The other worker stuck a knife into the wriggling armadillo's belly, and again, until the animal lay still. Then they dragged it over to the huts. Wagner followed them. They put it down near the two large brick ovens. Here two or three men were preparing the meal for the midday break. There were two large kettles on the two fires. A man was sitting on the ground with a large wooden bowl in which he was crushing little yellow-brown kernels with a stick, obviously some spice. The man did this with a circling movement and with his left hand poured in more kernels. He pushed the powder to the edge, a yellow-brown powder that was finely grained and yet seemed to be damp. Wagner crouched in front of the man, took a little powder from the edge of the bowl between his fingers and licked it. In a wild movement the man threw the bowl over with the ground powder and leaped up. Wagner crouched astonished on the ground and saw the yellow powder spilled on the sand and then the man's face, distorted with hatred. 'Sorry,' Wagner said and got up, 'I'm sorry.'

He went over to the site office and thought how idiotic this 'sorry' had sounded since it couldn't even be understood by the person whom it concerned. He had fumblingly reached into the man's – and therefore everybody's – spice, and then even his apology had been overbearing. He had behaved like one of those stupid clumsy tourists that had always annoyed him and Susann wherever they had come across them, in Greece, Spain or Morocco. And yet, as well as the anger at himself and a piercing shame, there was the feeling of quiet satisfaction at the small sensation of having felt and tasted this powder, it was fine-grained and silkily sticky to the touch and with a peculiar harsh bitter taste that left a sweetish burning on the tongue. He went back to the site office. Hartmann was waiting there. He said: 'I'm pleased for you that you managed it.'

'What?' Wagner asked irritated, as he had a suspicion that Hartmann might have been watching him.

'The concrete's good', Hartmann said, 'and I can see that you want to make the factory unsinkable.'

'Yes, as it were, it's important you go over the figures again. It has to be done in a tearing hurry. We want to start with the concrete for the basement by the middle of next week.'

Outside the siren wailed. Wagner leafed through the concrete calender and copied out the dates of the mixing ratios. There was a knock, the door was flung open and a man came in. He was wearing khaki trousers that reached to his knees and high laced leather boots. He had pushed his motorbike glasses back slightly into his hair. He gave Wagner a telegram and asked him to sign for it in a book. Then he stood waiting a moment, until Wagner gave him a tip, but which he obviously considered too little because on leaving he loudly slammed the door.

Wagner tore open the telegram and read: THINKING OF YOU. RENATE.

He went to the window and looked out. The messenger came out of the door below, got on to his motorbike, stepped on the accelerator and drove off. Wagner stared at the telegram. It was a message from another world. And it confirmed his suspicion that Renate's visit that time in Lüdenscheid had not been an extramarital escapade, but an attempt to break away. It was an attempt to escape stagnation.

The siren wailed. Wagner folded the telegram and put it in his shirt pocket. He glanced over at the Nissen huts. But none of the workers were going to the sites. Perhaps they had gone earlier. But he could see no one on the sites. Then he saw them, half-concealed by the Nissen hut, standing near their canteen where the man had ground the spice. They were standing in groups. He was startled and at the same time suspected that the men down there were refusing to work. He remembered the man's face, distorted by hatred, when he had reached into his ground spice.

Wagner went into the canteen. Engineers and technicians had got up and were getting ready to go to the sites. 'What's the matter?' Wagner asked Hartmann. 'They're not going to work out there.'

Hartmann went to the window and looked out. The others also crowded to the window.

Steinhorst, who was at a table doing a crossword puzzle, now also got up. With his dark glasses he went to the window like a blind man, took off the glasses, looked out and said: 'They're striking.' Wagner went out immediately. Steinhorst and Hartmann followed him. In the fierce heat they went over to the huts. Halfway over a man came running towards them, a foreman. The man was bleeding from the mouth and nose. He was talking breathlessly and gesticulating, his face distorted by shock and pain.

'What's he saying,' Wagner asked, 'what's he want?'

The man talked, he shouted, he pointed to the Nissen huts, then to the site office.

'What's going on,' Wagner called, 'where's Juan?'

Neither Hartmann nor Steinhorst could understand properly what the man was saying in his excitement, only that it had come to the use of force.

Wagner wanted to go over to the camp, the foreman promptly stood in his way, folded his hands and with a theatrical gesture cried: 'No, no.'

Wagner pushed him aside and went on walking, then Juan came running. Juan talked to the man who was still so excited, he shouted his replies. Then he translated: 'The foreman was beaten by the Bolivians when he tried to make them work. He was then threatened with a machete after he booted one of the striking workers in the backside.'

'Why are they striking?' Juan asked the foreman. The man shrugged. Wagner went on walking and thought, no wonder you get a punch in the face if you try to make someone work with a kick in the arse. The kick in the arse probably started the strike.

The air shimmered in the heat, there were still small columns of smoke over the clearing like over a field of lava. There was a smell of burning. Wagner went to the cooking area, to the wooden tables and benches standing in the open. The workers stood there, none were sitting, and many took off their hats as Wagner approached. Wagner again noticed that almost all the workers were Indian, only a few were mestizos. All looked at him. Suddenly one of them raised a hand and with a calm gesture pointed at Wagner, without saying anything. All he did was stand there and point at Wagner.

'What's going on,' Wagner asked, 'what do they want?' Juan asked.

The man who had pointed at Wagner slowly let his arm fall, and the jaguar man took a step forward and answered.

'The jaguar man says they still have to talk among themselves.'

'What,' Wagner shouted, 'are they crazy. They're striking and still looking for a reason. Do they understand what this means? The damage would be inestimable.'

His eyes burned with sweat. But he didn't want to wipe them now. The workers might think he was crying. So he stood there with streaming eyes and waited for the workers to talk among themselves. They took incredibly long, though actually they didn't say much, in fact very little, hardly anything at all. He again decided at all costs to learn Spanish and to put all his

160

energy into it, and not forever stand around so helpless in this country.

'You had better go back to the office,' Steinhorst said, who as always kept his plastic helmet on. 'Or you may get sunstroke.'

Hartmann had put a large blue and white check handkerchief over his bald head. Wagner said nothing and turned to the Indians again. How we must look to them, the three of us, Hartmann with his blond-red beard and the handkerchief on his head, Steinhorst, fat and sweating profusely and with the plastic helmet that was much too small for him, and me, with streaming eyes and sunburned forehead. At the same time he was annoyed at Steinhorst's presumption that came in the guise of concern. Because by referring to sunstroke he was clearly alluding to his predecessor's nervous breakdown.

Juan said, 'They need more time to talk. What they mean is, they want to talk without us.'

'Good,' Wagner said, 'I want their spokesman in my office in fifteen minutes.'

On his way to the office Wagner wondered if he should have threatened them with the police. And with mounting rage he thought of the answer he should have given Steinhorst: You'd do better to worry about your liver. But of course that was idiotic, and now he was also annoyed at being annoyed at Steinhorst's remark. At the site office not only had all the engineers and technicians gathered in the canteen, but the foremen who had their canteen on the ground floor had also come up. Wagner asked Juan to tell them the workers were striking, but the reason for the strike was not known yet. He was asking them to stay in the building until the matter had been settled.

While Wagner was still talking Steinhorst went to his bag, took out a flask in a leather case and in the silence that followed called out: 'Cheers.' Then he drank. Wagner was on the point of saying: Alcohol will not be drunk during working hours, but as nobody could work that would have been ridiculous. So he said: 'So that nobody feels discriminated against the company is offering whisky, while the supply lasts.'

It was a fairly feeble joke. And his anger against Steinhorst rose again for bringing this on him with his unauthorized holiday mood.

Paper cups were passed round, ice cubes got from the refrigerator, then whisky poured and drunk. There was laughter, people talked over each other. Someone had turned on a transistor and some provincial South American rock group was singing in hideous English: I go on and you fuck off. The mood in the canteen seemed to be like at a topping-out party and Wagner was reminded of his farewell party twelve days ago (was it really only twelve days ago?), except that there were no women here. Pedro was serving whisky from a plastic tray and when Wagner declined Pedro took the paper cup and emptied it in a gulp before Wagner's eyes. His eyes turned up as he drank, so that Wagner only saw the whites.

In the meantime the fifteen minutes Wagner had given as time to consider had passed and he knew everything would slip out of his control if the workers' delegation didn't come soon. The first engineers and technicians had already begun to get tipsy. Worse still, what at present could be considered a delay would then, in the eyes of the military authorities, become an open strike. He would have to phone Bredow who would inform the colonel. Probably the military would move in. The consequences were unforeseeable and he was convinced the Bolivians in particular would not know what to make of it, if it came to a clash between the military and the workers (the worst of all conceivable possibilities), or whether they would let themselves be deported without resisting. In either case building would come to a standstill for days, if not weeks. A wildcat strike, it would have to happen to him, and in his second week. It was grotesque. It was good for a laugh. He tried to laugh, but only snorted. He absolutely must try and sort things out, and right away.

Hartmann called: 'They're coming.'

They all crowded to the window. Below three workers were approaching the building. The jaguar man in front.

Wagner asked Juan to bring all three to him and asked Hartmann and Steinhorst (he wanted witnesses) to be present at the discussion. He pulled up the blinds in his room and sat with his back to the window so that the workers, when they were negotiating with him, would have to look into the harsh light. Juan pushed the three into the room. They stopped at the door, straw hats held in their hands in front of them. The scars on the jaguar man's face glowed red. Wagner saw the dirty feet in the worn-out leather sandals. They stood there as in an old photograph, the straw hats, the tattered shirts, the wide cotton trousers. The fan wafted over the smell of earth and freshly dried sweat.

Wagner told Juan to ask the reason for the strike. To his surprise a regular debate developed between them.

It was a while before Juan could begin with a translation. They didn't want to go on working because one of their number had been arrested and no one knew where he was, because they were having to build an unnecessary latrine, because a foreman had kicked them up the backside, because a snake had been killed, because somebody had stuck his hand into their food.

They say somebody, but that somebody is me, Wagner thought, what a hotchpotch of reasons. For a long time already they had had good reasons for a strike, the wretched accommodation, the poor pay, the separation from their families and people, all this they had accepted, but the moment he had reached into their food, touched the fine yellow-brown powder their honour had been violated. Here they were hurt, in this small area that remained to them and that yet was so extremely important: You don't let someone dip into your food like an animal. The three men in rags stood there, calm, even relaxed, he could see no excitement in their faces. They were waiting to see what Wagner would say.

Wagner considered. 'None of this is a reason to strike,' he said finally. They could have come to him earlier to complain about all they were telling him now. Then he would have tried to remove the problems. Remove, Wagner thought as Juan translated, is actually wrong, after all what ought to be removed is me, and they all know it. I could say: I won't do it again, I promise, and make myself look ridiculous. No one would ever take me seriously again.

Wagner said: 'I promise I'll make enquiries again to find out where the arrested man is. I ran over the snake, but it was not intentional. It was an accident, pure chance. The carpentry for the latrine can be done in normal working hours, and will of course be paid. Please tell your colleagues (how false that sounded faced with these three men in rags) all this, and then start work again in fifteen minutes. The siren will go off a second time. Should you not start work I shall have to call in the military.'

Juan translated, and the three left the room. Wagner glanced at his watch. It was 15.40. They had already lost forty minutes. In twenty minutes exactly we'll sound the siren. We'll give them the extra five minutes as they have to get back first. Then they can all discuss it.

'You say it's pure chance you ran over the snake. But these people don't understand that,' Juan said. 'What is chance? Chance has to account for anything and everything, at least in their world, in which everything can be accounted for. What can't be accounted for is chance. Chance is the eternal remnant, not soluble. Chance is infinitely naive and simple. Chance is stupid. It's their blind spot. But these people have explanations for it. Explanations to do with forces working in different ways, in the stone, the snake, the forest, the sun, the lightning, the

164

clouds. A force, and not a good one, made you kill this snake, the car perhaps, I don't know, and the snake allowed itself to be killed.'

'No,' Wagner said, 'you can tell me all this some other time, but not now. Steinhorst, what do you think, will they return to work?'

Steinhorst sat at the table as if all this no longer had anything to do with him. He had gone on drinking and puffed his cheeks: 'Hard to say. Don't know, why don't you ask the man who spat in their food. He should go and apologize to the Bolivians, so should whoever kicked them in the arse, which more or less amounts to the same thing. Then perhaps there's a chance.'

Surely Steinhorst knew or at least suspected that he, Wagner, had put his hand in their food. He wondered if he should go with Juan to the camp and apologize. But if they were then to go on striking for some other reason, for example because of the snake, he would only have made himself ridiculous. 'I'll let Bredow know, in case they don't go back to work.'

Bredow answered brightly with a beaming hello and immediately asked Wagner if he felt like a game today.

'No,' Wagner said, 'that's definitely not possible, they're striking here.'

Wagner had to call hello twice before he could stir Bredow out of his speechlessness. Then he enumerated the reasons for the strike, as translated for him by Juan. He left none out, not even that somebody had put his hand into the workers' food, but didn't say he was that somebody. Bredow wanted no further explanation of the reasons, only said: 'A load of rubbish, get them working. Make it hot for them. Spell out what's at stake. Threaten them with the military. Tell them they'll be deported.'

'Already have.'

'Good. You absolutely have to get them back to work today, never mind how, and if they only work ten minutes tonight, or we're in an unbelievable mess. The military will intervene immediately. You know what the consequences are. In any case, we're already behind in our schedule. Do you get the impression they're willing to talk?'

'We'll see soon enough,' Wagner said, 'the siren goes off in ten minutes.'

Twenty

The siren went off. Wagner stood at the window and looked over to the camp. The workers were standing and crouching in the shade of the huts. None of them were going over to the building sites.

'Then we can go home,' Steinhorst said. Hartmann wanted to go over to the workers and talk to them, alone, perhaps he could change their minds before Wagner phoned Bredow.

From the window Wagner watched Hartmann go over to the Nissen huts. Hopefully he'll succeed.

The concrete lorries arrived on time and drove slowly over to site A. Wagner heard voices and laughter from the canteen. He stood at the window and waited till he saw Hartmann coming back. He could already see from Hartmann's walk that he hadn't been able to achieve anything. Otherwise he would have walked faster. Wagner went to the canteen. They had all in the meantime made themselves very comfortable. They sat there drinking, talking and laughing as if what was going on outside no longer concerned them. They no longer paid any attention to Wagner.

Hartmann came in, wiped his freckled bald head with his handkerchief and said: 'I can understand they don't want people spitting into their food, but how the snake comes into

167

it is beyond me. But that's what it's about, and about the person who stuck his hand into their food. As I said, I understand that, but I can't make out what they want, what they're after. Probably they don't know themselves yet. All these months they've kept very quiet, put up with everything, but now the barrel's run over.'

'What barrel', Wagner thought, 'what kind of comparison's he making?'

Steinhorst asked whether the concrete lorries were to be sent back, or should they just dump six heaps of concrete onto the landscape in enduring memory of this glorious day.

Wagner got up and said: 'Right, everybody put on rubber boots. Who can work a crane? Good, Hartmann, you do it. And you too, Steinhorst, take a concrete vibrator. Vibration's supposed to be good for liver complaints. Will the other gentlemen also kindly take spades and vibrators into their refined hands. Translate that!'

The engineers, technicians and foremen stood there and gaped at him as if he'd disrupted their pleasant party in a particularily outrageous fashion.

Wagner went to his room and phoned Bredow: 'They're striking. They didn't go to work. Now we're pouring the delivered concrete.'

'Who's we?' Bredow asked.

'We, that's the engineers, technicians, foremen, the big chief included, in short everybody. But we'll have to think whether to cancel tomorrow's lorries. I'd say no.'

Bredow spoke about the fines that could be expected for breach of contract. In any case they were already a month behind, this was all a disaster.

Wagner interrupted him, saying he needed to get to work. He said it deliberately: 'Work', because he could see Bredow in his blue silk suit sitting in the air-conditioned office, in front of him that enormous empty desk with the photogenic Christi

168

and children in silver frames, the maternally solicitious Mrs Klein in the waiting room, and in the reception the beauty stalking on silver stilettos.

Wagner put on the helmet, pulled on the rubber boots with the label BOSS which both his predecessors had worn, and went over to the site. The drivers of the six concrete lorries were standing in the shade of their lorries and looked over at Wagner. As he passed one of the drivers spat in front of his feet. Wagner hesitated a moment, wondering whether to punch his ugly face, but forced himself to keep walking. Hartmann was just climbing into the crane. A little later the first concrete bucket swung over to the lorries. Wagner went to the place where a section of the floor, 300 metres altogether, was to be poured. The factory was the length of a giant tanker but unfortunately, Wagner thought, without its buoyancy. At least that could be changed with the next factory.

'Right, let's get going,' Wagner said.

They worked until the light began to fade, until slowly and hestitantly the cries of the night began. Wagner had waded in concrete and taken turns at the vibrator with Steinhorst. He had had to relieve him with increasing frequency and for longer periods. Steinhorst was completely exhausted, but said nothing.

'Let me,' Wagner had said.

Steinhorst would then sit down anywhere, get covered in concrete, once pissed where he stood, with one hand holding onto a frame. The man was finished. His grey-blonde hair was soaked in sweat and stuck tangled to his forehead.

When the last lorry had been unloaded Wagner tapped Steinhorst on the shoulder. Wagner took a cigarette out of the packet, lit it and handed it to Steinhorst. He had seen how his hands were shaking. He lit one for himself and divided the rest among the others.

'One sees,' Wagner said, 'how few people it takes to put up

a building like this. That's something one mustn't tell Bredow, and management even less.'

'Well yes,' Hartmann said, 'the day after tomorrow we'll be ripe for hospital.'

They went over to the site office, the lights were already on. Wagner could feel his legs and arms and a dull pain in his back. The blisters on his hands had burst, the cuts went into the flesh. The workers had watched them from the camp, none sat, they all stood, like a chorus, Wagner thought.

In the canteen Wagner offered another round of whisky. He said 'Salud' and 'Gracias'.

The local engineers and technicians pushed their way out.

'I'll sleep here tonight,' Wagner said.

'Why?' said Steinhorst, who had drunk another bottle of mineral water. 'It won't help.'

And Hartmann tried to persuade Wagner, better to leave when they did, one wasn't to know how the workers would react. Juan kept silent. Secretly Wagner had hoped one of the three would stay. At all costs Wagner wanted to avoid occupation of the site office. Here were all the plans, drawings and regulations. Arson would hold the work up for weeks.

On the way out Steinhorst said something about site heroics and a lonely watch. Wagner would dearly have liked to kick his wide backside. From below he heard the roar of cars starting and driving away. He saw the buses and cars, their headlights on, driving from the site. The clearing was already dark. The fires were lit in the camp and Wagner saw figures sitting or walking about. He had taken up a position by the window so that they could see him, as he could see them, in silhouette. One of the neon lights on the ceiling flickered spasmodically. What would Luisa, who was now waiting for him, think? Of course he would explain tomorrow so that there would be no misunderstanding and nothing to cause upset. But there remained the painful thought that she might believe he'd only wanted a brief adventure and so shabbily taken advantage of her openness. He should have asked Juan to let her know. To distract himself he sat down at the electric typewriter. Now, after nine days – and it was only nine days since he had taken over the running of the site – to be writing a report on a strike he himself had brought about seemed like a nightmare. He switched on the machine on which the Tipp-Ex dribblings of his predecessors were deposited like guano and listened to the steady hum. He rubbed his hands and pressed them as if he could squeeze out the phrases that would remove some of the grotesque significance from the entire proceedings. He shivered – though it was suffocatingly hot – from exhaustion and tiredness. Then he wrote the first sentences, simple statements that described the course of events, the details of which – he gave time and place – relieved him because they were so far removed from any conjecture of whether he was to blame for what had happened. He listed the reasons given for the strike by the spokesman, exactly as Juan had translated them for him, those also for which he was responsible, the death of the snake (how grave it looked written) and the hand in the food. After this information and clearly separate from it he wrote down his suspicion that reasons for the strike lay elsewhere: in the poor pay, the wretched barrack-like accommodation, the overlong working hours, the poor food and the legal insecurity of the immigrant workers who in reality were only tolerated illegal workers, at any rate the majority of them.

He signed the report, put it in an envelope and decided to post it in the capital, together with his report on the water level and the poor concrete. He went to the coffee kitchen and looked for something to eat. He only found a tin of corned beef. The refrigerator was empty, the mineral water had all been drunk. But he found two bottles of orange juice. He drank one bottle. The juice tasted rather sweet. Then he pulled the lid from the tin and went to the window, though lit from behind as he was he could see nothing, only himself, his dark reflection, but he wanted those outside to see him. Let them see he'd stayed behind. He began eating the meat in the tin with a plastic fork.

It came in strands out of the tin, the fat yellow, in it pieces of tendon white like worms. He recalled what Berthold had said: 'It's a suicide mission.' For him it was an irresolvable chaos, a frightening, incomprehensible mixture of violence, open and concealed, and intertwined interests unknown to him. How had the building contract been awarded? Why these ground surveys that failed to correspond to the land? Who had given the money? Who owned this site? And who the original one? And where did the loan come from? (Germany apparently, the Federal Republic). He knew almost nothing. On the other hand he had thoroughly studied the plans, had had company management show him the model and had liked it. It was a beautifully proportioned construction, built for its purpose, with large glazed areas facing north. Wagner had wanted to be an architect. But he had studied structural and civil engineering without even attempting to apply to do architecture. He had had doubts that he would be a good architect, rooted in his belief that he was unable to draw sufficiently well. As a child, so he had been repeatedly told later, he had liked drawing and done a lot of it, but they were strange drawings, the teachers could never see the resemblance to the depicted object.

Finally he himself had become aware of the discrepancy between what he saw, and what he put down on paper. Not that he drew any worse than the other students, but unlike them he was plagued by doubts, and this made everything more awkward and hopeless. He should have drawn what he saw quite differently. But how? So he lost the pleasure in drawing and painting after nature. But he loved drawing with ruler and stencil. His delight in the precise, in symmetry.

The phone rang.

It was Bredow. Steinhorst had informed him. Bredow said he had just given the Intendente a full account.

'Why?'

'Every strike has to be instantly reported to the military. They'll clear out the camp tomorrow if the Bolivians don't go back to work. They'll all be deported. Then we're stuck for days on end. It's a real disaster.'

'No,' Wagner said, 'we have to try and find a remedy of our own'. He was thinking, as he said this, not so much of the fine for breach of contract as that he was implicated if the workers lost their jobs. 'I suggest we wait until noon tomorrow. Then we'll see what exactly they want. So far they haven't asked for anything. They've just stopped working. Then we can decide whether to meet their conditions or not. Perhaps they'll only want an apology.'

Bredow's laugh was decidedly forced: 'That would be nice. No, it's all gone too far.'

'But you could have waited until noon tomorrow.'

'No. Strikes have to be reported immediately. There's still martial law, a state of emergency. And nothing frightens the military as much as strikes. We'll wait and see what happens tomorrow morning. And listen, take care. The Indians are not predictable. You mustn't underestimate this business with the snake. I've not found anyone here who could explain to me what it's about. But there's something behind it. Barricade the doors. Have you got anything to eat?'

'Yes,' Wagner said, 'the menu's good.'

'Then good luck.'

Wagner kept his ear to the receiver a brief moment longer, then hung up. From outside he heard isolated animal calls, but they were still far away, only the throbbing of the unit was close. He went to a room that was dark to be able to observe the camp without being seen. The Bolivians sat at fires, black figures, flickering shadows. In the movements, the gestures, he thought he recognized excited discussion and immediately related it to himself, to the site office. Wagner went downstairs. The door to the staircase couldn't be locked, a swing door. He went out. The high wire fence that surrounded the building was lit at regular intervals by plate lamps. Wagner felt as if he were imprisoned in a camp. He went to the large gate. As every morning when he was the first to arrive, it was locked. But the guard was nowhere in sight. He went to his car which was the only one on the clearing. At first he thought all the tyres had been slashed, but as he approached he could see nothing out of the ordinary.

Wagner went back into the building. He stopped once because he thought he had heard a noise behind him, but there was nothing.

He decided to spend the night in the canteen. The place was large and full of tables and chairs, at least he could get away if they came here. And everything here reminded him of the others, the paper cups, the sand ashtrays spiked with butts, the rubber boots on the floor left carelessly where an exhausted engineer had taken them off. Wagner fetched binoculars, an S was scratched on the black grip, it was Steinhorst's. Presumably when he was in charge he had watched the workers from this room while drinking his whisky. Wagner looked through the binoculars across to the camp. Everything seemed peaceful and quiet.

Wagner sat by the window. Susann was coming from the school, pushing the bike over the paved path. Her face was red from cycling in the wind and shining wet from the light drizzle. She pulled the black sou'wester that made her look carefree off over her head, and with short but energetic movements of her head shook out her hair, her thick dark blonde hair. She hung her black oilskin coat up in the hall where the peasant cupboard was that she had bought in a junk shop and then painted, following a pattern she had traced from a cupboard in the Altona Museum. Then she went up the stairs where the copper baking moulds she had collected since her student days hung on the walls. She worked in the kitchen with the calm, economical movements he had always admired. Sascha arrived, about to bawl, but it was impossible to get out of him what had happened. He would rather bawl than name the reason, perhaps couldn't even name it because he didn't know it. Problems at school, problems with other children. Sascha's teacher, that sour-faced woman said the boy's as if driven. But why? What were they doing wrong, Susann and he, they both made such an effort. And even if he did always feel an impatience in himself that he turned against Sascha when he wasted time or lost something, it was an impatience that actually was directed against himself, because increasingly he felt time passing and with it the possible fulfillment of his desires. It was the passionate craving for experiences through which one became self-aware, new and unique, like being hungry when one was a child or freezing until one was numb, or the smell in autumn when the leaves were burned. Since those days things had lost their smell and colour. One had to give oneself a push to see them and smell them anew. Perhaps all sensory cells died – like the taste cells – with age, and all that remained was the memory of that wealth and the desire for it, because with each year one grew poorer. He could not remember when he had last spoken with Susann about his or her desires. How should life be? Different. And what one could expect of oneself and for oneself, that also diminished with time and became less clear. In the end there was only the desire for things to be different.

He fetched paper and a ballpoint pen and sat at a table in the canteen to write to Susann. He wanted to suggest they separate. At first he didn't want to write about Luisa because then she would be bound to think it was because of this girl. But his decision had been made much earlier, on the day they had phoned him and asked him if he wanted to take over the job. It was a trial separation, and Susann herself had immediately agreed, she hadn't even been surprised. How little he was needed, how unnecessary he was, how little he had come to mean to her. Then he thought he owed it to Susann to tell the truth, to hide nothing, therefore also to write about Luisa and about Renate and that only like this, without lies, would he come to terms with himself. He took the telegram, damp with sweat, from his shirt pocket:

THINKING OF YOU. RENATE

Probably he and Renate only shared the same desire. Suddenly the light went out. A moment later, after a slight shock he remembered the unit was switched off every night at this hour. He thought of Luisa and this drove out any feeling of possible danger.

His father had once locked him in a storeroom. First he had unscrewed the bulb. Wagner recalled for the first time in years how, after a moment of panicking fear that seemed to suck the air out of him, he had seen the darkness, a promise of stillness, his fear extinguished. The breath still comes in little sobs. Sobs like gurgling. Like gurgling that comes from the diver as he rises from the seabed, in his hands the pearls that he holds out to the white men in the boat, before the stone tied to his back drags his body into the depths again, where he breaks open shells. Again he shoots up, the fountain of blood — his scream, and already the stone has pulled him down, and so he disappears, his breath rises in pearls.

Twenty One

He was woken by a quiet clattering. The neon strip lighting shone above him. The motor in the refrigerator was making the bottles standing on it clatter. On the ceiling the fan was turning. It was still dark outside. In the distance he again heard the quiet humming of the unit. Wagner lay on the floor, heavy and stiff. Slowly he raised himself and was so dazed, he had to lean against the arm of the chair. He looked over at the camp through the binoculars. A few lamps were lit, fire under the ovens, figures wandering about.

Wagner went into the kitchen and turned on the percolator. From the ground floor he heard pop music. He drank the rest of the orange juice and watched the coffee forced hissing through the filter. In the chrome casing of the percolator he saw his face, grotesquely distorted, the nose huge, rings under his eyes and unshaven, hair sticky with sweat. He stank. He had to laugh. He didn't look like the manager of a major building project, more like a tramp, or if he wanted to take a romantic view of himself, a traveller after a strenuous expedition into the interior. He sat by the window and saw the red in the east slowly brighten and drank coffee. He was wondering how to proceed later that morning. Nothing had happened so far that made further work impossible. The concrete had been poured. The engineers and he had a few blisters on their hands, that was all. But if the consignment of concrete was not used now, that was it. Everything depended on the workers going back to work today.

He then went down to the gate. One of the guards came running, in blue underpants and black slippers on his feet. He carried a submachine gun like a doll in his right arm. Wagner would have liked to ask where he'd been last night. He went in the direction of the camp. The guard followed him. Wagner said: 'No,' and pointed to the office building. The guard looked at him anxiously. Wagner continued walking, the man followed him. Wagner turned again, stamped his foot, waved his hand as if driving away a dog running after him. Then he went on between the Nissen huts. At a tar barrel (was this the hut in which he had found the injured man?) a man was washing his chest and shoulders. He came to the wooden benches and tables standing in the open, where some men already sat drinking coffee and eating bread. They looked at him. There was no sign of surprise in their faces, but they stopped chewing, and as he walked past them they slowly stood up. There was nothing threatening about this, the effect was more that of a polite gesture with which one greets a guest. Wagner wondered if he should talk to them. He stopped and hesitated, then noticed the jaguar man coming over from the range fire, a tin cup in his hand.

Wagner said: 'Buenas dias,' and then in German: he was sorry about what had happened yesterday, he could easily understand their anger. He wouldn't let anyone put a hand in his food either. But he had been so attracted by the colour and the fine grain of the ground spice that he simply had to feel. It had been a momentary, uncontrollable compulsion. As for the man who had been arrested, he promised to again try and find out where he was. But probably he had already been sent back to Bolivia. And one other thing, he again wanted to stress that he had not deliberately run the snake over, all he'd wanted was to stay on the road, it might have been right but perhaps it was also a mistake, to think: protect tyres and axles, but not the snake. He asked them to start work again, otherwise there would only be trouble. For them, for himself and for the entire project. He also promised that no action would be taken against anyone.

Wagner said all this very forcefully and as if they were able to understand every word. And when he apologized for the death of the snake he did it with conviction and great seriousness because for these people before him, in rags and worked into the ground, who lived packed into these corrugated irons huts and separated from their families it had a meaning, one he didn't know of course and would also no doubt not understand, but that mattered a great deal to them. He looked at them, nodded to them and was about to turn when the jaguar man approached him and held out his steaming tin cup to him.

It was a big blue enamel cup, chipped in several places. Wagner held it in his hand for a moment, smelled the coffee, drank and almost let out a shriek because he had burned his mouth. He made an effort not to pull a face. But the jaguar man seemed to have noticed anyway as he stuck out his tongue and pointed to it with his finger. At this Wagner also stuck out his tongue. They stood for a moment facing each other with tongues stuck out and simultaneously began to laugh. It was the first time Wagner had seen one of the Bolivians laugh. The scarred face became contorted, the man laughed less loudly than Wagner, it was more a giggle such as one hears with children. The others standing there also laughed. Wagner gave back the cup and briefly raised his hand. He walked slowly back to the building where the first engineers and technicians were parking their cars.

Steinhorst was sitting in the canteen. He had been drinking, his face was flushed and badly bloated. Steinhorst grinned: 'We thought we'd find you very small.'

'Why?'

'Well, a shrunken head. You need luck, or it's a short life.'

Wagner left Steinhorst sitting and was in his room when Hartmann burst in, breathless, sweaty, his bald freckled head glowing red: 'Military's coming.' On the way to the site he had seen three military trucks with soldiers and two jeeps. Wagner should phone Bredow instantly and Bredow should phone the colonel.

'The military must not be sent in!'

'It's also no longer necessary,' Wagner said, 'the workers are going back to work today.'

'The will reigns supreme,' Steinhorst said and belched.

Hartmann asked how Wagner could be sure they wanted to go back to work.

'I talked to the men.'

Hartmann looked at Wagner as if he'd gone mad overnight.

Steinhorst laughed, 'Your predecessor had conversations with St Paul. He stood on the site and screamed. And the man was a protestant.'

'How did you talk to them, in Spanish?'

'No, in German.'

'Merry Christmas,' Steinhorst roared, 'we'll drink to that, cheers!'

The siren wailed. Wagner went to the window. It seemed to wail longer than usual today. He looked over to the camp. The first workers were coming, then more, they were going over to the sites.

Wagner could hardly control his delight: 'They're coming, you see, there, all of them.' Tiredness and exhaustion fell from him, and he cried: 'At last we can get moving.'

Today the workers came, not in the usual straggling columns,

180

but in large and small groups. 'Right,' Wagner said, 'now we'll get to work,' and turning to Steinhorst, 'if you still can.'

'Always,' Steinhorst roared.

Wagner was leaving the office building as the first small military convoy drove onto the site. A jeep in front, then three heavy lorries, then another jeep. The convoy drove straight to the camp. Two of the lorries were open, on them soldiers sitting packed tightly together in rows of four, helmets on their heads, submachine guns between their legs. The last lorry was covered by a tarpaulin. The convoy stopped. Commandos. The soldiers leaped from the loading platform and ran with their machine guns, spread out and surrounded the huts. Some stormed the huts. Another group ran in the direction of the sites.

Wagner ran over to the camp. Relaxed, cigarette in mouth, the captain who had previously been in charge of the search for the injured man came towards him. In broken German the captain said he was happy to be of assistance to Wagner. Wagner shouted at him: 'This is not necessary. What's the point of it? They're working. Call off your men. We're working here. Everything's under control.'

The captain threw away the cigarette he had just lit. 'No,' he said. 'I've my orders.'

Hartmann arrived with Juan, both talked to the captain. But he only repeatedly shook his head. Wagner saw that neither of them was achieving anything and ran to the office building.

Mrs Klein answered. 'Where's the fire?' Bredow was on his way to the site.

Without explaining further Wagner asked for the colonel's phone number. 'Quickly,' he said, 'please quickly.'

In the administrator's office a man answered who understood neither English nor German. Wagner kept repeating: 'My name is Wagner,' gave the name of the company and said: 'El Intendente por favor!'

At last he heard the voice of Colonel Kramer who, in his

cultivated German with the light regional accent, asked what he could do for him. Withdraw the troops from the site. The men all began work on time this morning.

'Sorry, but that can't be done. The report of the strike has been passed on to headquarters. News of any strike must be instantly passed on to the top. A strike, you see, violates the state of emergency. That's no trifling matter.'

'But surely it can be stopped. To take action is pointless, unnecessary and only creates ill will.' He heard the colonel laugh. 'Preferably ill will now, than corpses later.'

'But I persuaded the men to go back to work. I gave the men my word nothing would happen. That there would be no reprisals.'

'Aaah, your word of honour, they don't understand that. No need for any pangs of conscience. In this instance I really can't help you. Simply because the entire business has passed beyond my control.'

'Good,' Wagner said and hung up. As he ran over to the camp he saw four men being led away. The men held their hands clasped over their heads, behind each was a soldier, machine gun at the ready.

What a performance, Wagner thought, how frightened the soldiers must be of these little people in rags. The jaguar man was the first. He looked in Wagner's direction. Wagner was unable to see his eyes under the low hanging brim of the straw hat. This morning he had spoken with these men. They had not been able to understand what he had said, and yet they had understood him. He had drunk from the cup of the man with the damaged face, and that was like sealing the peace between brothers. It must all seem like cunning to them now, like a shabby trick.

The three other workers passed him. They didn't look at him but looked down at the ground at their feet, as if their path were traced out there. They went to the lorry hooded with a tarpaulin. A hand came out of the tarpaulin at the tailboard, part of a steel helmet was briefly visible, the hand pulled up the jaguar man, then the other three Bolivians, one after another. They raised their hands, the hand appeared and with a tug pulled them up, a helping hand that seemed to contradict everything else, but was really only help towards execution.

The captain came over, briefly raised his hand to his helmet, said: 'Thank you,' and went over to his jeep. The soldiers had climbed onto the two lorries, the motors started and in a cloud of blue exhaust the convoy drove from the site in the direction of the forest. At that moment Wagner caught a glimpse of one of the cranes swinging a bundle of steel rods. So building continued as if nothing had happened. And as the last lorry and behind it the jeep disappeared into the forest, Wagner thought, I've failed in a way that can never be put right. He walked slowly over to the office building.

Steinhorst was still sitting on the chair in the canteen. In the meantime he had even put a bottle of whisky on the table.

Wagner said: 'There'll be no drinking in working hours, is that clear, Mr Steinhorst.'

Steinhorst slowly raised himself against the table. He stared at Wagner with puffy bloodshot eyes. Then he said: 'You arsehole. You shitstirrer.'

At first Wagner didn't take this as referring to himself. It was not said very clearly and with a slurred tongue. Wagner turned round, but apart from himself only Juan and Hartmann were still in the canteen, Pedro was cleaning the coffee machine. Wagner looked at Steinhorst and realized that he meant him, and that because there were others in the room he could not simply ignore it.

Steinhorst growled: 'You've understood nothing. Nothing. Nothing. Nothing. You have to stick your paws in everywhere. You're a wise fart.'

Wagner hit him in the face. With the flat of his hand. Not

even hard. He briefly felt something damp, wet, it was Steinhorst's lip and Wagner was shocked and revolted. Steinhorst looked at Wagner dazed. His lip began to bleed. He felt his lips with his fingers, then looked at the blood. He ran the tip of his tongue over his lips several times. There was suddenly something thoughtful in Steinhorst's face, as if he had to concentrate on the taste of the blood. Then he went out, in a straight line and without any unsteadiness in his walk.

Twenty Two

In the evening Wagner parked outside Luisa's house. He had come straight from the site, dirty and unshaven. He wanted to explain to Luisa why he hadn't been able to come yesterday, and wanted to ask her to come home with him. He had prepared sentences in simple French on the way. What depressed him was that he hadn't been able to write to Susann before Luisa moved in with him. What Sophie might say didn't bother him. He decided to simply ignore her and hoped Luisa could do the same.

The wooden shutters on the house were closed as always. The front door stood half open as if someone had just left the house, and the door to the ground floor flat was ajar.

He climbed the creaking stairs. At the top he listened a while and as he heard nothing knocked on the door, first quietly, then hard. From inside all he could hear was the chirping of sparrows, as if they were sitting in the kitchen. Probably going out she had left the windows open. The chirping made him think of home. He knocked again but knew she was out and took the telegram, curled with his dried sweat, from his shirt pocket.

'Telephone moi. Je t'aime.'

He tore off the piece he'd written on. On the other side was:

THINKING OF YOU. RENATE. He tore off the RENATE and put the note in the door.

He sat in the car and kept his eyes on the front door because he had taken it into his head she would come at any moment.

On the street children were burning an old tyre. Green flames were devouring the tyre. He thought of how she had stood at the oven. The gas there had burned that strange green.

It had grown dark and there was a smell of burning rubber. Bredow had come to the site in the afternoon, long after the military had left. His pale blue shirt had dark patches of sweat under the armpits. He gave the impression of being morose, yes, even nervous, something Wagner had never noticed in him before. He listened only inattentively as Wagner told what had happened. He kept looking at his watch. And finally said he'd come after all to talk everything over quietly.

Wagner said the behaviour of the military was unbelievable. He intended to complain.

Bredow gave a laugh. 'Very funny, where?'

'Listen, I never joke about these things.' Wagner tried to sound caustic and determined.

'I'm sorry, I didn't mean it like that. But everything's taken a stupid course. Only the military don't understand jokes when it comes to a strike. They're very sensitive there. Understandably. It puts the wind up them, something like that could spread and the next thing, you've got a revolution. I mean, they arrested all trade union leaders, but it could still begin from below, spontaneously, a spark's enough, some factory makes the first move, something trivial, it spreads like wildfire to other factories. No, they're pretty scared.'

'I gave them my word not one of them would be arrested if they returned to work.'

'Listen,' Bredow said, 'that's all very honourable of you, but we're not with the boy scouts here. Here it's not a matter of doing good deeds, but of getting this project off the ground.

Circumstances are such, at least here, that you can't promise something like that, because you can't keep it. In these things the military decide.'

'And what happens to the men?'

'They'll be deported. Put across the border.'

'Are you sure they won't simply put them in jail?'

'Quite sure. That would only cost money. Anyway, since the coup the prisons are overcrowded.'

'And how do I replace the four missing men? Now we're already five short, with the one they came for last Saturday.'

'Yes,' Bredow said, 'I'm afraid you'll have to get by without them. The men are all signed on at the same time, you can't just bring in others. There'd only be arguments. Imagine it, one lot worship snakes and the other lot eat them as a delicacy. Being the big hunter, you no doubt would belong to the second group.' Bredow laughed and, as Wagner didn't laugh with him, slapped him on the shoulder. 'I have to get back to the city now.'

Then he had got back into his BMW and driven off.

Wagner at first couldn't understand why he had come to the site at all, and only later thought he had found the reason. He wanted, as it were at the place of Wagner's defeat, to tell him there were no replacements for the men. Here, as Wagner admitted to himself, he was more ready to make concessions. Perhaps there was sense after all in this very exaggerated military action: it intimidated and forced down the cost. Bredow had saved on five men, among them three foremen, which at least helped balance the figures. He and the men were stuck with it: he would have to put even more pressure on them to work.

Luisa's house lay in darkness. He was so tired, he slapped his face with both hands to keep himself awake. Finally he drove over to the hill. He parked outside the bungalow. There was a removals van on the street lit by a mobile spotlight as if someone were filming. A piano was being carried from the house next door. Four men struggled with it. Walking beside them was Wagner's neighbour, in knee length trousers with a large check pattern. He was talking in butchered Spanish to the porters. When he saw Wagner he waved and called: 'Let's move uphill. You must come and see us one day.'

Wagner called: 'OK.'

As Wagner was about to open the door, it opened from inside. There stood Sophie. She was wearing her grey hair loose, it fell far down over the shoulders of her white overall. In her hand she held a sharpening knife like a short sword. He asked her if the Americans next door were moving out and where.

'They are fleeing. For great is their fear, here at the wall. But it will avail them nothing, no matter how high on the hill, let them choose the highest mountain in the land. For it stands written, the abyss will open, and from the abyss smoke shall rise as from a great oven, and the smoke shall darken the air and the sun itself. Come to us, join our community. For as was prophesied, the time has come, and everywhere there is murder, theft and whoring. The creatures of the air lament, as do those of the forest. The day is nigh. A great flood shall come, engulfing all, and smoke shall plunge all into darkness. And there shall be ice. Then he who is acquainted with God shall sit at the side of Jesus.'

'I'm hungry Sophie,' Wagner said, 'please understand, and tired.' He stared at her, this woman in the white overall and huge plastic sandals on her feet, and in her hand a sharpening knife. She stood there like a gloomy avenging angel. Perhaps after a good sleep and in a good mood he might have been amused, but now secret revulsion crept over him.

'I shall give unto you two witnesses and two thousand and two hundred days shall they prophesy. So it stands written. They are two olive trees and two blazing torches, standing before God.'

'Yes,' he said, 'good, I'll look it up.'

'What?' Sophie asked surprised.

'In the bible. But first I'd like to eat.'

He sat down at the laid dining room table. As she came in he thought he could see a dress made of sackcloth under her white overall. He thought of the four workers that had been arrested, and of Luisa. But now it disturbed him to think of Luisa, and of the four men, and of Susann and Sascha. He would gladly have driven them from his mind for a while; it would be like getting his breath back.

A man came from the garden through the veranda door. He was wearing blue overalls and went through the living room and out through the door to the hall. He had gone through the room without taking any notice of Wagner. When Sophie returned with the soup bowl Wagner asked who he was.

'It's the workmen, they've been sent to make the wall higher. But it shall fall. Would you like tea? There's lime blossom, that stills the heart.'

'Yes,' Wagner said.

'Let the heart be still.' He ate the soup, a meat soup with sweet potatoes, pieces of squash and root vegetables. It was a magical soup: it tasted good and he immediately felt fortified. He asked her to bring the tea to him in the bedroom and went into the garden again where men were at work under floodlights fixing a roll of barbed wire to the top of the wall. Why this urgency? Why did they have to work into the night as if they were about to be attacked?

He went into his room, carefully locked the door, drank the lime blossom tea as he undressed, and lay down on the bed. He immediately fell asleep.

Twenty Three

In the morning the siren went off as he drove onto the site. He saw the workers go over to the sites and felt relief.

In the office Steinhorst came to meet him and said in an emphatically lively way: 'All clear on the Andrea Doria.'

Wagner sat down at sketches and plans for the basement. He called for Hartmann and discussed statics with him. He felt Hartmann was limiting his answers to strictly technical matters.

Wagner didn't ask whether he blamed him, whether he could tell him what he had done wrong, and what he would have done in his position. He knew the answer: 'But I'm not in your position.'

But for the fear that after the midday break there could still be a strike, nothing would have kept him here longer and he would have driven to the city, to Luisa. But even after the midday break the men went back to work.

In the afternoon he gathered together all the drawings and calculations for the basement he would need in the capital for a permit. When the siren signalled the end of work, an hour earlier than usual because it was Saturday, Wagner raced from the room, through the canteen, past an amazed Juan.

He drove to the city.

190

Like yesterday, the door to the ground floor flat was open. He looked into the empty room and through the window into the yard. He stood still and listened to the silence in the house. Then he switched on the light, a bulb hanging from a cord, and climbed the well-worn wooden stairs. As he climbed he was already certain she was not in. His note was stuck in the door. He pulled it out, this rolled piece of Renate's telegram: THINKING OF YOU. He didn't even knock first, but pressed the handle. The door was not locked. He went through the dark hall, carefully feeling his way, because suddenly he had taken it into his head someone might be lying on the floor. He came into the kitchen. The shutters were half closed. Light fell through a crack. He pushed open the shutters. The two glasses from which they had drunk the orange juice stood next to the cast iron sink. they had been hurriedly washed. Dried orange fibre still stuck to the inside. Curiously the three chairs were tipped forward with their backs against the table, like in bars after closing time. Wagner went into the bedroom, both wooden doors were open. Nothing had changed. Only the case he had seen lying half-packed on the bed had disappeared. There were some white specks on the floor by the doors to the roof terrace, bird shit.

The room looked as if it had already been uninhabited for weeks. Wagner went to the bed and pulled back the cover. It had not been stripped. On the white sheet he noticed a yellowish spot – his dried semen.

He went out onto the roof terrace, confused and helpless. He stood by the stone balustrade and looked into the yard where the darkness was gathering. Her embrace: the movements with which she had helped him. Her eyes, as he lay over her, had slowly moved beneath the closed lids. In the distance he heard the screech of tyres of a car starting. A few chickens pecked in the yard. In a lit doorway hung with plastic strips a bowl appeared, with a short circling movement a hand tipped out the water. The chickens scattered.

Something unexpected must have happened, something that had taken her by surprise, as otherwise she would have let him know. Perhaps she had had to leave as abruptly as yesterday he had been prevented from coming to her. Someone in her family could have been taken ill. But the case had already been lying packed on her bed. Did she already know that evening that she would have to go away? Or was she so hurt and angry that he hadn't come yesterday, or perhaps – she had been arrested.

In the bushes growing out of the top floor of one of the houses opposite a night bird was singing, a delicate melodic tremolo. The windows of the flat were brightly lit and Wagner saw people in the room, adults and children. They were sitting at a long table and eating. He wondered how he could enquire after her parents' address. He thought of Bredow with his contacts among the authorities, but then said to himself it would be inadvisable to ask him of all people, who had warned him against the girl.

He left the room, in passing glanced into the kitchen where it was now almost dark. He was on the way to the front door when he stopped and went back again. An object on the floor had caught his attention. He turned on the kitchen light and saw it was the pomegranate that had been on the table on his previous visit. When he bent down he saw another pomegranate under the cupboard. It must have been lying there for some time because it was shrivelled, its skin wooden. Wagner put it on the kitchen table, on the bright yellow plastic cloth. He took the fresh red pomegranate with him as a momento. Why had she kept it? And why had it fallen from the table? And how long had the other one been lying there under the cupboard? He pulled the door to the flat shut behind him. In the hallway there was a smell of saltpetre.

Downstairs he clapped his hands and shouted: 'Hello.' A shout that in these surroundings seemed not to be his own, and was eerie. He strained to hear. He heard a strange sound, like small knives being sharpened, and from afar: radio music, a car, voices. He went through the open front door into the ground floor flat. It was empty. The rooms lay in darkness, only dimly lit by a lamp in the yard. The wallpaper hung from the walls in rags. There was a smell of mould and cat piss. The old woman he had seen sitting outside on the first day could not have lived here. He walked slowly through the dark rooms. Then again he heard that sound of something being sharpened. As he entered the large room that must once have been the living room he saw the rats running along the walls, unusually large animals that, as he took another step, suddenly plunged into a hole that had been torn in the parquet floor. It was rather a large hole, like the entrance to an underground tunnel. He heard the rustling of the rats. There was a smell of rotting flesh in the room, a heavy sweetish stench. He quickly went out and for a moment remained standing outside the front door of the house. Then he got into the car, put the pomegranate in the glove compartment and drove round the block again in the quite senseless hope that Luisa might at that very moment come round the street corner.

Wagner knew from the papers at home that since the coup people disappeared in this country, guerillas and their sympathizers, or those who were taken as such. Except he couldn't imagine that Luisa might have anything to do with the guerrillas, though then again he had to say to himself that he had no clear conception of any such radical group and its aims. Among his acquaintances only the architect Moll counted as radical, an unusually tall man with flaxen blonde hair, who constantly pestered with his demands for nationalization. Wagner stopped outside the flats where Juan and Hartmann lived, a new building with postmodern oriel windows.

Wagner asked the porter where Juan Augitiri lived.

'No está,' the man replied.

Wagner was about to go when he turned again and asked for Hartmann.

'Cinco,' the porter said and raised five fingers. Wagner went up in the lift. Hartmann was standing at the top waiting. The porter had obviously phoned him. Hartmann was wearing jeans and a red and blue check flannel shirt as if he were going on a mountain hike. He went ahead of Wagner. On his feet he had sandals of strong leather. The soles were folded over the feet and tied with leather thongs, presumably the sort of sandals Indians made. Hartmann's flat was a large five cornered room that ended in an oriel window. On the desk there was a small electric typewriter. Hartmann turned it off and with a jerk pulled out the inserted page. On the wall hung a large black and white cloth with a strange assymetrical pattern.

'I've been collecting Aurakan ponchos,' Hartmann said, 'they no longer weave them like this. They still have the patterns, but the patterns are now woven symmetrically, and you can buy those at the airport. The assymmetry has been lost.'

'They're very beautiful,' Wagner said and looked round the room that was filled with the same furniture as his bungalow.

But there was something homely about this room, the ponchos on the wall, strange fossils on the shelf, in a glass-fronted cupboard small clay bowls and vases with delicate incised drawings, the patterns bearing a certain resemblance to the large hangings on the wall.

'I'd have done better to take a flat here,' Wagner said, 'this bungalow I'm living in with its six rooms is depressing. It keeps reminding you that you're alone.'

'That wouldn't have been possible, the manager has to live in the bungalow. That's what it's been specially rented for by the company. You can't have any cocktail parties here.'

'I don't give parties.'

'Your predecessor also said that. Would you like something to drink? Juice, whisky, tea?'

'A whisky, please.'

Hartmann went in his archaic sandals into the kitchen and came back with a bottle and ice. As he poured for Wagner, he asked: 'What can I do?'

There was a slight hesitation in the question, as if he had actually wanted to say: Can I help? Wagner would then have said: Yes. Please stay. But instead he talked about his Spanish teacher who was suddenly not to be found.

'Has she gone away or disappeared?'

'I don't know. Bredow warned me a few days ago. Apparently she had contact with the guerillas.'

'You know of course how they silence the opposition here. People disappear. A suspicion is all it takes. Somebody gets arrested, they find his phone book, go through the names and addresses, and everybody under thirty disappears. Enquiries are pointless. The police know nothing and naturally don't want to know anything. People simply disappear as if the earth had swallowed them up. It can happen to anybody, to you too and to me. You always think as a foreigner you're safe. But that's nonsense. The company protects us. A little. After all, they have contact with the military.' Hartmann rubbed his finger against his thumb. 'Take care. Don't get involved. It's deadly dangerous.'

'Is that why you're quitting?'

'No. I didn't get involved here. It can't be done, even if one wanted to. The battle takes place outside our air-conditioned bungalows and flats.'

'Then why are you going?'

Hartmann smiled and shrugged his shoulders.

'But you must have a reason you can name?'

'Yes. One can't force an alien logic on things, and on people even less. Or you rape them. Then they're broken, things as well.'

Wagner pulled a cigarette out of the pack. It was an effort to hide his excitement. He broke a match lighting it. 'But logic asserts itself of itself,' he said after drawing on his cigarette, 'what's more, without violence. It's the desire for something different, something extra, the transistor, the stainless steel knife, Coca Cola, a universal desire, the desire for enjoyment and comfort. Nobody wants to work the ground with a hoe after having seen a motorized plough.'

'I know,' Hartmann said, 'that's a widely held view amongst us. It's what those who always know what's needed say. First they knew exactly what was good for people, namely progress and civilization, and now what's not good for them, namely progress and civilization. Yesterday they laughed at people because they didn't want Corbusier high rise buildings, today they laugh at people for wanting precisely those buildings. They're the eternal smart guys who know it all, even when they criticize themselves as eurocentrist.'

Wagner wondered if that included him, but thought Hartmann couldn't mean him as he hadn't criticized the people.

'But I'm for industrialization here,' Wagner said. 'Where people are starving the problem of the disposal of atomic waste is totally academic. Whether there's still radiation from the waste in a hundred or even a thousand years is a matter of comparative indifference to the person starving today.'

But Hartmann had not even been listening. He said: 'The people themselves would have to take over. They know far better what they want and what they don't, I mean those that haven't yet been bribed by us.'

'Do you think they'll be happy about a factory that lists? After all, it's a state contract.'

'Exactly. The people pay for everything. We give them the loans, build them the factories, deliver the machinery, cut down

196

the forest and then wipe our arses with the paper. What we leave behind is a red desert, a useless paper factory and debts. And don't tell me as you did the other day that you love the moon. The moon is uninhabited. But people live here.' He smiled at Wagner as if to apologize: 'I'm for the factory sinking into the mire, the sooner the better. And you're the man who wants to set things right. And I think you'll succeed.'

Hartmann got up, went in his leather slippers into the kitchen and came back with a bottle of champagne.

'This was a present from the company to celebrate when I started this job almost a year ago, time it was drunk.'

He put two tumblers on the table, opened the bottle. There was a bang and the cork shot to the ceiling.

'We'll drink to the sinking ship, cheers.'

'No,' Wagner said, 'it'll float.'

'We consider ourselves the bearers of happiness, but it's happiness that rests on widespread misery.'

'And you think that doesn't apply back at home?'

'Yes I do, there especially.'

'And what do you want to do?'

'I don't know yet.'

Wagner went to the oriol window and looked out. The street below was lit by big whip-shaped lampposts. A few men and women sat at a bar. A huge red neon staff of Asculepius glowed on a house front opposite, around it curled a white neon snake. Written beneath it in white neon lettering: Farmacia.

'Did you know,' Hartmann asked, 'that Juan is working on an ethnological study?'

'No. What's he doing?'

'He's studying us. He's doing field work at the site. He's observing you, me and Steinhorst. And the Swiss agronomists and Americans that live here in the city. I expect great things of it. It's sure to be of considerable interest to us all.'

Wagner sat down again. They drank to Juan and his work. Then they sat in silence together.

When Wagner said goodbye, he said: 'A shame you're going. I'm going to miss you here.'

Twenty Four

Wagner drove south on the country road. He had left already on the Saturday evening and slept overnight in a motel. Now and then he passed a few lorries or buses, rarely private cars. He was stopped three times on the road by military controls. But his car was always waved through after he showed his passport and work permit, while in the waiting cars even the seats were taken out. They were obviously being searched for weapons. On one occasion a man on horseback in a billowing black cloak had ridden past Wagner, like an image in a film.

Yesterday he had phoned Bredow as soon as he had got back from Hartmann, and had asked him to ask the colonel if he could find out where his Spanish teacher might be, as she'd suddenly disappeared. Bredow had replied with a coldness unusual for him: 'The Intendente's not a detective, you know.' He, Bredow, neither could nor would involve himself in this matter. And also advised him to keep out of it.

Bredow only promised to phone after Wagner had said then he would make enquiries himself.

Barely an hour later, Wagner's travelling bag packed for the journey, Bredow had phoned back. The colonel only knew that the girl had been dismissed from the teaching profession.

Apparently because of contact with left wing groups. She had not been reported in the city. But that wasn't so unusual.

'If none of this is so unusual, why all the excitement? What exactly is all this about contact with the guerilleros?'

'All he's doing is warning you. They've become cautious, that's all and don't want to see another manager kidnapped.'

'Well, all right,' Wagner said, 'but I'll drive to the capital today in any case. On Monday I'll make some enquiries about the basements with the building authorities and get a permit for the alterations in the plans. We'll begin building factory B by the end of next week. I'll go to our company representative, somebody there can come with me to the authorities.'

'Do that,' Bredow said.

Wagner had actually expected Bredow to ask him why he of all people wanted to go, it was a journey for a messenger. At most the job of a local engineer. He would have replied he wanted to compare ground surveys at the Building Authority.

'Enjoy the city, go to the El Punal, you can eat well there.' He also gave the name of a deputy, in case any problems should arise with the authorities, in particular the police. 'The man's under contract to the company as an advisor. Write down the name: Fabrizi.'

The land to the right and left of the road was flat and he remembered how disappointed he had been on the drive here, those flat fields could just as well have been in Schleswig-Holstein, only the grass was burned brown and dry by the sun. For kilometres the road ran dead straight. So he had time to think of Luisa, and always he saw himself with her: how they stood in the kitchen, she at the stove, the water for the coffee hissing, how she held out her hand to him, how they looked at each other going up in the lift to the restaurant, how she recited vocabulary and corrected him with a slight shake of the head, how she undressed, simply and with purposeful movements (no hesitating, no fumbling), how she lay down on the bed and watched him trying to pull out the knotted shoelace, until she laughed and he kicked off the shoe. And he thought of Susann. In his memories he always saw Susann separate from him. He had to think really hard before he found a situation in which they were both present. He had met Susann at an open air swimming pool. She was lying on a red towel. He had lain down next to her on the closely mowed lawn that smelled of chlorine, not because he had noticed her, but because there was still space there. He had lain down and begun to study for his exam (statics), had looked up, and there she was. There she lay, propped up, reading. He saw the pronounced curve of her breasts rising a little above her red and black check bikini top. But that wasn't what caught his attention, it was the way she was reading, concentrated, or more accurately, sunk deep into herself. But from time to time she touched the bridge of her sunglasses with her finger to push them higher on her nose.

He intended to write to Susann as soon as he got to the hotel. Driving through suburbs that stretched far into the countryside he had come to a motorway on concrete stilts that passed two-storeyed houses. There was a smell of burning rubber and exhaust. He drove past the windows and balconies of houses where the stucco had largely fallen from the yellow-brown limewashed facades. He had carefully made a mental note of the city map and while concentrating on the cars driving wildly, counted the various exits until he came to a concrete bend that led onto a wide road. The houses changed their appearance, became taller, were covered with marble, everywhere windows and shutters opened on to a late, peaceful Sunday afternoon. In the streets there were trees flowering red and white like huge bouquets.

He recognized the hotel from a distance by its orange sun-blinds. He was expected. Mrs Klein had ordered a room. He found a message from the company representative who wanted to call for him at the hotel. A boy carried Wagner's case and they went up in a lift lined in mahogany. The boy stared at Wagner. Suddenly he raised his thumb and finger and made a sign. Wagner shook his head in irritation. On the fifth floor the boy went ahead, opened the door to a small suite. Wagner gave him a note. The boy took it and again made the sign.

Wagner asked: 'What's the matter?'

The boy quickly said something in Spanish and Wagner indicated that he hadn't understood, said something in English that was probably intended to mean: take care. But Wagner wasn't sure. The boy left.

Wagner showered and put on his beige linen suit, knotted a tie and took the lift down to the lobby.

He only realized the hotel was air-conditioned when he stepped out on to the street, into the mild evening warmth. He followed the street which led to a wide boulevard. Here people were strolling. The floodlit goods shone in the shop windows. The noise of the car's engine still rang in his ears like a distant roaring. He felt a sudden hunger for adventure, a desire to get to know one of these lightly clad women who all looked as if they had just come from a beauty parlour; they looked so cool and fresh as they walked in this accumulated heat. It was as if everything were on display: the women approaching him, the cafés and restaurants that extended outdoors and spread over the pavements. He wanted physical closeness, her close to him, to touch her now, her skin, hair, that blue-black hair, her throat where he had felt her heartbeat. He walked quickly down the almost endless boulevard until his feet ached, he walked back and only slowly, because his shoes hurt, came to his senses. He bought a German newspaper at a kiosk and sat to read it in a café on the street. The paper was already three days old. He read everything: the advertisements, the news from the provinces, the dispute over waste disposal, the questions in Parliament. He had drunk two beers and eaten some peanuts and sat in the warmth of the night, watching the passers-by and enjoying his detached observation. He asked himself how he had been able to bear these last years, this aimless agitation, all the hectic activities that had only turned everything into a bleak here and now. He walked back to the hotel and in the intense fragrance from the flowering trees, in the chance contact with a woman's naked arm, the laughter of some young men, his tiredness and exhaustion were transformed into euphoria. Where it came from he couldn't have said, perhaps purely and simply because he'd not seen all this for some time, but perhaps also from the hope that here, tomorrow perhaps, he might find out Luisa's address.

In the hotel he turned off the air-conditioning and opened the windows. He sat at the desk and from the writing case pulled out a sheet of paper with the hotel address: *Hotel Cecilia*. In the distance he heard the city, a monotone roaring, and nearby, now and then, a passing car. A light wind carried the warm air into the room. He wrote: 'Dear Susann,' and stopped, as he usually called her darling. Dear Susann, that sounded woundingly official, on the other hand the old form of address seemed like an impermissable intimacy. And now he realized how idiotic that form of address was, had always been. In all the years he'd not even found a nickname for her that he could have used even now, in this situation. He wrote that what he was about to say he should have said a long time ago. That in the last two years and ever more frequently he had had regular suffocation attacks in this normality they had both got into because of their tiredness of each other, in this dullness for which they both took revenge on each other through hateful little squabbles, in this waiting for the reactions that were to be expected, one's own and the other person's. That he was not interested now in blaming or making excuses. That now he had come to the conclusion that there must be more than this mute hopeless life, for her and for him. That lately when he thought of the life ahead an image always came to him of a road that led in an absolutely straight line over a few little hills, through a landscape with which he was thoroughly familiar. It ought to be different, quite different, how he couldn't say, but to know it was enough. It would be best to separate. He offered her the house of course, would also continue to provide for Sascha. Sascha. Sometimes he came and rubbed his forehead against Wagner's stomach, a brief trusting gesture. Filled with this memory, this gentle trusting, an uneasiness overwhelmed Wagner that was so painful he was unable to continue writing, it forced him to get up and pace the room until he had calmed down a little. He sat at the open window and looked out. In a flat in the house opposite a light had come on. He saw a woman walking in the room, then a man, two children. He was glad he didn't have to be in one of these flats, and at the same time wished he could be together with Luisa. Of course not locked in a living room, as he had locked himself in with Susann. And his grief was grief at failing to come up to the expectations he had had of himself. But what expectations had they been? Those mutual explorations of their own needs, of their own desires; the attempt to state them clearly, not to lie to oneself. This mutual journey of discovery into the interior of one another, and therefore of oneself. But perhaps, after a certain point in time, there was nothing more to discover, everything had been explored, each now had experiences that curiously no longer allowed themselves to be communicated. Why, Wagner asked himself, and when had it happened?

Until his exams they had lived almost a year in a converted attic. They would lie in bed and tell each other about themselves. Each time her uncontrolled shrieks frightened him. He always thought the people in the house would be sure to come running, convinced that he was murdering her. Her shrieks had grown quieter over the years, until at last — by now they lived in their own house — they lay knotted together quietly groaning.

He undressed and got naked into bed; a moment longer he listened to the unaccustomed noise from the street, then he sank into a black stillness.

Twenty Five

The Prefecture was in the centre of the city, a large six-storeyed building, in style comparable to the Paris Opera. Tattered sun-blinds hung in orange strips above the high windows. In front of the entrance was an armoured car, next to it a jeep. The ground floor windows, all the size of barn doors, were barred, in addition sandbags were piled behind them. Wagner had taken a taxi from the Department of Building to the Prefecture. He had got through with the authorities much sooner than he'd expected. In the morning the company representative, a Mr Weise, had called for him at the hotel. Weise had been living and working in the country for years, like Bredow, and was responsible exclusively for contact with the authorities and government agencies. They had driven to the Department of Building, a dark dilapidated nineteenth century house, in danger of collapsing. An office boy in a blue uniform led them to a large office. Behind a bulky old fashioned desk sat a young man wearing glasses that hugely magnified his eyes. Wagner laid the building plans on the table and Mr Weise laid a thick envelope next to them. The man, who repeatedly and with exaggerated politeness addressed Wagner in Spanish, though he must have known Wagner didn't understand, took the plans and the envelope and left. As he went out he winked at Wagner as if at an accomplice.

Wagner hadn't yet finished his cigarette when the man came back into the room, bringing with him the building permit and the statics certificate. Obviously the amount in the envelope had been big enough to make checking superfluous. But the man should at least have allowed more time to pass, not to pretend that the plans were really being examined, but to demonstrate his own importance. Wagner then asked them to show him the entry in the land register and the exact measurements of the building site. The ground surveys revealed nothing that indicated the high water level. But the building area had been moved by 500 metres. Why? Weise translated the question. The man shrugged his shoulders. And who had sold the land to the paper factory. 'The land now being built on belongs to a consortium,' Weise translated, 'the man doesn't know who, a notary represents its interests.'

Wagner had thanked the company representative and turned down his invitation to visit the city office, indicating that he still had business at the Prefecture.

At the Prefecture entrance stood a long queue. Wagner went past those waiting to the two guards at the door. The soldier leafed through the passport and tried to decipher some of the visas and stamps. Wagner showed him his company's work permit. The soldier saw the company stamp and called out something through the entrance. An officer came out. He took a careful look at Wagner. Under his left eye he had a nervous tic. Then he glanced at the letter and waved to Wagner to follow him.

They plunged into a sticky heat, a stench of sweat, urine, sour milk and naphthalene. On the wide marble steps that led into a domed lobby people sat and stood waiting, tightly packed the way Wagner remembered it on the last day of signing in at the Technical University. They crossed a long corridor of people queueing four abreast, packed together amid a constant fluttering of newspapers and forms. What was strange, even uncanny was the silence of this crowd. No loud talking, no laughing, only a whisper now and then. Somewhere in a side corridor a child could be heard whimpering. In a corner a nun knelt and said a rosary. She turned as Wagner stepped over her legs; her tongue came fleshy rose out of her mouth, quickly circled her lips. The officer, who went ahead of Wagner, pushed aside a beggar who showed him the stump of an arm, a lump of raw flesh in which Wagner, horrified, thought he could see white worms. At last they stood in front of a high folding door. The officer knocked, and at a call from inside opened the door. They entered a narrow, but extremely high room. From the ceiling hung a fan that slowly stirred the sticky heat. At the end of the room, in front of a high window, an elderly man sat at a small desk. He wore his greying hair like Bredow, combed straight back. His pale blue shirt had dark sweat stains under the armpits. He had stuck his tie into his shirt like a rope. The officer spoke to the man who remained seated behind the desk and absent-mindedly smelled the end of a chewed pencil. From next door Wagner heard a strange scraping and whispering. Wagner only now noticed how the room was divided. Probably a part of the queue ended in the next room. The man at the desk had put the pencil aside and begun to leaf through Wagner's passport, which the officer had handed him over the desk. Then he read the company letter and immediately pointed to a wooden chair.

'What can I do for you?'

Wagner said he was looking for the home address of his language teacher. The woman, Luisa Casas, had left unexpectedly. But he still had to pay her the outstanding wages.

The man twisted his face into a small, dirty grin. He said: 'I'm sorry, but I can't give addresses to foreigners.'

'Yes, I know,' Wagner said and pulled the envelope from his

jacket pocket. It contained an empty page, apart from the company letterhead, in which Wagner had put a hundred dollar note. The man unfolded the page and behaved as if he were reading the letter with interest, but nothing betrayed that he had seen the money. He held the page in his hand, quite openly and clearly. Wagner thought the money had fallen out unnoticed. He wondered if he should say there had been something else in the letter, which naturally would have been grotesque: first to try and discreetly bribe the man, then point his finger at it. The man looked up and with a short wave of his hand sent the officer from the room. He handed Wagner the letter and envelope over the desk. Wagner immediately noticed the envelope was empty. The man said that the company warranted that in this case he could make an exception. He got up and asked Wagner to follow him. They again went through the high, filthily grey corridors and passageways in which people were waiting and pushing. Now and then Wagner saw a file carrier, men in grey overalls who carried large bundles of papers. In a corner a woman crouched and ate a yellow pulp from a tin bowl. There was a smell of food and burning charcoal, as if she had just cooked the pulp over a fire. A family sat on the floor, father, mother, a baby at her breast, three children next to her. They were asleep, heads sunk forward. Next to them, clothes drying on the bars of a window. On a wooden bench sat an old man, his head hung heavily on his chest, a pince-nez dangled from a cord, on his lap a straw hat. The face was chalk-white. The man sat there as if he had died fifty years ago and in some mysterious way become mummified. The office manager, who had gone ahead of Wagner, climbed some steps and knocked at a door covered in iron plating. A small iron window opened from the inside and behind it Wagner dimly saw a pair of eyes. The office manager called a password, the door opened. They entered a wide, windowless room faintly lit by a few lamps. The room was filled with wooden book shelves metres high. File carriers wandered with torches in the narrow passageways and searched among the thick files stacked in layers on the shelves. The office manager gave one of the file carriers a note on which Luisa's name was written. Wagner stood next to the office manager and waited. He kept having to look at the manager's ears, finely shaped ears, but from them sprouted thick grey tufts of hair. The face reminded him of an exotic animal, the protruding teeth over which the mouth closed, the narrow nose with the large nostrils, the greying hair stuck to the skull. But he couldn't remember the name of the animal. Then the file carrier came with a bundle of papers. The office manager leaved through the files, pulled out a form, put it back inside the file, tearing it as he did, and said no one of that name had been reported. Of course the duty to report had been very feebly practised before the national revolution.

Wagner asked if a woman of the same name was wanted by the police or had been arrested.

'I can't say.'

Wagner took out his wallet and for the first time the man gave a slight, spontaneous smile, a smile hinting at a secret understanding.

'Impossible,' he said, 'it isn't payable.'

Wagner took the note from his pocket with the name Bredow had given him, in case there were any problems with the authorities.

The man's face showed his astonishment. His manner, so far affable, turned into an exaggerated desire to oblige. He held the iron door open for Wagner and then led the way, stooping slightly, back through the passageways and corridors, past the people waiting, until they came to a section that had just been painted. Here no one waited. A footbridge covered in bullet-proof glass led over to a new building. Under the glass bridge there were several dead birds. A tree stood in the middle of the concreted yard, an unusually tall and widespreading tree. On the other side of the footbridge they came to a steel door that opened only after a long discussion between the office manager and a screeching voice on the intercom. The corridors in this building were bright, the offices newly furnished in natural wood. Some young people were standing in the corridor drinking coffee, evidently officials, girls that looked as if they were at college, in jeans, white socks and flat shoes, the men in Lacoste shirts. The office manager led Wagner to an office equipped with steel furniture, here sat a young man in faded jeans. Metal shades dimmed the light. The man pointed to a metal chair by a glass table. He read the company letter and sent the office manager from the room with a nod of the head. The man got up, shook hands with Wagner, 'Fabrizi,' he said and sat down on a linen covered sofa.

'How's Bredow?'

'Fine.'

Fabrizi asked if the Bredows were still unbeaten at tennis. Fabrizi spoke German with a Swabian intonation. He had also played the Bredows and lost. Then he apologized because Wagner had come by that dreadful detour via the registration authorities, a route through a bureaucratic hell. Fabrizi laughed: a prejudice widely held was that the Germans had the largest bureaucracy, in actual fact the prize belonged to many South American countries, this one in particular. At last everything was being computerized. This year they had received delivery of a giant computer for the fight against crime. After a great deal of wrangling they had decided on a German computer, it was now being programmed by German specialists.

Wagner only occasionally noticed, because of small grammatical mistakes, that Fabrizi spoke acquired German. To the question, where had he learned German, Fabrizi answered that he had studied computer science in Stuttgart. Then he had been in Wiesbaden again. He had done his practical training there, in the Federal Crime Squad. He praised its efficiency. Now, at last, they'd also acquired a computer here. Now terrorism could be fought to some effect, because the previous method of screening had suffered due to the painful mindlessness of some of the military. That way everyone disappeared who had long hair, a beard and glasses, wore jeans and read a book. Fabrizi laughed. 'According to those criteria all of us here at National Security would have to be liquidated.'

He offered Wagner a brandy and asked what he could do for him.

Wagner handed him the note with Luisa's name and said she was a Spanish teacher who had suddenly disappeared.

A small fold suddenly appeared between Fabrizi's eyebrows. 'We can see,' he said, 'if the name's been entered yet. Come with me.'

They went through bright corridors laid with wall-to-wall carpeting. Wagner asked what the tree in the yard was. 'A snake tree,' Fabrizi said, 'at least literally translated. It was planted over a hundred and seventy years ago to commemorate the country's independence. The prison where interrogation took place used to be here, right behind the Prefecture. And if a prisoner never came out again, then people said he'd been bitten by one of the snakes that apparently lived in the tree. Now the military want to cut the tree down, allegedly to fight this sinister superstition, in actual fact out of fear the tree could become a symbol for those that have disappeared.' He laughed again, 'it's all strangely naïve.'

They had come to a large room without windows. Here stood the giant computer. Fabrizi spoke to a young man, gave him a note. The man fed in the name.

'Here,' Fabrizi said, 'you can convince yourself.' Wagner saw the display. A word lit up: Unknown.

'You see, we've no record. Do you know if the name is correct?'

'I think so.'

'Date of birth?'

'No, I don't know it.'

'She's not in the computer, at least not under this name. But that doesn't mean anything. We have the ones about which there's no doubt, as far as we know. But in the provinces the authorities all go their own way, as does every provincial garrison commander and town governor, and in the end even every company commander and patrol leader. It's a hopeless mess. Everyone does as he pleases. It's stupid and permits tyranny. And we constantly have these regrettable mistakes. Our work here is more exact and more effective. We could fight terrorism at the roots and limit the measures we take to the real activists. It would be a clean surgical operation. But this way the informers are eliminated before we can even establish their dates. Do you know the woman's place of birth?'

Again Wagner could only say no. He asked himself why he had even come, as naturally it had not been for the permit for the basement. Sixteen hours driving, only to have to answer no to the first obvious question. He had seen an old, begrimed registration office and a new building with a computer for tracing people. That had been the outcome of this journey. What had he been looking for? Perhaps only the utterly insignificant assurance that they were not looking for her, because then – if this was her real name – there was a chance that she really had only gone away. On the other hand, as he had just heard, anyone could in fact disappear on whom only the shadow of suspicion had fallen. The disappearance was then confirmation of the suspicion.

Fabrizi must have read something quite different in Wagner's disappointment, namely distrust of the new crime department. He asked Wagner for his full name. Wagner saw on the display:

Friedrich Leopold Wagner (these old fashioned names that had led to everyone, since his school days, calling him simply Wagner, even Susann when she called him always reminded him of the chemistry teacher: 'Wagner, come to the blackboard!'), then his passport number appeared and the day of his entry into the country, the place of residence and the date of his birth.

'Your birthday's soon,' Fabrizi said.

'Yes,' Wagner said, 'yes, soon.'

'Is there anything else I can do for you?'

'No,' Wagner said, 'no thank you.'

Fabrizi accompanied Wagner to the lift, said goodbye and asked him to give his regards to Bredow. Wagner looked over once more at the big tree in the yard, its shadow lying across the light concrete like a black cloud, then he stepped into the lift and went down.

Twenty Six

A cattle transport drove in front of Wagner. The trailer, from which cattle horns stuck twisted through the bars, swung from side to side. The shit that flowed down squirted onto Wagner's windscreen. Wagner turned on the windscreen wipers and overtook the lorry. He wanted to drive through the night and hoped to be at the site at about noon the next day. In the north a storm was brewing, a long cylindrical blue-black bank of cloud. His shirt and trousers stuck to him. He searched for music on the radio and finally found a station on which the St Matthew Passion was being transmitted from Munich. So he drove through the heat and thought of Christmas.

He stopped once, drank a bottle of mineral water and an espresso, peed and drove on. Heat haze lay across the street in the distance, the asphalt seemed to be under water. At some point, quite unremarkably and quietly, the absence of anything to say had overtaken him and Susann. In summer, on Sunday mornings, they had breakfast on the terrace. Sascha dripped honey on to his trousers, Susann sat there, eyes narrowed inspite of her sunglasses as if bad temperedly giving him a hard look. In the garden next door sat the senior consultant who six months earlier had separated from his wife and three children.

He was sitting with his girl friend at a table laid with a white cloth, a physiotherapist, twenty-two years old. Both of them in top form, they sailed, played tennis, skied in winter; in the mornings he jogged in the fashionable residential district, a young face but, under the suntan, senile. He was no more than two or three years older than Wagner. The physiotherapist sat on the garden bench, brown legs crossed like a fakir. Wagner stared across when she nimbly got up, in shorts, the wide trouser legs rolled up so he could see the gentle curve of her buttocks, and teetered into the house. She always wore sling-back high heeled shoes – even when sunbathing naked. She came back, holding the garden hose, and began watering the garden. She wore a white net vest from which her nipples peered out inquisitively, as if they wanted to check that Wagner admired them. Susann in the meantime had sat down again at one of the tables in the shade, where she corrected exercises. She sat on the garden chair as if about to leap up. She had long dark hair on her legs. Since the winter she no longer shaved them, although she knew he didn't like hairy legs. He thought of Herbert who had turned up one day, in the evening. He had come in a taxi, drunk, and told them he couldn't bear it any longer at home. He had rushed from the flat or he would have stabbed his wife, the quiet, friendly and generally cherished Sigrid, with a breadknife. He had already had the knife in his hand. Not that there had even been a quarrel. All she'd said to him was: 'You'll manage,' after he had told her his job totally and utterly nauseated him; this endless talking, talking, talking, to sell people the definitive computer. 'You'll manage,' she had said in that quiet way that everyone loved. At that he'd lost his head. Three years now they lay in their large beautiful double bed without anything ever happening, every two months an attempt, blind drunk, that always ended in exhausted wrangling. He laughed: 'We both make an effort, the greatest conceivable effort, and that makes everything impossible. And

we hate each other because we have to make an effort.' Wagner
had taken him to the guest room. Then he had had to wipe up
the piss in the bathroom.

Herbert had begun weeping, had wept until he was in bed.
So they lay in their desolate beds, in their desolate rooms, in
the desolate houses one on top of another and next to each
other, wall to wall, sleeping cells, eating cells, copulation cells.
One Sunday afternoon Wagner had stood in the garden looking
at the lawn, this lawn as if cut with nail scissors (he mowed it
every Saturday), the small carefully trimmed hedges, the birch
tree and the idiotic blue spruce, and had felt a dismal, dull ache
in his chest.

Why was he standing here seeing this, he could just as well
not stand here and not see it. So he went to the chopping block
and took the axe, went to the blue spruce and before an
appalled Susann and a weeping Sascha chopped it down. He
was breathless but relieved, indescribably relieved when he saw
the spruce lying on the ground. It was the only time in all the
years that he had lost his self-control.

Why he had chopped down the spruce he was unable to
explain either to Susann or to Sascha, whom Susann had drawn
to her shocked. Because Sascha believed the rubber dwarf had
his home in the blue spruce.

How unfair I am in my memories, Wagner thought, to
Susann, to our life together, while every thought of Luisa
instantly turns into the desire to be near her, and he thought
he understood why devotional kitsch showed silver hearts in
flames. But this was not solely a desire to be with Luisa, but a
desire for a different life, a new beginning, a longing to become
someone else; it was with this desire, of which he had not been
fully aware, that he had left home.

When he thought of Susann, it was the memory of the paral-
ysis that had set in over the last few years. Years ago, they had
just met, he had gone with Susann to the Hamburg Art Gallery

where he hadn't been since his schooldays. They were standing in front of a painting by Klee: *The Revolution of the Viaduct*. While Susann looked at the painting, the aggressive dissolution of technology, as she called it, he had examined the alarm system on the painting and out of irresistible curiosity to find out how it functioned fingered it, which had set the siren off, painfully loud, and two guards in the room came rushing. After the initial shock, Susann had laughed and said to the guard: 'My friend's an engineer.' Three months later, after he had passed his exam, they had flown to Tunisia on money borrowed from his father. They stayed at a hotel by the sea. In front of it was a palm grove. They had picked up some of the fallen dates, sweet sun-warmed fruit. Susann had told him about the Vandals whose fate had concerned her ever since she was a child, because they had simply disappeared. A people that had roamed through all of Europe, crossed over to Africa, founded a great empire, and then simply disappeared without trace.

Wagner said, 'I know the reason.'

She looked at him intrigued.

'The Vandals crept away in their sandals.'

She grabbed him and twisted his arm (she had learned jiujitsu as a schoolgirl), till he was on his knees and laughing kissed her bathing sandals.

Later, after they had swum they lay side by side and ate the dates. He watched the drops of water run from her hips. Susann put a small date stone in his ear because he hadn't been listening to her. When she then tried to take the stone out of his ear it slipped in deeper. Wagner shook his head, he hopped about on one leg in front of Susann who watched him anxiously – in vain. Suddenly it was as if Wagner had water in his ear after diving, everything sounded muted and distant. Susan wanted to immediately take him to a doctor. But he'd said, it can wait till we're back home. He quickly got used to his woolly hearing and finally forgot the stone. Until two years ago when he was on holiday with Susann and Sascha on Amrum. He had been swimming for some time in the surf, come onto the beach, shook his head, the date stone flew out of his ear. A small black plug that in the meantime had become soft. His hearing was new, bright and clear, a thrilling awareness of the wind, the surf, voices, as if everything muted and dull had fallen from him. An experience that only lasted for that day. The next day he had already grown so accustomed to it, only memory told him it had once been different.

Dusk had set in. On the horizon there was an area lit yellow like a stadium or a shunting yard. As he approached he saw it was an intersection, of astonishing size with curving feeder roads and underpasses as if two motorways crossed here. The four-lane motorway in fact ended under the bridge in a dirt road. Wagner looked for the intersection on the map and discovered he was on the wrong road. He must have missed an exit, or it hadn't been marked. The road he was on led north, to the waterfalls. He had already read about these falls as a child, how they had been discovered by the conquistador Cabeza de Vaca who had travelled widely on the continent, always in search of gold, and had lived for seven years among the Indians of North America, one of the first Americans to do so, until he had gone south again and after a march of several weeks found the Iguazú Falls. Cabeza de Vaca had fallen onto his knees in his rusted armour: he had seen the day of creation. Wagner wondered if he should simply go on to the Falls. They were expecting him at the site on Wednesday. He thought of the groundwater, the concrete, but said to himself there was nothing he could do about the groundwater, at least not yet, and the concrete was good, so he decided to go. He wanted to take this detour. In the last few years he had only ever done what had to be done. Now he drove on. The further he drove the less he doubted that he could justify this detour.

After an hour he came to a lay-by. There were some lorries in the parking lot. He took the jacket with his wallet and went over to the open charcoal fire where meat and sausages were being grilled. The lorry drivers were sitting at one of the long wooden tables. Wagner sat two tables away from them on one of the wooden benches, stretched his legs and waited. As no one came to serve him he went over to the iron grill where a man in a bloody apron was turning pieces of meat and sausages with a huge iron fork. Wagner pointed to one of the large steaks. The man took a cracked china plate, put the steak on it and pointed to the table where Wagner had been sitting. A waiter covered the table with a strip of white paper and put an open bottle of red wine, white bread and the steak in front of Wagner. Wagner cut into the meat from which the blood oozed dark red. He drank, it was a simple local wine. He dipped the white bread in the juice. Suddenly a man stood by him. He had got up from the lorry drivers' table. The men looked over and grinned. The man wore a dirty check shirt and was saying something to Wagner and kept pointing at Wagner's head. Wagner didn't understand and shrugged his shoulders, a gesture the man took to mean something else, as he came closer to Wagner, reached for his hair and with a little jerk pulled out a few hairs. Wagner leaped up in surprise and clenched his fists, but the man gave a friendly laugh and said: 'Gracias.' Then he went back to the lorry drivers' table. He showed the men the hair and then put it carefully in the breast pocket of his shirt. Wagner wasn't sure what he should do. What did the man want with his hair? Perhaps it was just curiosity because he had never touched blonde hair. From their table came laughter, not contemptuous laughter but warm, even friendly. Wagner sat down again. They raised their glasses. So he raised his and drank. Slowly the tension left him. He drank and drifted into a placid apathy. He heard the raging of the cicadas, and now and then a lorry on the motorway and laughter from the neighbouring table. And he always laughed with them, relieved and aloud, as if he were taking part in the conversation. He was so tired his head kept sagging forward onto his chest. He waved for the waiter and paid a sum that seemed very high, but said nothing, put the change into his trouser pocket and went to his car. He turned down the seat, locked the doors from inside, set the alarm on his wrist watch and lay down on the cushions with his legs drawn up. He quickly fell asleep.

Twenty Seven

It was still dark. When he pressed the light on his wrist watch he realized the alarm had not woken him. He sat up. There was a dull pain in his right arm. In front of the windscreen he saw a wall and only slowly in the dim light of a street lamp recognized it as the bonnet. He got out. Everything was still. The fire under the parrilla still glowed. Some distance away a figure sat slumped at a table and snored. Wagner walked round the car, but there was no one in sight. He got the torch from the glove compartment and shone it on the engine. He immediately saw the dangling ignition leads. The distributor cap had been removed. Wagner's wrist watch began to bleep. He wondered whether to get into the car and lock himself in and wait for the sun to rise. Then he said to himself his only chance of finding the thief was now. Presumably the noise of him at work had woken him. He walked slowly over to the restaurant and stopped outside. After all the thief (or thieves) might be lying in wait for him inside the building. But he could more readily count on help there. He decided if he was threatened or attacked he would instantly scream with all the force he could muster.

It stank of cold smoke and grease. He felt his way along a corridor and quietly opened the door to one of the rooms. In the soft light shining in from a lamp outside Wagner saw a man and a woman lying in bed. The man was naked, his chest covered in black hair. The woman was wearing a black slip that had come up round her waist. She was lying on her stomach, her buttocks shone white.

They both lay there as if dead. The next room was empty. In the one next to it, on a mattress on the floor lay a man with a large belly. He was wearing light trousers. His bare feet hung over the side of the mattress. A huge bug crawled on the floor. In the distance Wagner heard the roar of a lorry passing. He felt his way out of the dark house. Fat insects swarmed around the lamps. Bats shot through the air. Suddenly he saw a match flare in the driver's cabin of one of the lorries parked at the side. Wagner hesitated for a moment, then told himself the man had in any case already seen everything. Perhaps he knew who the thief was, unless of course he himself was. Wagner went over to the lorry and stepped onto the running board. When he looked through the window into the driver's cabin he had a shock, there sat the man who had pulled out his hair. The man looked at him in silence. He was smoking and blew the smoke, almost gently, in Wagner's face. Then he grinned and said something in Portuguese. Wagner asked in German and in English if he'd seen who had removed the distributor. But the man only shrugged his shoulders. He understood nothing. Then he pointed at Wagner's hair. Wagner waved to him and the man got out. Wagner went over to his car, but took care not to walk in front of the man. He pointed to the uncovered engine and the missing distributor. The driver bent over the engine. Then he straightened and with a shrug of the shoulders indicated he couldn't help, or perhaps that he didn't know who had stolen the distributor. But if he'd been awake at the time he would have had to see the thief. Now he was talking to Wagner again. He gesticulated in the direction of the road. Wagner wondered if he should mention the Falls, but said to himself it would be more sensible to go back by the quickest route. Then the company could worry about the car. He named the city. The driver grinned, repeated the name and with a gesture invited Wagner to get in. Wagner took his jacket from the car, took out his car keys from the jacket pocket, but was unable to find his wallet. The letter to Susann was still there, but the wallet with his papers, the company letter and the work permit had disappeared. Luckily he had put his money in his trouser pocket. He searched the cushions with the torch. The driver lifted the mats. The wallet had disappeared. Should he go with him without his papers? Perhaps it wasn't advisable to stay here as the thief had not found any money and would know he had it on him. It didn't surprise him that his travelling bag had also disappeared. He had been robbed clean. He took his jacket and went with the driver to the articulated lorry. It was an old lorry, some American model, brightly painted. On the tailboard a naive picture, the archangel Michael fighting a dragon. The back of the lorry was empty except for some wood splinters and pieces of bark. Wagner got into the driver's cabin. The seat was tattered. Some mangos lay on the floor.

Wagner again looked over at his car standing in the light of a gently swaying lamp. Every movement in and around the car could be seen from here, but perhaps the driver had been asleep.

Wagner made a mental note of the name of the lay-by; pantera negra, the black panther.

They drove on the country road in the direction of the Falls. Wagner told himself at some point they would have to take a road to the east, where he could see a red streak. Soon the sun would rise. The driver winked at him, looked for music on the radio and sang to it in a gentle deep voice. He was in his early twenties, the face deep brown, black curls, a head like a Moroccan. He had taken off his check shirt and now sat at the wheel in a sleeveless t-shirt. A lean, hairy body with muscular arms. The gear shift came out several times so that the driver had to keep it in place with his right knee. Wagner pointed to the gear shift and held it. On the horizon the sun slowly raised itself above a broad hill. Wagner watched things slowly acquire outline. He kept the jacket on his lap, in it the letter to Susann. He held the vibrating gear shift with his left hand, the vibrations crept from his hand to his arm to his shoulder, from his shoulder to his head, steady vibrations that slowly shook every thought from his head. People were sitting inside the drums. The drums were turning. He was sitting in a drum and at the same time he could see the other people in their sections of the drum. He had got into the drum as an experiment. The point was to prove a distortion in perspective. Things were supposed to grow larger or smaller at will. Things in fact grew larger and larger until the whirling in his head merged with them. He himself was calm, but things rotated at a tearing speed. They grew smaller and smaller until they suddenly disappeared down a black hole.

When he woke it was daylight. Still half asleep, he wondered where this flight of things would have taken him, then saw the driver grinning and again holding the gear shift in place with his knee. They were now driving on a dirt road. In the side mirror Wagner saw the reddish dust like a long flag fluttering behind them. They drove through a slightly hilly landscape in which sugar cane was being cultivated. The landscape, Wagner thought, could be that of the city outskirts. What irritated Wagner was that the man was not driving on the asphalted country road. But perhaps he had taken a short cut. Wagner again named the city. The driver nodded. He laughed. He pointed ahead, as if to calm Wagner. Nevertheless Wagner began searching for a map in the compartments by the dashboard. He wanted to find the place on a road map. The driver watched him, then offered Wagner a cigarette. Wagner took it. He pointed to the gear shift and again held it in place with his left hand.

They continued like this into the afternoon through a landscape that Wagner compared constantly to the one through which he had driven on his way out. Sometimes he found it quite similar, then again not at all similar. He had been so sunk in his thoughts on the way out that nothing in particular had stuck in his memory. And the sun's position confused him, rather than allowed him to deduce an approximate direction.

As they drove through a banana plantation they saw a group of people standing in the road. Bunches of bananas were stacked at the roadside. The men and women were shouting something to them and gesticulating. At first Wagner thought they wanted to sell them bananas. The driver stopped and got out. Wagner followed him into the dusty red heat. Dust that reminded him of the city outskirts and the excavation. Perhaps they were near after all, as he could see the green bulge of the rain forest in the distance. The people spoke to the driver in Spanish, which he clearly couldn't understand. Wagner only slowly realized the people were excited. In their midst stood a man who appeared to be injured or ill, as he was supported by two men. Wagner pushed his way through and saw the man was spattered with blood. With his right hand he held his blood-smeared left, from which the index finger was missing. Blood ran along his arm, but it only flowed slowly and the tracks of blood were already dry with dust at the edges. Someone spoke to Wagner. Wagner asked: 'What happened?' No one understood him. A woman made a snake sign in the air and then with the edge of her hand a blow to the left index finger. If Wagner understood the mime correctly, the man had been bitten by a snake and then chopped off his finger with the machete. The man stood there quietly, almost relaxed. There was no pain, no horror in his face. Occasionally he turned the hand a little and looked at the wound. And oddly enough Wagner too felt no revulsion or disgust. The strange light, the people gathered and now calm again, the man's composure, the matter-of-fact way in which one woman gave him something to drink, another wiped the blood from him, took whatever was alarming from the scene. The driver got in, then Wagner, and, without there being any need to discuss it, the man. Many hands supported him and pushed him up. Now there was the smell of blood in the driver's cabin.

The driver turned on the engine, Wagner put it in gear and held the gear shift in place. He changed gear at a nod from the driver. They had by now learned to work as a team. He felt the man next to him and something coming damp and sticky through his trouser leg, his sweat. Until he realized it was blood dripping from the man's elbow. Involuntarily Wagner moved a little away from the man, who noticed, and also that he had stained Wagner's trousers with blood. With a quick movement he pulled the shirt out of his trousers and holding an end with his teeth, tore off a piece and stuffed it between himself and Wagner to save him getting any dirtier. He said something, probably an apology, and smiled at Wagner. He was missing an incisor in front. His face had grown pale but he still laughed, and not even in pain. On his right hand he wore a narrow gold ring. Wagner would have liked to ask him about his family, if he had children, and how many. He wanted to show him a photo of Sascha, but it was in the wallet.

They drove along the reddish dirt road in which were deep, dried-out ruts, so Wagner kept being jolted against the man. He looked at him now and then because he thought the pain was sure to show in his face, at least with the jolting and shaking. But all he saw was concentrated self-possession.

Wagner had once, years ago, driven with Susann to the Elbe. She was six months pregnant (and at that time had been really beautiful). She was walking along the shore. In the willow bushes hung plastic bags, tattered, remnants of the last high tide. It was a warm, slightly windy day. The Elbe: small choppy waves in which the sun sparkled, and on the shore the white froth of waves trailed by a harbour ferry. In a sandy hollow a couple lay naked. The woman, a blonde, had dark black pubic hair.

'It comes out in the sun,' Susann had said, and they had laughed so loudly the couple had sat up in alarm. He wished she were sitting next to him now so he could talk to her.

After a good hour's drive on the dirt road they reached a small town. The man now sat leaning against Wagner, his eyes deep and shadowy in their hollows, but the wound no longer bled. He was close to fainting, but still directed the driver through the streets until they came to a hospital, a new building painted white with a huge red cross on the facade. The driver stopped at the entrance and reversed a little. He nudged Wagner's shoulder in recognition because he had put the gear shift in reverse. Then he helped the injured man from the driver's cabin. They took the man, he hung heavily onto them, under the arms and led him into the hospital. A sister with a large coif, white as a yacht, came running and brought a wheeled stretcher, and as they lifted the man onto the bed he lost consciousness.

A doctor, a youngish man with a full black beard, had Wagner explain in English where they had found the man. Probably he was bitten on the finger by a snake, then presumably cut it off himself with a machete.

The doctor said: 'Wait please. In front of the hospital you will find a bar.'

Wagner sat down with the driver at a table outside the cafe. He ordered water. The driver spoke Portuguese with the waiter.

Wagner looked across the square that was the town centre. Next to a monument that depicted a bearded bronze head were two benches on which some old men were sitting. An iceman was pushing a cart across the square and ringing a small brass bell.

Wagner wondered if he should simply rent a car and drive back that very night. But where were they?

There were many Indians there and also blacks. Some children were hopping in squares drawn in the sand, standing on one leg they bent down, picked up a stone and hopped back. They were probably playing hopscotch and Wagner would have liked to know what the game was called in Spanish and how it had come here. He remembered how he had wanted to live with Luisa, a plan as if from another life.

Dusk set in. Men put their chairs outside front doors and sat there talking and smoking. In the bar the television was on. The head of the Junta was talking. He wore a narrow fitting uniform that for some reason made him look like a gentleman's tailor. Perhaps it had to do with the thick black moustache.

Wagner saw the doctor cross the square, the long unbuttoned overall flapping. He joined Wagner and the driver at the table. 'He's ok, and this finger' (he raised his index finger) 'is only important for soldiers and doctors.' He ordered a beer and asked Wagner what he was doing in the country.

Wagner told him he had been to the capital and on the way back someone had stolen his distributor. Now he was on the way to the building site.

The doctor asked him to repeat the name of the city. Then he laughed and said: 'You're totally wrong.' He called something over to the bar in Spanish.

The waiter came with a street map. The doctor showed the place where they were now, then pointed to a place further northwest. Wagner's site was there. The two places were approximately 300 kilometres apart. Wagner looked at the driver, the driver stared at the map and shook his head. He obviously couldn't read. The doctor spoke to him in Portuguese. The driver pointed to a place that was on the other side of the border, Barracão. As pronounced by the doctor, the name sounded only remotely familiar. The driver looked at Wagner, his face showed regret. Then he suddenly got up and went over to his lorry. At first Wagner wanted to run after him to tell him it was all right, but the doctor said the driver only wanted to get something. It was all a misunderstanding.

He had ordered a scotch and held his glass to Wagner's.

Wagner wanted to know if he could rent a car here. 'No. Impossible. This is the end of the world.' Then he began to explain the quickest way for Wagner to get to his building site. There was a bus connection, but you had to change twice and in between ride on a donkey. Wagner took this for a joke.

'No, it's true, you have to go by donkey?'

'But why?'

If Wagner understood the man correctly, the road led via a motorway bridge over a deep ravine, but it was really not a proper motorway bridge.

'I don't understand.'

'I understand. This country is a miracle. Because there's a continual transformation from rational structures to shit and then from shit to fairy tales and finally to real miracles. You'll see it on the road.'

Meanwhile the whisky had stupified Wagner, and that had taken the edge off all problems. He had to laugh at the thought of Steinhorst wading in rubber boots in the excavation to mark boundaries. The driver had got into the lorry and driven off. He drove round the square and stopped right outside the bar. He climbed from the driver's cabin and carried something, lightly covered, in one hand. With a quick movement he put the distributor on the table in front of Wagner. Without looking at Wagner, he said something to the doctor. 'He's sorry. He wishes you good luck.'

Wagner stared at the piece of machinery which, as if in derision, had even been cleaned.

The doctor translated that Wagner's wallet and travelling

bag had been stolen by another lorry driver when Wagner had gone into the restaurant to look for the distributor.

Wagner laughed, laughed as if to free himself of the stress of the past hours, the heat, the noise, the dust, the roaring that was still in his ears. He held the distributor in his hand and laughed. At first they both looked at him surprised as if he'd gone mad, then they also began to laugh, cautiously at first, as if by laughing they might hurt him, then without restraint and loudly. After Wagner had regained his self-control he shook hands with the driver and said: 'Gracias.' He asked the doctor to ask the driver why he had torn out his hair. The doctor made sure he had understood the question correctly. Wagner saw a slight, cunning grin on the driver's face. He took the hair from the breast pocket of his shirt and showed it to the doctor, saying something that made him laugh aloud. The driver had pulled out his hair to prove to a friend that he'd slept with a beautiful blonde.

The driver embraced Wagner. And Wagner was immersed in the sunlit, dirty smell of his childhood. Then the driver got into his lorry, turned on the engine and drove, hooting, once round the square and away.

If Wagner still wanted to get the bus tonight he would have to hurry, the doctor said. He would take him to the bus stop. Wagner wanted to pay but the doctor insisted he was his guest. They had already gone a distance when the waiter came after them bringing the distributor which Wagner had left lying on the café table.

Twenty Eight

With its engine roaring the bus drove slowly up the incline. It rocked with crashing axles over potholes. It was dark, there were only two red emergency lights on the ceiling. People stood tightly packed in the aisle. Many were Indians, they slept standing. The old woman who sat next to Wagner had wrapped herself in a wide black shawl and in her sleep had sunk against him, her head on his chest. A white hen lay on her lap. She had carefully put the bird, its legs tied, with its back on her lap, and there it lay as if hypnotized. But now and then it moved its eyes. Behind him a child was crying. In the net luggage rack two piglets grunted. Occasionally the bus stopped, and always more people got on. Once those in the aisle had to get out because a woman with a baby tied to her back wanted to get out. She crouched in front of the bus, lifted her skirts and peed. Then she got back in and after her the others that had waited outside. The bus roared on its way through the night. Suddenly flames lit the landscape, gigantic torches, in the light they gave a treeless and shrubless plain could be seen; oil pumps moved in shadow on it like pecking steel birds. The old woman next to Wagner had woken. He saw the light gleam yellow on the wrinkled face. The woman reached into a basket standing on the floor and took out some bread. She broke off a piece and handed it to Wagner. It was corn bread. She took a dented tin bottle from the basket, unscrewed the lid and handed it to Wagner. For a moment Wagner hesitated. Then he took the bottle and drank. It was lukewarm juice, but its strange grainy flavour made it taste cool. Then the woman drank. She tore pieces from the loaf and stuffed them into her toothless mouth. The hen lay as if dead on her lap, but its eyes followed the bread in her hand. The old woman again held the tin bottle out to Wagner. But he didn't want to drink like this, straight from mouth to mouth. He thanked her, waited until the woman had finished eating, took out his cigarettes and offered her one. She carefully pulled out one and then a second. She put one behind her ear, the other in her mouth. They sat in silence next to each other, smoked and were thrown against each other by potholes.

Sitting next to this old woman who smoked like a sailor, holding the cigarette in the hollow of her hand between thumb and middle finger, he asked himself what there was still left for him. What did he actually want? Aside from his work, which was fun, he couldn't answer the question why he'd gone to all the trouble over the years: why is the banana bent? He laughed out loud. The old woman gave him a quick look and nodded as if to say: Go on. If he thought back, then a few memories drifted past, the painful, tormenting ones in sharp outline very close and clear, the so-called beautiful ones isolated, far away and in a faint mist. But there was no land in sight. Somehow, almost imperceptibly, his desires had got lost. They had been worn away by the many little habits and the many little needs.

They drove through forest and he immediately thought the site must be near. Which of course was impossible. Then the bus stopped. Something was lying on the road. There was a movement in the front of the bus. Some men got out, also the driver. He could hear them calling excitedly. A hectic commotion began, a babble of voices, one on top of the other.

Wagner thought it must be exactly like this on a sinking ship. He heard the calls and snarls of the forest animals, the many-voiced cry of the hunted and of death that even drowned the dull roar of the engine. Then they all got back in and the bus drove on without Wagner having seen what had happened on the road.

He dozed off and a little later a new commotion in the bus woke him. Everyone crowded out. Wagner went to the driver and showed him the note on which the doctor had written the name of the town for him. But the driver only pointed to a house and said: 'Fin de viaje.'

Wagner pressed the distributor into his hand and waved to him. The man stood there, astonished, as if Wagner had put an Easter egg in his hand. Wagner went over to the hotel to which the driver had pointed. In the bar a man lay across a table asleep. He had put his head on the table, stretched his arms wide, and lay there as if taken off guard and shot dead while drinking beer. It was just after two and Wagner didn't know whether to wake the man. Then he noticed a bell above a table. He rang. After a while a morose man in pyjamas appeared.

'Wagner asked: 'Do you have a room for me?'

'No,' the man said and shuffled away. Wagner wondered whether to sit at the table with the man, but then went outside. There was a cane chair right by the entrance. He sat in it. He left one hand in his trouser pocket where he had his money. He covered himself with his jacket. From behind some bushes came a strange snorting and groaning. But Wagner could see neither animal, nor person. He would have gladly explained to somebody why he was sitting there, filthy and unshaven. How it had begun with a crazy idea, because naturally he had driven out in the blind hope of discovering Luisa's address at the Prefecture (the hope of meeting Luisa again in the city), how he had taken a wrong turning, and how after that he kept finding himself further from the destination he actually wanted. Tiny coincidences piled high to make an irrevocable inevitability. Renate would have called it an adventure. But it was only an adventure from the perspective of a Hamburg suburban villa's front garden with its blue spruces. Susann would have described it far more soberly as a strange lack of success. Already half asleep, the crackling of the cane chair made him sit up in alarm.

Children screaming woke him. It was daylight. Some children were standing behind a yellow flowering bush and throwing small red berries at him. When Wagner got up they ran away.

He went into the hotel and sat down. The proprietor came. His face was still morose, which Wagner immediately realized was due to his waking him in the night.

'Café y pan, por favor.'

The proprietor looked in distrust at Wagner, then rubbed his finger and thumb, a gesture, Wagner thought, found wherever we've been. Wagner showed the proprietor his money, a bundle of notes, more or less as revenge because the man had taken him as being unable to pay. At the same time he realized it was a mistake to show him so much money.

The proprietor brought coffee and bread, some jam and rancid butter. Through the open windows Wagner saw the sun rise over the forested range of hills. He thought of the site, of the groundwater in the excavation for factory B, but he thought of it as if it no longer had anything to do with him. A piece of past history, distant and strange, his problems, his efforts. What had Hartmann said: Wagner was the one who would put things right.

None of it mattered to him, only thinking of the strike he felt a pang, and the uneasiness was back. Not because he felt guilty about the contractor – what a crazy mistaken idea – but he was ashamed on account of the workers, on account of the four men who had been dismissed and deported because of him. What must he look like to the other workers: a clumsy giant, face red with sunburn, bright blue eyes that, so he was told, could hide nothing.

The proprietor came, spoke to Wagner and pointed outside. There stood a donkey and next to it a man wearing a large straw hat that shaded his face. The proprietor indicated that Wagner should go. Wagner held a note out to him. The proprietor pocketed it without giving change. Wagner told himself perhaps the ride on the donkey was included in the sum. He went outside and got onto the donkey that the man, who wore a poncho despite the heat, held with one arm round its neck. The proprietor came bringing a straw hat for Wagner, for which he wanted to be paid. He refused a note Wagner held out to him, choosing one from the wad of money. It was for a fairly high sum and in Germany Wagner could have bought a Borsalino for it. But he didn't protest because he told himself he had only himself to blame, he shouldn't have shown the money. At the same time he was overcome by the fear that he would be led into an ambush on the donkey, to be robbed, if not actually murdered. The man clicked his tongue and pulled the donkey after him down the village street. The children ran alongside Wagner and again threw the small red berries at him. One of the boys made a V sign. Wagner didn't know if this was an offer or only intended to annoy him.

Without paying any attention to the animal, the man pulled it after him on a rope. They entered the forest which began just beyond the village and plunged into a green world above which the sky was no longer visible. It was the first time since being in the country that Wagner was so physically close to the forest. Occasionally one of the lianas that hung like rope from the trees brushed against him, stems with a finely rippled bark, the colour of mustard and a good twenty metres high, next to them palms, bushes in half shade, spear-shaped leaves of delicate bright green; but even the attempt to see the variety of leaf shapes and shades in this green world completely confused him and he thought how poorly language was able to define this thrusting, light engulfing vegetation, and therefore to perceive it. He had once read about an Amazon Indian tribe that had more than two hundred words to determine green. The donkey quietly followed the path, a thick dry layer of leaves, the man in front in his poncho, straw hat on his head so that Wagner had still not been able to see his face. Hadn't the jaguar man also worn a hat like that, frayed and torn at the side? A branch brushed against Wagner, and he was showered with grey-blue pollen as if from a small explosion. Wagner wanted to see Juan as soon as he got back, only he would be able to answer the questions on his mind: what were these giant trees called and through whom had he met Luisa, because Juan must at least have heard from somebody that she wanted to teach Spanish, that she needed money. A tree several metres in diameter lay toppled; it could only have happened recently, it had struck a path through the vegetation. Wagner saw the sky, veils of cloud in the startling blue. But what Wagner had not expected at all was the silence in the forest; he could hear no animal call, no water, no wild life. The guide went in sandals of the kind Hartmann had worn, and though the man went so purposefully uphill Wagner heard no panting, not even breathing. Only the donkey snorted now and then. Its coat was drenched in sweat. Suddenly the man turned. Wagner looked into the old face of an Indian. A face that didn't fit the tenacious movements of the body. The man forced the donkey back a little and pointed to a tree trunk lying on the ground, on which lay a green snake, of the same kind Wagner had run over on the first day. The man waited until the snake had disappeared, then he dragged the donkey past the tree trunk. Wagner sat soaked in sweat but shivering on the donkey. Having seen the guide's face he now sank into a listless apathy, an indifference to time and place. For a while it disturbed him that the donkey stumbled several times going uphill so that he kept having to cling to the saddle. Then the path became so narrow the guide could no longer walk beside the donkey, but had to go ahead. Suddenly a howling storm broke out in the trees above Wagner. A group of monkeys were doing gymnastics in the tree tops.

The donkey was tired and panting, increasingly the man had to drive it with blows of a stick to its front legs. Then the vegetation thinned, and they stepped out of the forest — before Wagner lay a six lane motorway bridge. The bridge spanned the precipitous valley in a bold arc. And on both sides it ended in the forest, in small paths.

It lay before Wagner, mighty, wonderfully pointless and without purpose, unless it bore a purpose in itself. Wagner noticed a pedestrian on the bridge. If he had come here in a Landrover he could have smiled at it as a curiosity, a monument to bad planning and corruption, as Hartmann had described it; but like this, drenched in sweat, thirsty, with insect bites like huge boils and a tick the size of a dung beetle in his arm, he rode onto the bridge in great amazement. At the edges stood rusted machinery, compressors green with parasitical life, a tar machine, machine parts lay scattered everywhere, a cement mixer, its large drum wearing a green beard, a crane wreathed in creepers, the white flowers foaming from supporting beam to beam like a waterfall.

Then they plunged into the forest again and it seemed to Wagner as if his pulse had slowed down. Apathetic again, it was already late afternoon, nearly dusk, he rode on until they reached the place. It was immediately evident the town had once been the centre of a large building site. Because here too everywhere were rusted lorries, bulldozers and cement mixers. And also heaps of pebbles and sand and two mounds of cement set in formations that resembled the Dolomites. After this, dilapidated Nissen huts — that for the first time made Wagner think of his own site – and some caved-in prefabricated houses in which the engineers had probably lived. Then came some old residential buildings in colonial style, and a whitewashed church opposite a yellow-brown two storey house with heavy columns. The word 'Hotel' had been painted on the facade in tar-colour. There was also a Chinese laundry in the same building. The man stopped the donkey – it was the first time the man had stopped since they had set out in the morning, and immediately sat down on the ground.

Wagner went into the hotel.

The lobby, supported by cast iron columns, lay in a dim light. There was a penetrating smell of perfume. The wood panelling on the walls was warped. An officer and a woman were sitting at a round smoker's table.

The woman looked at him closely, especially his trousers, then she said: 'No.'

The officer sat in the armchair, his uniform jacket unbuttoned and his tie loosened. He grinned.

Wagner reached into his trouser pocket and pulled out the money. The woman stared at the sweaty crumpled wad of notes, put her cigarette out in the ash tray and got up. She went to the counter and took a key from the board. She gave Wagner some soap and a towel. She walked ahead decidedly slowly, along a corridor lit white by neon lights. Wagner saw her small round behind in her narrow skirt, her black stockinged legs, her high heeled cork shoes, and thought perhaps she had misunderstood him. He had landed in a brothel. She unlocked the door to a room. In the bare, high ceilinged room stood a metal bed, a chest of drawers and on it a jug and bowl. A chipped mirror aimed directly onto the bed hung on the wall. The woman made the paying gesture with her fingers. Wagner held out the money to her. She looked, hesitated, finally pulled out a note. Wagner wanted to protest, then said to himself it wasn't a matter of money, the important thing was that tonight he would sleep in a bed. The woman left. He looked at himself in the mirror, unshaven, filthy with dried blood stains on his trousers. He looked like somebody on the run. He was surprised the woman had even given him a room.

'I've pretty well had it,' he said aloud to himself.

Wagner washed his hands and face in the bowl. Then he tried to wash the blood from his trousers. He would have liked to shave. He beat out his filthy jacket, then held it over his arm so it hid the wet spot on his trouser leg. He went to the hotel lobby where the woman was again sitting at the officer's table. The man looked at him closely with lively curiosity. Wagner handed the woman a note with Bredow's telephone number. She waved a finger, which no doubt was intended to mean it couldn't be done. He again showed his money. She got up, went to the counter, dialled a number and held the receiver out to Wagner. The line was dead. The bus?

'Mañana.' She wrote down the time. 7.30.

Wagner told himself a day more or less didn't matter anymore. He sat at one of the tables in the deserted hotel restaurant. A waiter in a white, carefully ironed jacket put a bottle of white wine and a grilled fish on the table, without him having ordered anything. Wagner ate some of the fish, a freshwater fish with many bones and white delicate flesh. Wagner wanted to pay, but the waiter gestured there was no need. Probably the evening meal was included in the price of the room. He went outside, the guide was still squatting on the ground. Wagner gave him a note. The man shook his head and took a coin out of a small leather bag. Wagner actually had to force the note on him. The old man took the money and continued squatting. Wagner crossed the square which was already lit by street lamps, though it was only just getting dark. In the centre of the square was a marble pedestal with two large bronze boots, spurs on the heels. Going nearer, he saw that the body that had once worn these boots had been torn down. On a bronze plaque, also shattered, the first name Domingo was still legible, and in Spanish and English that the great general, leader of the people, builder of the highest bridge in the country, had been born here.

Wagner went through the streets, past old houses. Pieces had broken from the flower and fruit garlands on the façades, everywhere cracks and fissures had opened in the walls. There was a smell of food cooking and of naphthalene, with which the inhabitants probably fought off the giant moths that fluttered in the air and kept hurling themselves against Wagner's suit. There was nobody in sight on the street. The roar of a televised football match burst from open windows. Dogs prowled everywhere, big creatures of a mongrel type he had never seen before, naked and rosy as pigs. They growled at Wagner as he walked past. Unusually large chickens ran about on the street and took powerful leaps into the air, their claws drawn high like eagles. Wagner saw they were catching grasshoppers almost the size of a hand, but were only able to tear and swallow them after a regular battle in which the chickens used their claws. Everything in this palce seemed to have mutated to giantism. A man lay under a van as if run over, his legs stuck out from beneath the vehicle as if the driver had simply braked and let the person he had run over lie there. The man didn't move, and as in the meantime it had grown almost dark Wagner couldn't think what the man might be doing under the van.

He came to a district where there were huts hammered together of wood and corrugated iron, tiny houses, all of them surrounded by small fences made of crates and slats of wood. In these huts too the television was on. Behind the huts the land rose a little and above were houses that resembled farmhouses in Lower Saxony, at any rate they stood on posts. They were half-timbered and built of brick. Wagner was looking at a draw well, of a kind he hadn't so far seen in this country, when suddenly a mob of blonde children rushed at him, calling:

241

'Greedy guts, greedy guts, give us a sweet.' They held hands out to him that, he noticed horrified, had six fingers. "Ave a look,' they shouted.

They were clean, blonde children who spoke Low German as if they were somewhere in North Germany.

A man's voice called, and in an instant they all disappeared. At the door of one of the half-timbered houses stood an old grey-bearded man, a giant, as tall as Wagner, but broader and bulkier. He was holding a lamp and behind him stood a young woman with light blonde hair. The man asked Wagner in German where he was from and where he was going. It was old fashioned German, and Wagner immediately thought of Sophie.

Wagner said he was an engineer, came from Germany and was here in the country to build a paper factory. The old man gestured to Wagner to come into the house. They entered a large kitchen, but it was only lit by two oil lamps. There was a large wooden table in the middle of the room, around it chairs of rough wood. By the wall an old cast iron stove, above it hung ladles and copper pots. The old man pointed to one of the chairs. 'We bid you welcome,' the old man said, 'but consider, for they who praise the Lord and think they never shall behold grief, they shall awaken and lament. The plagues shall come, and soon, yes, soon, there shall be death, calamity and hunger. And in a great fire all shall burn, for the Lord shall pronounce judgement upon the whore of Babylon, her whom you also serve. Look unto yourself, repent and pray, that you shall be spared eternal darkness.

'This is my daughter Rebecca, she will bring you a jug of beer.' Wagner asked the man if he knew a woman by the name of Sophie.

'No,' the old man said, 'I know everyone here, I am their preacher, I don't know the woman. But there are many communities here. We came over a hundred years ago from Pomerania.'

The woman brought a jug and a glass and poured Wagner beer. Wagner saw she also had six fingers, the old man's hand was normal. The young woman hid her hand behind her back and stared at Wagner. He drank the beer which was heavy and a little bitter. The old man had sat down at the table opposite Wagner and also drank.

'It is written: A mighty angel raised high a great stone, as big as a millstone, threw it into the sea and said: So shall a storm thrown down the great city of Babylon and never again shall it arise.'

Suddenly Wagner was overcome with dizzyness, the exertion of the last few days, the heat, the beer, again this talk of the destruction of Babylon, it all confused him and left him depressingly listless. He wanted to lie down and sleep.

He got up, aware that he swayed a little, said 'thank you' and went out and down the steps. The moon shone bright and clear. There was nobody in sight on the street, only the dogs ran free in the night, naked and gigantic. Then he saw a small dachshund, as he approached to stroke it he saw it was a fat rat. In the hotel lobby the woman sat on the officer's lap. Her dress had slipped to the top of her stockings, stuck between her legs, wedged there, was the officer's hand. But the woman only pointed to the key board and the officer left his hand where it was.

Wagner went to his room and locked the door. He slipped the shoes from his feet and lay on the bed without taking off his shirt and trousers. In the corridor he heard footsteps and a woman giggling, a little later, further away but clearly audible, bed springs squeaking, moaning, a woman moaning, a man groaning, or rather grunting; though he resisted the thought it made him think of the dogs running free outside in the night.

Twenty Nine

Voices. Light. He sat up in alarm. There were men in the room. Somebody screamed. He recognized uniforms. He was pulled up. At first he stood stupified, then felt pain, his hands had been forced into handcuffs behind his back. He screamed.

He was pushed through the door, dragged along the corridor. The receptionist was standing outside one of the rooms in her dressing gown, distraught. It was still dark outside. He was pushed into a police car and thought this was how they had come for Luisa, exactly like this. He sat on a wooden bench. Then the car started and he was thrown to the floor, where he was left lying. After a short drive (they had turned off the siren) the car braked sharply. The door was flung open, he was dragged out. He was led into a house, a villa. The facade lit by two floodlights seemed to be of wood blocks. Standing at the entrance two guards with submachine guns, a large hall, a flight of stairs, marble rippled blue-white, sandbags, a machine gun in the corridor, an iron door, two clouded mirrors, then down some steps to a basement, a long whitewashed corridor, a boiler (why this boiler, big enough to heat a multi-storeyed building?), a steel door was unbolted, Wagner was pushed into a small room. The door was bolted behind him. He was in a cell, two metres by four. On the ceiling a bulb in a wire basket, a bucket for faeces, a plank bed, no window. Wagner sat on the bed. He listened. He heard his blood roaring.

He thought everything would quickly sort itself out, his company and nationality would protect him, but then he remembered he had no passport and he felt the fear in his throat. In his jacket they would find his letter to Susann, and he was glad he hadn't posted the letter because, he hoped, then they would see he was a foreigner. At the same time he remembered that many foreigners had disappeared, untraceable despite every alleged effort by the embassies. Wagner had always thought these people were in fact in some way connected to the guerillas, if only through sympathy. But Fabrizi had said that every department acted independently, even the lowliest. What a word, he thought, the lowliest, but it fitted his situation, he had arrived at the very bottom, come right down, filthy, he was scum. The thought of the door being flung open, that they might drag him out and shoot him, made his teeth chatter. He was trembling. He stood up, leaned against the wall and tried to regain control by concentrating on his breathing. He wanted to distract himself by trying to imagine what Susann and Sascha might be doing. Would they still be asleep? Had they just got up? Were they having breakfast? They had taken his watch. Not knowing what time it was brought him to a new state of nervous uneasiness, as if his life depended on knowing the exact time at that very moment. Probably they were having breakfast, as always in the kitchen, Susann's collection of copper pans on the wall. The check table cloth, blue and white. Susann already had her make-up on, the eye-liner carefully pencilled in on the tired face that for months now looked more tired in the morning than at midday, that dear trusted face. In the evening there would be the smell of baking apples, because it was Advent – while he sat in this oppressive heat on this plank bed that smelled of disinfectant. Susann scattered sugar over the apples that then caramelized in the oven. A transparent brown glaze. Love apples.

He remembered the pomegranate he had found in Luisa's kitchen and that was now in his car. And the other pomegranate that lay under the kitchen cupboard, shrivelled small, turned into wood. How long could it have been lying there? Hadn't Steinhorst said that from the small room in which his kidnappers had hidden him Ehmke had seen some pomegranates under a kitchen cupboard? Was it two or three?

But Wagner had not seen any small room from which he could have looked into the kitchen. Or was there perhaps a store-room off the corridor opposite the kitchen? No, Wagner thought, I'm driving myself mad, and at the same time thought, they wanted to kidnap me. They, who are they? It's this cell, this narrow oppressive cell that's making me think these deranged thoughts. He tried to think of something else, but he thought: Did she want to lure me to the flat? 'That's crazy,' he shouted, 'crazy.' He tried to control himself, he pressed his fists to his temple until the pain brought him to himself. He lay down on the bed and pressed his arm against his eyes to blot out the light. He had taken a few deep breaths when the door was flung open. A soldier beckoned him.

Now, he thought, now.

He got up quite automatically and went out. He decided to scream, he would not let himself simply be slaughtered. They led him up the steps. Outside there was a grey, diffuse light. So it was morning already. He was led along a corridor and pushed into a room, a large high-ceilinged room. Through big folding doors that led onto a balcony with a wrought iron railing (probably this had been the living room) he could see a park. In the room a desk, a massive desk from the turn of the century. Next to it, a small office desk. An officer sat behind the big desk, a youngish man, a civilian stood next to him. The civilian stared at Wagner, his red face bloated, fat, eyes glazed.

How do such faces come about, Wagner thought.

The civilian lit a match and Wagner saw his hand shake. The officer, who wore three stars on his epaulettes, had the crumpled letter to Susann in his hand. Before either of them could put a question to him Wagner began talking in German, as if to prove he was a foreigner, that he had nothing to do with the underground struggle. Wagner gave the name of his company, said he was in the country as a civil engineer in charge of building a factory, named the place, also gave Bredow's name, and said he had lost his way.

The civilian began to grin. Clearly he understood German. The officer folded the letter and pulled out a sheet of paper, probably on it was the translation of the letter. He's reading what was only intended for Susann, Wagner thought and was filled with rage, he shouted: 'I want to speak to the Intendente, Colonel Kramer.' Then he shouted the company's name, but thought many who had stood here had named some well know foreign company in their despair. The civilian said something to the officer who sat thinking and at the same time quite uninhibitedly bit the nail of his middle finger, the habit of a school boy who doesn't know what to do next, but this minor bad habit along with his silence betrayed who was in charge here. The officer got up abruptly and called out something in the direction of the door. While two soldiers pushed and pulled Wagner the officer reached for a file. They led Wagner down a corridor past two girls and a young man sitting on a bench. They held Wagner in a well-practised grip that was not painful if one surrendered to it. The three waiting on the bench had looked at him with expressions of fear and pity. He had tried to smile at them. The soldiers led him down the steps and he thought they were going to lock him in his cell again, but they went past the door. The corridor made a sharp bend. Wagner was astonished at the corridor's length, at the extent of the cellars under this old villa. They stopped outside a heavy iron door. It was an iron door like those built into air raid bunkers that could only be opened by two heavy iron levers.

Wagner was pushed into a brightly lit room, the floor and walls of which were tiled. There was a white enamel bed, a cupboard in which lay chrome-plated medical instruments, so strangely shaped he had never seen any like them before. A red cross was painted on the cupboard, for outpatients, he thought, then the words torture chamber shot through his head.

He turned, wanted to get out through the door, to escape, screamed, struck out, they grabbed him, dragged him to the bed, a third soldier came running, a struggle followed, then Wagner felt a fierce pain in his arms, his shoulders, a pain that made him bend forward, they had twisted his arms and raised them. Now he lay with his chest on the bed, his face pressed into the plastic cover, a revolting stench that made him choke; from behind someone unbuttoned his trousers and pulled them down. Wagner saw the door open, a man came in, in an overall, under it a uniform, a mixture of doctor and officer. Wagner watched as the man slowly and carefully pulled on rubber gloves, how, pedantically accurate, he pushed the rubber down to the base of the fingers of the other hand with the tips of his fingers, then stepped behind Wagner. He tried, in his speechless horror, to turn his head to this man who now stood behind him, but a fist pressed his head onto the plastic cover, his legs were pulled to one side, and with animal fright he felt someone drive a finger into his anus. Then the pressure on his neck eased. Wagner can get up. He sees the doctor put down a small torch, roll the gloves from his hands and wash his hands. With a brusque gesture one of the soldiers makes it plain he should pull up his trousers. But his legs are trembling, his hands, his whole body trembles, the trembling even reaches his head. Two soldiers grab him by the arms, and he is led back, half supported, half pushed, to his cell. He sits in the cell which has grown even hotter, his bare feet on the concrete floor. He remembers how, it was last autumn, he ran barefoot on the sand. It was a Saturday afternoon. Susann had gone with Sascha to a children's birthday party. He had sat in his study and tried to read the paper. But nothing held his interest. He had sat and listened to the silence in the house, and suddenly it was as if everything had stopped. Here he sat while outside the clouds slowly drifted in the sky. He had got up simply to interrupt this numbness. He had roamed through the much-too-big house with its straight lines and right angles. Finally he had left the house. He had driven to the Elbe and walked along a stretch of the embankment. Then he had taken off his shoes, put them by some willow bushes, he had an urge to run barefoot on the sand. He had actually only wanted to go down to the water, but had then kept on running just as he had run here when he was a child, his eyes longingly on the river that made its way, broad and black, to the open sea. He had walked almost an hour before turning back. The shoes had disappeared. Susann had laughed helplessly. To warm him she had made him mulled wine.

He tried thinking of Luisa. He tried to recall her as clearly as possible, the way she spoke, her intonation, her skin, her hair, her movements when she pointed to things and named them, he tried to recall her in minutest detail. But he couldn't do it. He had to admit to himself he hardly knew anything about her, neither what she thought, nor what she liked or loathed. And again he remembered the letter that was upstairs on the officer's desk. This letter to Susann to clarify everything, that now was unlikely to ever reach her, as also his request that they separate. He regretted not having posted the letter in the capital. Because now a fortuitous event prevented Susann from knowing what had been written, but which others, at least the officer, already knew. And it was clarity he wanted, for himself and for Susann. Even if the tenacious hope remained of a new beginning for himself and Susann. That had made

249

him hesitate to post the letter. But he wanted no illusions, no keeping silent, above all no false grief. If she cried, which she did only rarely, sometimes when they quarrelled and occasionally after school quite simply because she was exhausted, she got into a breathless state that frightened him because she always tried to control herself, to keep back the tears, until finally she sobbed aloud.

Those sobs that finally set free.

Thirty

The door was flung open. Two soldiers stood in the doorway. Now they're coming, he thought, now they'll get me.

The soldiers gestured to him. He got up, slipped his feet into his shoes and took his jacket. Slowly he went out. He was surprised at himself for being so calm. He saw every detail clearly and in sharp outline. The lights behind a grating on the basement corridor ceiling. The patch on the uniform jacket of the soldier walking in front of him. A piece of denim had been sewn on the back and stitched several times. With this patch on the back the uniform looked as if somebody had already been shot in it. They went past the boiler that was far too large for this house, even it if were necessary to heat day and night. But there was no need to heat at all. He thought of Luisa's body that had been so hard to imagine in the cell, here as he climbed the steps and at the top saw the strips of sunlight in the corridor he had it before his eyes. There were many people crowding the corridor now, women and men of all ages. And that calmed him because he said to himself, they can all see me and the more that do the better. He was pushed into a large, but shabby room. The officer immediately came up to him, pointed to a chair by the desk and said: 'Sorry. I really am awfully sorry. It was a misunderstanding.'

He led Wagner to the desk and handed him the receiver. A broad ray of sunlight fell through the closed heavy velvet curtains. The light hurt his eyes. He heard Bredow's voice: 'What are you up to? You're lucky they took the trouble to phone us. Let me talk to the captain!'

Two hours later Wagner was sitting in an army helicopter. He had had a shower at the villa. The captain had even wanted to lend him his electric shaver. But Wagner declined. The pilot was fairly young (the army, apart from the Junta, seemed to consist of young people). He winked at Wagner from beneath his pilot's helmet. A familiarity that had something obscene about it. 'I'll take another way. It's a little bit longer but more beautiful.' Then he winked again and took the helicopter lower over the primeval forest that lay beneath them like a green blanket of cloud. It was through this that Cabeza de Vaca had fought his way. Steaming in his rusted armour, tormented by the bites of giant insects, his skin covered in boils. From the trees the pollen drifts down blue-black. Pale and sunken the face beneath the iron helmet. Puz oozes from an arrowhead in his right arm. The stench of the pus attracts the iridescent blue-black carrion flies that sit on the filthy bandage like a black grape.

For days he has heard the mysterious roaring, gradually growing louder, the further they fight their way through this green night.

The horses sink into the ground that exhales the damp of many thousands of years, then suddenly the forest opens. Foaming, the torrents plunge from the sky. They wash the blood and dirt away, they wipe out all the deserts of the earth. Mist, foam and a rainbow rise from the water. Cabeza de Vaca falls to his knees. These roaring torrents are the spilling of God's fruit bearing seed, they are the everlasting first day of creation. To discover God's rain Cabeza de Vaca has roamed one half of the earth and sailed round the other. He was born with eyes that he might see this. What remains of his life is a gift. They follow the gorge of the Falls, the pilot has put the helicopter at a slant so that Wagner can get a better view of the plunging water. An hour later they landed on the Green Hill. Bredow stood on the lawn, his trousers fluttered in the turbulence as the propellers slowed down. Wagner climbed from the helicopter without thanking the pilot.

Bredow shook Wagner's hand and said: 'Good luck!'

Bredow had parked his car on the lawn. Wagner got in. In his jacket pocket he felt the letter to Susann. The captain had returned it to him torn open, again with an apology. The letter, he said, had made him realize Wagner was clean. After that he had made them phone Wagner's company.

Bredow started the car and after a quick sidelong glance said: 'You don't look well. Have you got a temperature? There have been a few cases of Legionnaire's Disease here. For some reason only Europeans and Americans get it, which is why they call it Atahualpa's revenge.' Bredow laughed. For the first time he laughed again.

'But seriously,' he said, 'It's a horribly dangerous disease. And often fatal.'

'I think I'm getting a cold.'

'Exactly,' Bredow said, 'that's how it begins, with a harmless cold, then pneumonia, and before you've time to look around you've had it.'

'I'm ok.'

'Take care, see a doctor.'

They fell silent. Wagner thought Bredow was trying to find a way out for him. Wagner could now go sick and return to Germany. They stopped outside Wagner's bungalow. The neighbouring bungalow in which the agronomist from Texas had lived had disappeared. The house had been torn down.

Where earlier only knee-high wire mesh divided the land there was now a concrete wall the height of a man, with a roll of barbed wire on the parapet.

'You'll have to move out,' Bredow said. 'We've already rented a new bungalow for you, higher on the hill.'

'And why?'

'Straightening the front line,' Bredow said and laughed again, though, as Wagner saw, he had intended to remain serious. But he simply could not repress this bubbling cheerfulness. Wagner said he wanted to go on living in the house, he didn't feel he was in danger.

'Wait. First get a good night's sleep. Think about it again tomorrow. Living at the border here for any length of time is rather uncomfortable. Come to us tomorrow evening for a meal. They'll bring you a car tonight. They'll simply leave it outside.' The front door opened and Sophie appeared in her white overall. She had put up her plaited grey hair.

'I've already put a warm meal out for you. You must eat warm food. Warmth takes away the shock.'

'Yes,' Wagner said, 'perhaps.'

Sophie had cooked stuffed cabbage. For a moment she watched him as he pulled away the threads wrapped round the cabbage.

In a minute she'll say the sun will grow dark, and I shall answer her: Yes, the sun has grown dark.

'Eat slowly and chew properly. Shall I bring you a beer?'

'Thank you, Sophie.'

She left in her large plastic slippers, and Wagner resolved to buy her a pair of the dark blue canvas shoes he saw everywhere in the city.

He took the letter from his jacket pocket and put it on the table while he ate. He wondered whether to write it again but then thought its appearance, crumpled and torn open, was a part of his history and that he should only put it into another envelope. If, that is, he still wanted to send it. He ought to write a different letter now. He decided to leave the letter for the time being.

Thirty One

 In the morning he overslept, something that had never happened to him before. He was woken by Sophie knocking. Wagner saw that the alarm had already been bleeping for ten minutes. He remembered a dream in which this bleeping had been a going-to-sleep machine that had to be controlled by counting with it. What had woken him, he thought, was that he had become entangled in a monstruous counting labyrinth. When Sophie brought him coffee he asked her what community she was from.

Her people were Russian Germans, she said, that had come to the country in 1930. She belonged to the community of the Day of Judgement. And the day was not far off. And then the beast with seven heads would rise from the sea. She stared at Wagner with her blue eyes with their small, never changing pupils. The city shall be smoke and fire, happy the dead that had died in the Lord. She shuffled into the house and a moment later came back with a booklet she handed to Wagner. Perhaps he would like to read it. Not much time remained.

The picture on the title page showed a naive drawing of the globe of the earth breaking apart. Over it hung a cloud from which a hand came, the size of the globe, as if it had just given the earth a push and broken it. The smoke cloud that came puffing out of the crack looked like a small atomic mushroom. Underneath was written:

And the angel I see standing upon the sea and upon the land raised his hand to the sky and swore to the living eternal God, Creator of Heaven and all therein, and of the Earth and of the Sea and all that dwell there, that henceforth time shall cease.

He allowed himself time on the way to the site. The rented car was a rather decrepid Chevrolet. For the first time Wagner looked more closely at the region, this red-brown land turned into a plain with deeply eroded watercourses in which – it must have rained in the meantime – there was still water. He only gave a passing thought to the excavation for factory B because memories of the last few days crowded in on him. He would have to change his life. It was as if he had got out of step, it had sometimes happened to him before, a sudden feeling as he walked that he was walking wrong, it was not his usual stride, and the more acutely he became aware of it, the more impossible it was to get back in step. So his walk became inhibited and he imagined the sight of his comical efforts would bring people to a halt. And he only succeeded in again walking properly after he had quickly selected a destination, only that brought back the simplicity of walking correctly. But what destination should he set his eyes on now? He had always seen himself as sitting at the engine of progress, perhaps now was the time to move to the brakeman's cabin. But how? In any case the train had already reached a frenetic speed. And was there still such a thing as a brakeman's cabin? He laughed out loud. His neck felt heavy the way it always did when he was getting flu. He decided to send the letter to Susann with a brief explanation of why it was torn open. He wanted no compromise because of any vague hope, any timid sentimentality, neither for himself nor for Susann. He wanted clarity, it was to be goodbye to the comfort that stifled, to the timidly familiar, to all half measures. Awaiting him would be insecurity, doubt, breakdown, in other words suffering, but that was the price of growing richer in himself.

He thought of the magazine Sophie had given him with its naively depicted breaking globe, and the angel's words: Henceforth time shall cease. But it was completely and utterly inconceivable that time should stop because there was no one left. It was possible to imagine oneself as no longer existing because there was always a consolation in the thought – though also something dismaying about it – that everything else continued. But one thing was unimaginable: Henceforth time shall cease.

He arrived almost an hour late at the site. Everyone was already at work. In the office, where he could feel the gradient beneath his feet, they greeted him as if he had come back after a trip of several weeks. As he climbed the stairs he thought the local technicians and engineers would grin, because seen from the outside there was something ridiculous about his journey: to lose his way, intend to drive to the Falls, let them steal his distributor, ride across the eighth wonder of the world on a donkey, and finally be arrested. None of them knew that. And none of them would ever find out that his dignity had been wounded, that hands had been laid on him.

The engineers and technicians from the site office came to meet him. They laughed, they slapped him on the shoulders and nudged him in the side. Juan was not there. Juan had been missing for days.

'Juan has disappeared,' Steinhorst said. Steinhorst had been drinking. But there was nothing aggressive in his manner, only a friendly concern.

'Where is Juan?'

'Disappeared,' Steinhorst repeated. 'No one knows where he could be. Not even the police, which is not surprising. The manager and his interpreter both suddenly disappearing, that would be too much.'

'Is it definite he hasn't gone away?'

'Fairly. The day you were at Hartmann's and asked about Juan he disappeared. He'd gone down to get himself cigarettes. The light was on in his room, and so was the radio.'

Wagner went to his room. The sketches and calculations for the basements were there. He was convinced there was a connection between Luisa's disappearance and Juan's. He thought of the dried pomegranate under the kitchen cupboard. Was it a coincidence? Were they both after all in contact with the guerilleros? Or had they become victims of suspicion?

Wagner went into the canteen where Steinhorst was sitting at a table, his legs up on a chair, smoking.

'Can you remember what Ehmke said, what was it he saw from his hiding place?'

'Ehmke? Yes. You mean the two pomegranates.'

'Was it two? Are you sure?'

'I think so.'

'And where were they?'

'On the floor. He could see into a kitchen. He could see part of a kitchen floor through a gap under the door. And two pomegranates. Why?'

'I saw some too on the floor. In a kitchen.'

'Well, that's not exactly unusual. In how many German kitchens do you suppose there are apples lying on the floor in October?'

'Perhaps. Where's Hartmann?'

'Bredow gave him time off two days ago to sort out his affairs. We're the dregs, you and I.'

'Don't include me.'

'Suits me. But we can drink to the return of the prodigal son. We should raise our glasses to that, all of us. You've had the luck of the devil. Bredow's already told the tale.' He called out something to Pedro. Pedro came running with glasses and paper cups and handed them out to the engineers and technicians.

Wagner saw the crack in the corner of the canteen, quite a wide crack that ran along the ceiling and both walls. Steinhorst grinned. 'It's rained. One day. Not even hard. We're used to quite a different sort of rain here. And we put down gravel, but as you can see, the concrete can't take the strain. If you'll allow me to make a suggestion, I'd have the gravel shovelled out again. Then the place'll not fall down so quickly on our heads. All we have to do is get used to the incline. The management of the paper factory will have to get used to it. I can already see those sweet cunts tottering at a slant through the place.'

Wagner touched glasses with everyone.

'And the basement?'

'We've already begun. According to Bredow, the building permit's only a formality.'

Wagner smoked and slowly drank the scotch. Formality, Wagner thought, naturally also means I needn't have gone. Which is correct. He asked for another drink. Only a week ago he had run around like a guard dog, ears pricked, eyes alert. But that was a long time ago. The actual number of days meant nothing. Outside there was a fine haze in the air. The sun as if behind frosted glass. Slowly the cranes swung into his field of vision. They were moving even more slowly than usual, but perhaps that had to do with the whisky. He went to the window from which he had a view of the camp. There it was, deserted. Only a dog scratching wildly in the earth. Probably it was digging for one of those little animals that looked like guinea pigs and made a strange tock sound. He saw the concrete lorries arrive and drive slowly over to excavation B.

'Have you heard anything more about the jaguar man?'

Steinhorst shrugged his shoulders.

260

Wagner thought how he had reached into the workers' food and how that had started a strike. But the thought was no longer painful. But there was still the fact that he was to blame for the fate of the four men who had been deported. He had behaved in such a clumsy, such a demented and stupid way. A blue-black bank of cloud was coming up from the northwest. He would miss Juan. He had always wanted to talk to him, instead he'd allowed himself to become embroiled in a battle for good concrete. And played tennis with Durell and Bredow.

Steinhorst had got up. He was so drunk he had to steady himself against the window sill.

'The big rain's on the way. Then we'll have to put on our life jackets.' He saluted and shouted: 'Aye aye, sir, to a seaman's grave.'

All I need is for him to start weeping, Wagner thought. Steinhorst did in fact begin wiping his eyes.

'What is it?' Wagner asked.

'The poor bastard,' Steinhorst sobbed, 'a good man, Juan, but a poor bastard.'

Most of the local engineers were still standing about in the canteen. They stared at Steinhorst sobbing. Wagner found weeping men repellent, he would have liked to calm Steinhorst down with a few slaps. He took the plastic helmet and said: 'Steinhorst, come on, we're going to factory B.'

The concrete lorries stood by the excavation. Concrete was being poured on metal shutes. At the bottom were workers with spades and concrete vibrators. As Wagner appeared at the edge of the excavation some took off their hats. How ridiculous, he thought, I'm standing up here like a general. But then with a shock he thought that perhaps they were afraid of him.

Esposito, the young engineer spoke, saying something to him.

'What does he want?'

Steinhorst translated that the man was saying something about the quality of the concrete. The concrete was poor.

Wagner went to one of the shutes and felt the concrete. He could tell immediately, it was wretched concrete. It should have had a particularily high density. The workers had stopped working. They looked up at him. If it would have done them a favour he would have said: It's shit.

But that didn't matter to them down there. They wanted to work in peace and get their money.

'Shall I send for the gauge?' Steinhorst asked and sat on a bucket.

'No, not necessary,' Wagner said, 'the concrete's ok.'

Steinhorst grinned: 'We'll drink to that. Coming?'

'With you, no.'

Wagner rubbed his hands clean and made a sign to the workers to continue working. The concrete slid into the excavation, at the bottom spades and vibrators dealt with it. The young engineer who had complained about the quality of the concrete stared at Wagner and in his face Wagner saw first disappointment, then contempt, finally something like hatred. Wagner turned and went back to the office. The bank of cloud slowly made its way across the sun, a cool dark veil fell over the clearing. Wagner should have explained to the man it was not out of fear he had given the order to continue working, nor because he had been bribed, no, nor because he was afraid of chaos, because out of chaos came good work. It was much more out of curiosity at what would happen now, a secret pleasure in disintegration, a disintegration that had taken hold everywhere; yes, it was already in the system. He saw things as if from a great distance and through the eyes of a giant: curious about what would happen next. He wanted to do what had to be done, but no longer wanted to intervene. He wanted to let things take their course, not in the hope that he would carry them along, but they him, and that like this he could find his way to a destination that he could not yet see, unless this disintegration, this falling apart were itself that destination.

He was almost at the office building when the first drops of water fell from the black bank of cloud, drops of a size he had never seen before. They struck the reddish earth like small grenades, each time sending up a little dust.

'The flood,' Steinhorst shouted behind Wagner. Wagner turned round. Steinhorst lay stretched out on the ground. He held his mouth open wide. He lay there like a huge beached fish.

Thirty Two

Though early afternoon, it was already dark. The windscreen wipers threw up the water. The red-brown plain had turned into mud flats, rivulets everywhere, gullies that fed torrents that stopped at the roadside where the embankment was raised to a height of at least two metres. In the heavy rain Wagner saw something black, massive, a lorry blocking the lane. Its rear wheels had broken through the asphalt surface. Wagner drove carefully past the lorry on the opposite lane and saw that here the water had overflowed the embankment. The asphalt surface cracked like thin ice. Wagner pulled up past the subsidence, where the road seemed safe. He went back to the lorry. The rain was like a warm shower. The lorry's rear wheels had broken through the road's surface. The driver was standing by the lorry. He didn't look at Wagner, but stared at the water rushing under the road and increasingly sweeping away the soil. The asphalt cracked across the entire lane and broke away in lumps. The lorry sank deeper into the subsidence. Suddenly the door opened and a girl jumped from the driver's cabin. She stood in the rain in a thin dress. Luisa, the thought raced through Wagner. He ran to her. She turned as he was about to touch her. It was the face of a stranger, heavily made-up. Presumably a street prostitute. She wiped the hair from her face and Wagner wondered if she was crying. He pointed to his car, she could get in, but she only shook her head. A jeep came out of the rain from the other direction. It stopped. Soldiers with rain capes pulled over their heads got out and went to the edge of the subsidence. They stood there like alien headless beings from another planet, and Wagner was very glad to be separated from them by the subsidence that was getting wider all the time. Muddy brown water streamed through the gap. The city could no longer be reached from the north. So no lorry would be coming with concrete to the site tomorrow.

Suddenly the lorry slid with a roar from the edge of the road into the subsidence that was now at least six metres wide. For a moment it dammed the mass of water, then slowly tilted and was pushed to the side. The water tore increasingly large clods of earth from the embankment. The asphalt surface was rapidly breaking apart. The soldiers had to reverse their jeep. The lorry driver had watched his lorry subside without the least excitement, as if it had nothing to do with him. The woman said something to the driver, then she went up to Wagner and pointed to his Ford. In the meantime the rain had washed the make-up from her face. She now looked much younger and really did resemble Luisa, the long thick eyelashes, the wet black hair, the brown arms, the dress that clung wet to her childlike body. Wagner decided she was at most sixteen. Getting in she hesitated for a moment, then quickly pulled up her wet dress, wrung it out and let it lie on her thighs. She had narrow brown thighs. They drove through the rain that was in no way comparable to rain as Wagner knew it in Germany. The water fell flatly from the sky like large pieces of rag.

She only answered his questions, even those he tried to ask in Spanish, with a quick shake of the head. As soon as they got to the city she pointed to a street corner for Wagner to stop.

She said: 'Gracias,' and got out.

He saw her run barefoot through the puddles, high heeled shoes in her hand. He drove on. The streets were empty. There was nobody to be seen in the doorways. Remarkably all the doors and shutters were closed, iron roller blinds had been lowered outside the small stores. Wagner drove to Luisa's home. He parked the car directly in front of the entrance. He ran through the rain into the house. In the hall he felt for the light switch. The door to the ground floor flat still stood open. He saw light reflected on the floor that was under water. He climbed the stairs. At the top he knocked on the door, but at the same time opened it. He looked for the light switch in the hall. Here, too, the light was still working.

There's an abundant supply of electricity in this country, he thought. Nothing had changed in the kitchen. The dried pomegranate still lay on the table. It had rained into the room because the doors onto the roof terrace were open. The rain pattered onto the terrace. He carefully closed both doors. He went through the hall again, but there was no other room and no cupboard. And he could see no other door in the kitchen either. He put the pomegranate back under the cupboard where he had found it, went into the hall, closed the kitchen door and knelt on the floor. Through the gap under the door he could actually see the pomegranate lying on the floor. But it made no sense because no one could have been held prisoner in the hall. He shut the kitchen window, turned off the dripping tap and the light. He would not be returning to this flat. In the ground floor flat he heard a splash, he was about to go and see, then he heard croaking. Probably some frogs or toads. In the car he again looked at the house to which soon the forest would be returning.

On the way to the Plaza he came to a roadblock. A military lorry had been parked across the road. Soldiers stood in the rain, rain capes pulled over their steel helmets. Two soldiers came to Wagner's car, one held his submachine gun with the safety catch off pointed at him, the other checked the identity card Bredow had got for him. To Wagner's surprise he immediately handed back the company letter as if it were a trivial scrap of paper. Now he kept looking from Wagner to the photo on the identity card. Obviously the photo did not bear sufficient resemblance. He indicated that Wagner should wait. Wagner felt the uneasiness rise in him like a weight in his stomach. The soldier had gone over to the jeep where one of his superiors sat under the lowered hood. Wagner looked for his cigarettes, offered one to the soldier who still held the submachine gun pointed at him. But the soldier only shook his head and chewed his chewing gum, so that there was only the same unchanging dull movement in his face. When Wagner lit his cigarette his hands were shaking. The soldier noticed; he grinned. Wagner was convinced that at a sign from the jeep the man would simply press the trigger. Probably he would only interrupt his chewing for a moment to take the recoil from the gun. The other soldier came back with Wagner's passport. Wagner could go through. On the Plaza there were three tanks. Their guns pointed at the streets leading to the Plaza. Wagner drove over to the hill and was again checked. He had never seen so many soldiers on the streets. And three barriers of sandbags had been put up to close the entry road at the foot of the hill. He had to slowly curve round them as if in an obstacle race. The sergeant who normally gave him a friendly wave this time stopped him, greeted him formally but was embarrassed, and asked for the car papers and his passport. An officer stood watching the control in the small guard room, which had also been made more secure with sandbags.

'What happened?' Wagner asked.

'I don't know,' the guard said. Then he waved Wagner through. As Wagner stopped outside his bungalow Sophie came out. She was wearing a suit and held an umbrella in her hand. She had obviously been waiting for him.

'What's going on?' he asked, soldiers everywhere.

'Today is the day of wrath and reckoning,' she said, 'I have put a meal out for you.'

'But where are you going, everything's shut.'

'We are going to pray. You should join us. For the Lord said: Come! And let him who thirsts come; and he who would, let him take of the water of life.'

'But you won't get to the city.'

She had opened the umbrella and hurried away, and Wagner thought she was probably going to some house on the hill to meet with her own people and pray.

Thirty Three

When he entered Bredow's house already sitting there were the colonel and the black-haired beauty from Bredow's office, sunk deep in an armchair. The director of the concrete factory was also there, with him his wife, small, round, very pregnant and always smiling. Christi had immediately put her arm through Wagner's and said, 'It looks bad. One should never go with strange people.' What she meant by that he wasn't sure, he supposed it was a mistranslated Danish saying.

The colonel shook hands with Wagner (a warm, damp man-to-man handshake) and said he was glad Wagner had got off with only a black eye.

Wagner said: 'Yes, yes.'

How ridiculous these attempts were to put what had happened to him into colloquial turns of phrase. Christi sat him opposite the black-haired beauty who looked deep into his eyes, as if she had been asked to. This was obviously meant to be a promise. Christi sat next to Wagner and they all drank to him for having come back unscathed, but also for having made such good progress at the site. The initial problems had now been solved. A girl in a white apron brought in a soup tureen. Christi served the soup with a silver ladle. 'Wagner needs to get his strength back,' she said. He would see to it, Bredow immediately added, that Wagner got danger money. As could be seen, under these conditions the job wasn't exactly without its risks. The pregnant woman laid a hand on her stomach in which the foetus visibly moved. There was no need, Bredow continued, to declare the money. The internal revenue knew far too much anyway. Wagner would be paid in cash.

Slowly it dawned on Wagner that it was not his return that was being celebrated here, but the fact that he had accepted the poor concrete. They thought they now had an accomplice in him. And so this was the initiatory celebration.

'On principle I shall not accept any extra payment,' Wagner said.

The colonel interrupted his conversation with the director and looked over at Wagner. Bredow's face showed a helplessness that, because it was so unconcealed, made him look stupid.

'What do you mean by that?' Bredow asked.

'Nothing complicated, I act out of conviction.'

At this they all laughed loudly and were visibly relieved, the colonel, Christi, Bredow, and after Bredow had translated for them, the crooked-mouthed director of the concrete factory, his pregnant wife and the black-haired beauty. In the meantime the main course had been served, roast beef. Wagner ate only a little. For some strange reason his teeth ached. And he had no appetite. He asked the colonel what the troops in the city signified. Guards and roadblocks everywhere. With this rain the rats always come out of their holes, the colonel said. A police guard had been shot in the morning. At midday there had been a strike at the sugar refinery. The strike was not yet over. And at the cement works it had come to a strike. The administrator spoke in Spanish to the director, who looked concerned as he replied. Then he fixed a grin on his crooked mouth. Even Bredow smiled. For a moment Wagner was tempted to ask what there was to grin about, but he let it pass.

'Prevention is better than treatment,' the colonel said to

Wagner, his dentist in Blankenese had always said that. He wanted to drink to Hamburg with Wagner, but Wagner said he couldn't drink anymore. The officer hesitated a moment, but decided not to take it as an affront and talked about his training in Germany, how once during manoeuvres on the Lünerburger Heide he had lost his way and finally found a shepherd who, as if he belonged to the Russian secret service, knew all the troop movements of both sides and was able to immediately send him to his unit. And then, shortly after his arrival in Germany, a Hamburg business man had invited him to a house party and asked him if he had danced with his daughter yet, at which, being proud of his idiomatic German, he had replied, 'I've not done her yet.'

Wagner laughed despite himself, probably because he already knew the joke. With a napkin the colonel dabbed the avocado purée he had splattered on his white uniform jacket while laughing. But then Wagner was angry with himself for having joined in the laughter and contributing to the friendly atmosphere. When the conversation turned to the weather and the colonel thought the heavy rain might continue for another two or three days, Wagner said in that case the office building at the site would probably float away like a cork. Christi began to laugh, but she laughed far too loudly and shrilly, as if at a dirty joke.

'It's no joke,' Wagner said. 'When the groundwater level reaches a certain height buildings can definitely be compared to ships, they either float, but are properly anchored, or they capsize and sink.' Christi laughed again and put her hand on Wagner's thigh.

'It doesn't often happen,' Wagner said, 'but it does happen from time to time, and always for the same reason: shoddy work or corruption.' Bredow looked at Wagner, his face showed strain. He held his fork between plate and mouth, as if undecided whether to eat another mouthful or put it down.

'For example, in Bremen it was never possible to move into a fifteen-storeyed office block because only its own weight, not its live load had been calculated, that meant, fully furnished and during office hours the building would slowly have sunk, would probably then have started to lean and then would have collapsed. That however would have been no great loss, as the building was extraordinarily ugly. What's more, they had forgotten, or rather, the architect had forgotten to put any toilet facilities into the building. In this office block certain needs could only have been taken care of in some corner.'

Christi laughed and laughed while looking across at Bredow who still sat grimly, fork in hand. The director, his wife and the black-haired beauty stared at Wagner, silent and uncomprehending, as no one had translated anything. But Wagner spoke to the director of the concrete factory as if this account referred to him, and to him only. 'However,' Wagner said, 'it was not the architect who had received this contract through his contacts who was particularly upset, but the structural engineer who should have checked the plans. The man was so upset that one day he had climbed to the top of this building that now stood there useless and had thrown himself off it. Do you know,' Wagner said to the director who once again had twisted his mouth into a grin of embarrassed incomprehension, 'I was always very impressed by this man with his almost Japanese code of honour, even it it seems rather ridiculous now.'

'And the architect?' Christi asked.

'The architect lives on in peace in his bungalow that's ruined the landscape, and if he isn't dead he's still building.'

'But the building, what happened to the building?'

'Stands there: grey, dark and empty. You come out of the station in Bremen, there it is, a hulk, for a long time it was used for nothing but one advertisement. On the top floor in gigantic neon letters the words: Coffee Hag. For the heart, and next to it a red neon heart.'

Christi began translating the story for the director. She had drunk a great deal and her face was red and patchy. Wagner suddenly had an attack of shivering. Bredow, who had put back the mouthful of food onto his plate and stopped eating, said: 'You're ill. You really must see a doctor. Shall I send for a doctor?'

'No,' Wagner said, 'it's all right.'

Then suddenly the light went out. The wife of the concrete factory director shrieked, everyone began to talk at the same time. Christi lit two candles.

'Perhaps it's the main fuse,' Bredow said and went into the garden.

'One never knows here if it's a short circuit or if the light's gone out forever,' Christi said.

Bredow came back and said: 'The entire hill's dark. Perhaps some overland cables have collapsed because of the rain.'

'Or the dam's burst,' Christi said, 'but the fifty metre tidal wave hasn't reached us yet. But we're on the hill.' She laughed. 'We would have had to turn the light out anyway. As we're having flambéd cherry ice cream.'

Christi got up and Wagner saw she was swaying a little.

At that moment the light went on again and they all cried: 'Bravo' and 'Ah.' Christi sat down again next to Wagner and asked him why he was looking so grim.

'Not grim,' Wagner said, 'only curious.'

'Why curious?'

'To see what happens next.'

The maid brought in a large bowl with ice cream on which there were deep red cherries. Christi turned out the light. A long blueish flame could be seen in the bowl.

The ice did Wagner good, for a moment his mouth was cool and moist. The telephone rang. Bredow went out. The ringing had given Wagner a shock, it had made him start, not that he could think why. Bredow came back immediately and said

273

something. The colonel threw the napkin onto the table and left.

'What is it?' Christi asked.

'The colonel has to go to the city immediately. It's begun. Tell them to make him coffee.'

'What's begun?' Wagner asked.

But Bredow was not listening, he was saying something to the director of the concrete factory whose wife kept nervously stroking her stomach, as if to convince herself of its size. Christi had put her hand on Wagner's thigh again. Now she was drunk. Her face glowed and the buttons on her white silk dress had come undone. Wagner saw a suntanned breast and thought that she probably sunbathed naked.

'What's the matter,' he asked her, 'why the excitement?'

Christi drank the full glass of wine as if it were water. Now she was having trouble speaking German. Danish words kept coming into her sentences. If Wagner understood her correctly, there had been a coup in the capital or there had been demonstrations, or both, apparently the PIR had played a part. 'The guerillas have taken a radio station,' she said, 'perhaps it's revolution, perhaps all our dreams are over,' she laughed, 'or perhaps it's only the world going under.'

Wagner got up and in getting up pulled Christi, who was hanging onto his shoulder, with him. The way she clung to him embarrassed him.

'Stay here,' she said. 'You can sleep here. Your house is down by the wall. That's dangerous.'

'Yes,' Bredow said, 'it would really be better if you stayed with us tonight.'

Wagner thanked them and said he preferred to go, yes, in fact he should go.

'Why should?'

But then they all listened because they could hear the

274

colonel's voice outside. He was shouting something. They stared at the door, a stare filled with hatred.

Wagner simply left without saying goodbye. The colonel was making a phone call in the entrance hall. He had unbuttoned the white uniform jacket and loosened his tie, he shouted some orders into the phone and several times repeated: 'Adelantarse hasta la fábrica.'

Meanwhile his cigarette burned a black mark into the small lacquered table by the phone.

Outside the rain continued unabated. Wagner ran over to the car. The rain cooled his forehead and cheeks. He got into the car. The rain drummed on the roof. He lit a cigarette.

Opposite him the door opened and the colonel came out of the house. He walked slowly through the front garden, despite the rain, as if he were enjoying it, suddenly stopped in the street as if he were standing under a shower. Wagner saw he was swaying a little, but then he unbuttoned his trousers and began to piss. Despite the rain Wagner clearly saw the stream of piss in the light of one of the outdoor lamps. Wagner started the engine. He wanted to drive into this pissing man. The colonel turned round towards him, not in the least alarmed. He even nodded. Then a headlight came on from a car on the other side of the street. The car turned and stopped by the officer, who had pulled his prick back into his trousers with a swinging movement. He came over to Wagner's car.

'Be careful down there, in your house, on the demarcation line. Better to stay here. There's all you need here, even someone to make you happy.'

Wagner looked at him and thought, I should have run him over.

As Wagner said nothing, the colonel said: 'Good, then to work, duty calls.'

He went to his car. The driver, a soldier, got out, held open the door for him and slammed it after him, got in and drove off. Another car drove in a screeching curve across the street and followed the Mercedes. Four men sat in the back, bodyguards.

Wagner felt no satisfaction at not having run the colonel over. Conjecture at what might have happened to him neither horrified him, nor caused him to rub his hands in gratification at having got away with it once again.

But if he had done so everything would have been different, of that he was sure. He could feel he had a temperature, shivered pleasantly, a childhood memory came of being allowed to stay in bed and having every wish granted. His mother brought him warm milk with grated almonds. He slowly drove down the street. There were lights everywhere, in the houses, on the streets, even trees, bushes and borders were floodlit, as if the only assurance of one's existence were visibility – as if darkness could swallow everything. So the hill lay glaringly lit, but as if dead. Lower down an ambulance with a revolving blue light came towards Wagner. The siren had been turned off, presumably because it was driving through an expensive residential area. The ambulance raced past and Wagner was sure they were taking their victims away inside.

When Wagner passed the exit road to the city he saw that in the meantime two tanks had taken up positions there, scrap metal from previous wars. Trenches were being dug on both sides of the street. The engine of one of the tanks began to roar. The tank slowly turned on its tracks and rolled over the lawn. Either they're very frightened or the danger's real, Wagner thought, if they roll across this trimmed lawn. Slowly the tank turret swung the barrel of the gun to the street that led from the city.

The city was in darkness.

Wagner drove slowly towards the barricade of sandbags.

'What happened?'

'I don't know. You better return home quickly.'

The street was deserted. He had trouble concentrating on his driving. Outside his bungalow the lights were also all on, the entrance was lit, the front of the house spotlit, the lamps were on on the lawn. He ran to the front door. As he unlocked it the harsh wail of the alarm gave him a shock. He felt for the switch and because of the screeching noise panicked at not being able to instantly find it. At last it was quiet. He went to Sophie's room. He listened at the door. Not a sound to be heard. He looked through the keyhole. It was dark in the room. Probably she had stayed with her people.

He went to the bathroom to run a bath. But a reddish brown jet shot from the tap that then ran dry with a slurp. From somewhere in the pipes came a mysterious belching and banging. He heard the quiet monotone whirring of the air conditioner, otherwise everything was still. He went to the veranda door, pulled up the blinds, unbolted the door and went out. For the first time since his return he went into the garden. To right and left, where earlier knee-high wire netting had marked the boundaries on the one side to his neighbour's land and on the other to a public area of lawn, now stood the concrete wall. On its parapet iron frames had been set in concrete. From the frames hung barbed wire. The garden now jutted like an overhang over the plain, especially as the rain had swept away the soil from the neighbouring plot where the American agronomist's bungalow had been. Standing on a garden chair peering over the wall, all Wagner saw were the remains of the foundation walls. There was a smell of wet rubble and plaster. The flowers, the lawn, the borders had disappeared.

Up on the hill dogs began barking, probably Klages' sheep-dogs in their kennels. Ferocious barking that intensified until it was completely frenetic, as if the dogs were being approached by something completely unfamiliar, horrifying. Then it suddenly stopped. Wagner went to the front wall from which he had often looked out at the plain, and stepped onto the ledge. He got a shock: the huts were immediately below the wall. But there was nobody in sight. The entire plain lay under water, a dark wide sea from which the hill rose like a brightly lit island. Wagner stared into the streaming darkness, but could see nothing. There was a shot in the distance – at first Wagner couldn't tell where – then another, one, two bursts of machine gun fire, an explosion, then another, then the lights went out. Now the hill was also in darkness. The shooting had stopped, the only sound was the thundering rain. Now they're coming, Wagner thought. He listened. Sporadically, hesitantly, the voices of the night began, the croaking, squeaking, snarling, then grew louder. Wagner heard a noise behind him. As he shot round he saw a figure clinging to the iron frames on the wall that bordered what had been the American's plot of land. For a moment the figure stayed in sight, like someone taken by surprise. Very slowly it slipped from the wall. So the area in front of the wall was not as deserted as it had appeared. Wagner went cautiously back through the garden to the house. Floating in the pool was a fat toad and a shapeless parcel. He was about to prod it with a stick. But then thought perhaps there was a body in the parcel, a body tied up in a plastic bag. He quickly went into the house and locked the veranda door. Although the air conditioner had only stopped working a few minutes ago, it was hot and sticky. He felt his way to the kitchen where there were two torches on a shelf. He heard a strange rasping sound on the parquet floor in the hall, he has heard it before, but doesn't know where. He takes the larger of the two torches, goes into the hall. In the beam of the torch he sees two rats running across the hall. They probably came into the house while he was in the garden and the door was open. He goes – in the beam sees a fat beetle crawl across the floor – to Sophie's room. He knocks. He calls: 'Sophie.' Not a sound. He turns the handle and shines the light into the room. It is empty. He goes to the cupboard and cautiously opens the door, having suddenly imagined she could be standing inside, dead. But there are only a few dresses and blouses hanging in the cupboard. He goes to the entrance hall and lifts the receiver. He is not surprised to find the line dead. He goes to the kitchen and gets himself a bottle of beer from the refrigerator. For a fleeting moment his hand feels the cold. He drinks the beer in the dark. This, he thinks, could be his last bottle of beer for a long time. He again hears the rasping as if little knives were being sharpened, this time in the kitchen. He stamps his foot: scurrying, then it stops. From one of the other rooms he hears a strange noise, like the sound of a cork coming out of a bottle. The noise keeps recurring at regular intervals. He has drunk the beer without hurrying and gropingly puts the bottle down on the refrigerator. As he turns to switch on the torch the bottle falls to the floor and shatters. He ignores the broken glass and goes to investigate the noise. It leads him to the bathroom, the bath. It comes from the tap he turned on earlier. Unusually large and fat cockroaches are forcing their way through the tap, this is what makes the popping sound. He shines the torch into the bath. The bottom is covered in a black glittering mass. The chitin carapaces can be clearly heard scraping as the animals crawl over each other. They still slide down the smooth sides in their attempt to crawl out of the bath. But more and more squeeze out of the tap and soon the bath will be full enough for them to crawl over the side. From his bedroom Wagner hears a deep, satiated slurping, as if from a large animal. He quickly goes there, runs the beam over floor and walls, but can see nothing. The slurping stopped as he came in. He stands there, shaken by a bout of fever, and says aloud to himself: 'I must control my thoughts'. He lies on the bed, soaked from the rain and the sweat now running cold from his pores. It seems to him as if the ceiling of the room is also sweating, at any rate he feels large cool drops fall onto his face.

He tries to think of Luisa but sees Susann and Sascha walking through snow, fresh untrodden ankle-deep snow that muffles every sound. One day last winter he and Susann had lain in the snow together, silent, not touching each other. He gets up because he thinks it would be better to wait outside. If they haven't already climbed over the wall, if they're not already at the door. A host of hungry, worm-eaten figures, wracked by work, among them again and again he sees his workers, even those that were arrested. Then again he hears that noise from the bath, that popping, popping, popping. He runs to the bathroom. The cockroaches are crawling over the edge of the bath. He quickly slams the door, but knows the creatures will find their way to the other rooms. Kitchen and bathroom have the same ventilation shaft. He runs to the front door to take refuge in some other house, but even before he has opened the door knows that no one will let him in. They are all sitting rigid with shock behind their bolted doors. He wonders if he should drive back up to the Bredows, but then sees the people before him, the fish-mouthed director of the concrete factory, his wife, pregnant, face perplexed, slightly stupid, the glossy beauty, the drunk Christi, Bredow soaked in sweat and fear on his face. And Wagner thinks if the lights were to go back on again on the hill everything would continue as before, a power cut, but let it stay dark, he hopes for an abiding darkness in which the cockroaches will force their way into every house and every bungalow and the rats too, here on the hill but in Hamburg as well, there too, to feed on the refuse, on the accumulated wealth built on misfortune and suffering. No, the others would come, from the forest, from the huts, from the hovels of the city, and among them would be the labourer with the chopped-off finger and the man with the destroyed face. He could hold out his hand to them. He could help them over the wall. He freezes and sweats. He feels as if a fire has gone out inside him and that is why he goes into the garden, to cool in the rain. For a moment he hesitates, wondering if he should shut the door, then tells himself the rats would still force their way in, whether through the toilets or the walls. A strange fluttering and crawling and scurrying surrounds him. The pool is full of toads, but there also seem to be fish swimming in it, and sometimes a dark swell stirs the water.

In the distance, where the city is, he sees the reflection of a great fire. The rolls of barbed wire have been torn down from the walls, the iron frames jut naked out of the concrete.

Then, unexpectedly, the lights go on again. For a moment Wagner sees movement in the garden, it instantly stops. All the way up the hill the houses, the gardens, the streets are fully lit again, a light that gorges itself on darkness.

Wagner hears himself scream in rage and disappointment and at the same time thinks, I should be glad. He tries to look over the wall, but is blinded by a searchlight shining from the hill onto the wall. Slowly the cone of light moves along the wall down to the water whipped by the rain. A chill runs through him. His tongue feels swollen. Not too far away he hears the hammering of a machine gun, also from time to time the dry detonation of a mortar. The rain falls heavily, monotonously. He is on the way back to the house when the lights go out again, and the hill lies in even deeper darkness. He stands and listens. The silence is profound. No shooting, no screaming, even the animals have fallen silent, as if the world were holding its breath.

New Directions Paperbooks — A Partial Listing

For complete listing request free catalog from
New Directions, 80 Eighth Avenue, New York 10011

† Bilingual

The Smile at the Foot of the Ladder. NDP386.
Stand Still Like the Hummingbird. NDP236.
The Time of the Assassins. NDP115.
Y. Mishima, Confessions of a Mask. NDP253.
Death in Midsummer. NDP215.
Frédéric Mistral, The Memoirs. NDP632.
Eugenio Montale, It Depends.† NDP507.
New Poems. NDP410.
Selected Poems.† NDP193.
Paul Morand, Fancy Goods/Open All Night.
NDP567.
Vladimir Nabokov, Nikolai Gogol. NDP78.
Laughter in the Dark. NDP470.
The Real Life of Sebastian Knight. NDP432.
P. Neruda, The Captain's Verses.† NDP345.
Residence on Earth.† NDP340.
New Directions in Prose & Poetry (Anthology).
Available from #17 forward to #52.
Robert Nichols, Arrival. NDP437.
Exile. NDP485. Garh City. NDP450.
Harditts in Sawna. NDP470.
Charles Olson, Selected Writings. NDP231.
Toby Olson, The Life of Jesus. NDP417.
Seaview. NDP532.
George Oppen, Collected Poems. NDP418.
István Örkeny, The Flower Show /
The Toth Family. NDP536.
Wilfred Owen, Collected Poems. NDP210.
José Emilio Pacheco, Battles in the Desert, NDP637.
Selected Poems.† NDP638.
Nicanor Parra, Antipoems: New & Selected. NDP603.
Boris Pasternak, Safe Conduct. NDP77.
Kenneth Patchen, Aflame and Afun. NDP292.
Because It Is. NDP83.
Collected Poems. NDP284.
Hallelujah Anyway. NDP219.
Selected Poems. NDP160.
Octavio Paz, Configurations.† NDP303.
A Draft of Shadows.† NDP489.
Eagle or Sun?† NDP422.
Selected Poems. NDP574.
A Tree Within,† NDP661.
St. John Perse. Selected Poems.† NDP545.
J. A. Porter, Eelgrass. NDP438.
Ezra Pound, ABC of Reading. NDP89.
Confucius. NDP285.
Confucius to Cummings. (Anth.) NDP126.
Gaudier Brzeska. NDP372.
Guide to Kulchur. NDP257.
Literary Essays. NDP250.
Selected Cantos. NDP304.
Selected Letters 1907-1941. NDP317.
Selected Poems. NDP66.
The Spirit of Romance. NDP266.
Translations.† (Enlarged Edition) NDP145.
Women of Trachis. NDP597.
Raymond Queneau, The Blue Flowers. NDP595.
Exercises in Style. NDP513.
The Sunday of Life. NDP433.
Mary de Rachewiltz, Ezra Pound. NDP405.
Raja Rao, Kanthapura. NDP224.
Herbert Read, The Green Child. NDP208.
P. Reverdy, Selected Poems.† NDP346.
Kenneth Rexroth, Classics Revisited. NDP621.
More Classics Revisited, NDP668.
100 More Poems from the Chinese. NDP308.
100 More Poems from the Japanese.† NDP420.
100 Poems from the Chinese. NDP192.
100 Poems from the Japanese.† NDP147.
Selected Poems. NDP581.
Women Poets of China. NDP528.
Women Poets of Japan. NDP527.
World Outside the Window, Sel. Essays, NDP639.
Rainer Maria Rilke, Poems from
The Book of Hours. NDP408.
Possibility of Being. (Poems). NDP436.
Where Silence Reigns. (Prose). NDP464.
Arthur Rimbaud, Illuminations.† NDP56.
Season in Hell & Drunken Boat.† NDP97.
Edouard Roditi, Delights of Turkey. NDP445.

Oscar Wilde. NDP624.
Jerome Rothenberg, New Selected Poems. NDP625.
Nayantara Sahgal, Rich Like Us, NDP665.
Saigyo, Mirror for the Moon.† NDP465.
Ihara Saikaku, The Life of an Amorous
Woman. NDP270.
St. John of the Cross, Poems.† NDP341.
Jean-Paul Sartre, Nausea. NDP82.
The Wall (Intimacy). NDP272.
Delmore Schwartz, Selected Poems. NDP241.
The Ego Is Always at the Wheel, NDP641.
In Dreams Begin Responsibilities. NDP454.
Stevie Smith, Collected Poems. NDP562.
New Selected Poems, NDP659.
Gary Snyder, The Back Country. NDP249.
The Real Work. NDP499.
Regarding Wave. NDP306.
Turtle Island. NDP381.
Enid Starkie, Rimbaud. NDP254.
Robert Steiner, Bathers. NDP495.
Antonio Tabucchi, Letter from Casablanca. NDP620.
Nathaniel Tarn, Lyrics . . . Bride of God. NDP391.
Dylan Thomas, Adventures in the Skin Trade.
NDP183.
A Child's Christmas in Wales. NDP181.
Collected Poems 1934-1952. NDP316.
Collected Stories. NDP626.
Portrait of the Artist as a Young Dog. NDP51.
Quite Early One Morning. NDP90.
Under Milk Wood. NDP73.
Tian Wen: A Chinese Book of Origins. NDP624.
Lionel Trilling, E. M. Forster. NDP189.
Martin Turnell, Baudelaire. NDP336.
Rise of the French Novel. NDP474.
Paul Valéry, Selected Writings.† NDP184.
Elio Vittorini, A Vittorini Omnibus. NDP366.
Rosmarie Waldrop, The Reproduction of Profiles,
NDP649.
Robert Penn Warren, At Heaven's Gate. NDP588.
Vernon Watkins, Selected Poems. NDP221.
Weinberger, Eliot, Works on Paper. NDP627.
Nathanael West, Miss Lonelyhearts &
Day of the Locust. NDP125.
J. Wheelwright, Collected Poems. NDP544.
Tennessee Williams, Camino Real. NDP301.
Cat on a Hot Tin Roof. NDP398.
Clothes for a Summer Hotel. NDP556.
The Glass Menagerie. NDP218.
Hard Candy. NDP225.
In the Winter of Cities. NDP154.
A Lovely Sunday for Creve Coeur. NDP497.
One Arm & Other Stories. NDP237.
Stopped Rocking. NDP575.
A Streetcar Named Desire. NDP501.
Sweet Bird of Youth. NDP409.
Twenty-Seven Wagons Full of Cotton. NDP217.
Vieux Carre. NDP482.
William Carlos Williams,
The Autobiography. NDP223.
The Buildup. NDP259.
The Doctor Stories. NDP585.
Imaginations. NDP329.
In the American Grain. NDP53.
In the Money. NDP240.
Paterson. Complete. NDP152.
Pictures form Brueghel. NDP118.
Selected Letters. NDP589.
Selected Poems (new ed.). NDP602.
White Mule. NDP226.
Yes, Mrs. Williams. NDP534.
Yvor Winters, E. A. Robinson. NDP326.
Wisdom Books: Ancient Egyptians.NDP467.
Early Buddhists, NDP444; Forest (Hindu).
NDP414; Spanish Mystics. NDP442; St. Francis.
NDP477; Taoists. NDP509; Wisdom of the Desert.
NDP295; Zen Masters. NDP415.

For complete listing request free catalog from
New Directions, 80 Eighth Avenue, New York 10011

† Bilingual